call me him.

call me him.

a transgender coming-of-age story

River Braun

Cover design by Curious Ways

ISBN: 9798557679978

Printed in the United States of America

Sometimes, the greatest act of courage is simply breathing.
To those beautiful souls who have not felt loved for who you are—
may you find your voice and your tribe.

Trigger Warning

While I do not pretend to write for every person's experience, in an effort to write a novel that reflects the realities of life for members of the LGBTQ+ community, there are scenes in this story that may trigger some readers, including those involving transphobia, misgendering, body dysphoria, sexual assault, violence, bullying, self harm, anxiety, depression, and drug use.

If you fear you may be triggered by any of these themes, please read when you are in a safe space and in a good headspace to do so. If you are in need someone to talk to, consider reaching out to one of the following hotlines:

- National Suicide Prevention Lifeline - 800-273-8255
- The Trevor Project -
  https://www.thetrevorproject.org/ org
  1-866-488-7386

And, if no one has told you this today, I love you.

1

Wylie

"Get out of my sight!"

That was the last thing I heard my mom scream before I slammed the front door and ran down the driveway.

Gladly. I hucked my board to the ground and jumped on, wheels bumping over the uneven cement sidewalk. The perpetually dead lawns of my crappy SoCal neighborhood blurred into brown streaks in my peripheral vision. Most days began like that for me. Fight. Sleep. Repeat. Like the shampoo commercials. I couldn't wait to get out of this shit-hole town.

I slowed down to round the corner, coming to an abrupt stop in front of my secret spot. Nothing special, just an empty clearing hidden behind a giant oleander bush on the corner of two yards. I changed in the small clearing every morning before school—out of the stupid girl-clothes my mom bought for me and into the ones I stole from my older brothers' closets—the ones they grew out of and never wore anymore. Or the stuff I could find cheap at thrift stores. My brothers' clothes were baggy on my scarecrow-thin frame, but I didn't mind. I blended in with the other skaters.

I shrugged on the black NOFX t-shirt I bought for 25-cents and pulled on my brother Jared's, old boxers and black jeans. Done, I shoved the other clothes into my backpack and emerged from the bush. An actor, constantly changing my clothes—changing myself—for the role I played. With 'Willow's clothes' in my backpack, I emerged from the bushes as 'Wylie.'

I looked around. Had anyone seen me? I didn't want my morning ritual known or anyone to see me light a joint before hopping back on my board. I inhaled the pine-flavored smoke deep into my lungs, trying to forget the heinous dress my mom bought me for the upcoming family gathering. Pink and white. Puffy skirt. Really? It's the year 2001 woman. We survived Y2K. The '80s are over. Way over.

That's what we were fighting about. My mom and me. I told her I'd rather wear a black Hefty garbage bag to dinner. She threatened to take away all of my clothes and make me wear nothing *but* garbage bags. I told her to go ahead—anything was better than the shit she made me wear. I mean, really, I'm almost 15-years-old, I should be able to pick my own clothes. That went over about as good as I expected. She hates it when I cuss. At least it ended the argument and I got to leave.

So, I was just skating along, thinking about the morning's drama, when I skidded around the corner by the 7-Eleven. I kicked off to get more speed when I heard him.

"Hey, boy—off the board!" A rotund cop started walking towards me. His partner, a skeletal figure over six-feet tall, placed his paper coffee cup on the car he was leaning on and followed.

Startled, I jumped off my board and spat out my joint, crushing it under my foot as I grabbed my board and started walking in the same direction I was already headed, acting cool, but my heart was about to beat its way out of my chest.

"Stop."

I felt a hand on my shoulder. Tubby's partner was a little faster on his feet. I looked into his heavy-lidded eyes. His agro expression and the slight twitch in his mustache-covered lip made him seem a bit demented.

"What?" I tried to shrug off his hand.

The cop's grip tightened, digging into my shoulder. "Let's hear some respect coming out of that mouth."

Tubby caught up. "What's your name?"

"Wylie." I looked down, still trying to weasel my way out of the skinny-cop's grasp. "Let go of me."

"Settle down Wylie. Unless you want to take a ride with us. What's your last name?"

I stopped squirming. "Masterson."

"Well, Wylie Masterson, you know that skateboarding is illegal on these sidewalks? You could injure someone." Skinny cop loosened his grip a little.

I flipped my long bangs out of my eyes and scanned the street. No pedestrians in sight. This was such crap. These guys were always hassling us skaters. Saying we were "disturbing the peace" or some shit. Whose peace was I disturbing here?

"Thank you, officers, for helping me see the error of my ways. I'll just go ahead and get to school now." I tried to turn and walk away.

"Not so fast, son." Tubby put his face close to mine. "You smell like you been smokin' some of that mari-ja-wana. You high, son?"

I had to stop myself from laughing in the cop's face. His southern accent was funny enough, but the way he pronounced marijuana was too much. I looked him in the eyes and affected my best southern drawl. "Why no, I am not, officer."

Before I knew it, Skinny had me on the ground, hands

behind me, his knee in my back. My face was inches away from someone's abandoned grape chewing gum and I felt the tiny pebbles in the parking lot carving divots into my cheek.

My mom says my mouth has a habit of getting me in trouble. Her boyfriend says my mouth writes checks that my ass can't cash. I hate to say it, but they're kinda right. Why can't I keep my mouth shut? Could this day get any worse?

Then, Skinny put the cuffs on me. "Open your mouth." He put his face close to mine.

"Bite me." I felt a hand pressing on my head, grinding my face into the pavement even more.

"Yeah, I can smell it on you." He took his knee off my back and lifted me to a standing position in the small alley-way of the strip mall. "We're going to search you and your bag for drugs. Do yourself a favor—stay still."

For once, I did as told and stood stiff as a post while Tubby picked my bag up off the ground and started searching it. I glared at him. Skinny went through my back pockets, pulling my wallet out, which was attached to my pants by a long, silver chain. The Velcro made a ripping sound as he opened it up.

"Your school identification says your name is Willow Masterson." Skinny looked me up and down. "You a girl?"

Just then, Tubby pulled my clothes out of my backpack— red tank-top and white jeans, last season's K-Mart specials. He held them up, confused. To be honest, I liked the fact that I could make myself look like a guy. But too often, this is what happens —

"Are you a boy or a girl?" Tubby echoed the words directed at me time and time again throughout my childhood.

I didn't answer. Why does it matter so much to people? I wanted to tell them to fuck off, but I was on thin ice, especially given what was in my front pockets.

Tubby shoved my clothes back into my backpack. "You must be one of those ho-mo-sex-uals." The venom dripped from that last word as if it had been spoken by Satan—the unholy serpent, himself. "You know, it's a crime to lie to the police. Why would you want to lie to us, young lady?"

I liked it better when he called me "son" even though he was not my father. I would have liked it if my father had called me "son" but he left five years ago and hasn't called me anything since.

I seethed in silence as Skinny slid my ID into my back pocket. "Looks like butch here has lost her sense of humor."

The morning traffic buzzed by as Skinny patted me down, making a show of running his hands down my flat chest, working his way down my body before grabbing my crotch. "Nothing here, Sarg." He looked me dead in the eyes, not moving his hand away. "Looks like maybe you're missing some parts, Wylie."

Rage rose up inside me until I could feel the tips of my ears burning. I felt the heat of his hands coming through my clothes. My stomach twisted itself into knots. I thought I might throw up right there and looked around to see if anyone, was seeing this. But I was backed into the alley and Skinny was so close to me there was no way a passing vehicle could tell what was going on.

Tubby looked uncomfortable. You'd think it was his groin in Skinny's grip. He set my bag down. "Alright little missy, you watch yourself on that board from now on." He nodded his head at Skinny, a silent suggestion to let me go.

Skinny let go of my crotch and spun me around. He uncuffed me, leaned close to my ear and hissed, "Get your queer ass to school and don't let us see you causing any more trouble."

I wanted to shove him. Kick him in the balls. Anything to

relieve the anger and embarrassment I felt inside. Instead, I picked up my stuff and ran until I turned down the next cross street and out of their sight. I threw down my backpack at the base of a palm tree, choking on the tears and snot running down my throat. I set my board down and slumped down on top of it, my face in my hands, trying to get a grip. They couldn't hurt me. No one could. Then I threw up in the dirt at my feet, unable to swallow the line of crap I was feeding myself.

I stared at my vomit, growing angrier, still feeling his hands on me and hearing their derisive laughter eroding my pride. The Police—they were supposed to protect and serve. Not grope and humiliate. I choked down another sob, trying not to puke again. I cued up Rage Against the Machine's *Take the Power Back* onto my internal playlist—my way of steeling myself against the otherwise debilitating emotions trying to break me down.'

'Cause the circle of hatred continues unless we react
We gotta take the power back!

I closed my eyes and listened to the words of Zack de la Rocha screaming through my head, imploring me to take my own power back. Anger replaced humiliation. Anger was my power. The tears stopped. My heart rate slowed. I was in control.

I opened my eyes and looked at my watch—the one my Grandpa Frank gave me for my 14th birthday with a silver and black face and a black Velcro band. The fantastically-non-feminine watch said it was 7:25. I had to go. It was almost time for the AM meeting and, even though I wanted nothing more than to be alone today, if I missed the meeting, I'd get hassled by my crew. And I'd had about as much hassle as I could handle that day.

♠ ♥ ♣ ♦

"Wylie, hold up!" Cameron coasted down the curve of his driveway and down the block to catch up with me. "I've got a perfect fish for today's game. New kid. Name's Alex. Looks like he's got money." Cam was huffing and puffing like the big bad wolf at the third little pig's house, his blue eyes—just as wild. I let out a long exhale at the unwelcome intrusion, wishing I had just a few more minutes alone after the events of this morning.

"Yeah, I've seen 'im around. Alien skateboard? Matchstick Men graphic on the deck?" The sidewalk was about to turn to gravel, so we simultaneously hopped our skateboards off the sidewalk and onto the street. I wondered if our simultaneous board pops were a fluke or a function of our long history. For my money? A fluke.

"Same dude, man. I've got him first period." Cam confirmed, just as Chase, another member of our crew, rolled up behind us. He was more of a tag-along than a member, but we tolerated him most days.

"Uh, what's that? You got your first period? Uh, congratulations!" Chase blurted out, his two front teeth extending out from beneath his upper lip like a beaver. That, combined with his habit of saying "Uh" before every damn sentence, made him seem like a cartoon character who somehow got lost in reality. If you could call 9th grade 'reality.'

"Shut up, Chase. I swear to Christ I'm gonna kick your ass one of these days." Cameron faked like he was going to punch Chase in the face and almost fell off of his board. Chase feigned terror, but I know the little weasel's balls were prolly shrinking up. He ran from conflict faster than Flo-Jo, which was why we called him 'Tracky' when he was being particularly annoying. Which, was usually always.

I shook my head and pulled out a joint and lighter from my pocket. Officer Skinny was so caught up in what was between my legs that he forgot to search all of my pockets. So, he missed his chance to arrest me for possession. Asshole.

I lit up. The warm smoke replaced the cool spring air in my lungs. I pushed a few more times with my right leg to get more speed going before exhaling. I coasted about 100 yards as my body relaxed and I fantasized about winning another big pot at lunchtime. One step closer to leaving this shit town. One step closer to freedom. The farther away from home I got, the more I relaxed.

The three of us cruised through the neighborhoods on our way to Riverview High. No, we didn't go there. Not yet, anyway. My crew was all still in junior high school over at Chaparral. But every morning, we met under the football bleachers at the high school around the corner. We were the class of 2004, in our last semester of 9th grade. This had been our morning ritual since September. This is the AM meeting, where we started the day getting high and discussing our lunchtime game. Whoever brought in a good fish got a cut of everyone's winnings—ten percent. We'd had a lunchtime game of Texas Hold 'em going since 8th grade—a much better use of our lunch money than actually spending it on the crap they serve in the cafeteria. I mean really, have you seen the stuff they try to push on us? It's criminal.

Five minutes later we made it to the bleachers. We all popped up our boards and walked into the cool, shady hideout. Lamar was already there, his 8-inch tall afro waving impressively as he practiced pressure-flipping his board. He was the last piece of our four-member crew of skate hooligans. And the only black kid I'd ever seen on a skateboard.

The four of us sat on our boards in a circle on the ground, passing around the joint I procured the day before with some of my poker winnings. Weed was pretty easy for us to come by, especially in the canal, where us and some other locals skated every day. The canals were below street level and were as wide as a two-lane road, with angled, high walls—perfect for skateboarding without getting harassed. You could only get in if you knew where the entrance was, and the people that came to skate there were pretty selective about who they told. The canal was the site of the PM meeting, where twenty or so regulars showed off their skills and competed for bragging rights. Skateboarding and hanging with my crew were the only times I felt like I really belonged on this planet.

"Tracky, stop sucking on that joint like it's your tiny dick and pass it on!" Cameron held his hand out and Chase passed it, face red as he tried to hold his breath as long as possible.

Chase, tears bubbling from his eyes, finally released his breath. "Uh, someone woke up on the wrong side of the world today."

"Will you two give it a rest?" I was starting to lose my buzz. "Geez. Cam, do you think he'll play?"

"Yeah, I think so. I kinda mentioned that we like to play sometimes. He seemed interested. And, I've seen his wallet. There's always cash in it, so he's got the buy-in." Cam took a drag and passed the joint to Lamar.

The buy-in was ten bucks. I know—we rolled deep for 14-year-olds. We played as many hands as we could in the privacy of the 100-square-feet of concrete between the portables in the 45 minutes we had between fourth and fifth period. I won more than I lost, which kept me living at about the upper-middle poverty-class level.

"Yeah, but does he look like he'll keep his mouth shut when he loses everything?" Lamar interjected, smoke spewing from his mouth like a dragon that had lost its spark.

"Oh, he'll keep quiet. If he knows what's good for him. I'll make sure of it. Don't worry." Cameron rubbed his hands together, imagining himself more of an evil-genius than the dull brute that he was. Everyone's eyes rolled at that. Cameron liked to talk tough, but honestly, I'd never seen him beat up anyone in the almost-two-years that I'd known him.

Lamar, always thinking about the long-game, asked, "Ok then, how do you think we should play him? I mean, if he's got money, maybe we should string him along for a while, keep him coming back so we can keep skimming those bills off of him for longer."

Cam, as you can imagine, loved to see people broken. Fast. Sometimes, when I felt particularly desperate to get out of this town, I tended to side with Cam. But most of the time, like Lamar, I preferred the long play. Especially since we'd gone through just about everyone we could at Chaparral. It was nothing short of a miracle that no one told on us. We'd fried a considerable amount of fish in the past year and a half.

"I vote long play." I took the joint from Lamar and finished it off before squashing the half-inch long butt into the dirt.

"C'mon, let's break him today! Bet aggressively, drive up the stakes!" Cam was starting to look crazed again.

"Uh, uh, why so greedy, Cam? You got a hot date or something?" Chase's tongue was lolling around and his arms were embracing the air like he was making out with a ghost. He seriously didn't know when to keep his mouth shut. He could hold his own in a game of poker though. The little runt had taken a few dollars off of me, but I learned his tells since then and could always catch him in a bluff. Of course, he didn't know this.

"Why do you ask, Tracky? You jealous?" Cam flipped him off.

"You still sore I took your whole bankroll yesterday?" I shot Cam my best sardonic smile. "And the day before?"

Then he flipped me the bird. I held my smile.

Cam ignored me and pleaded, "Ok, if we're playing the long game, I say we bring out some mechanics. Maybe pull a double-duke."

I protested, "No way man. I'm not cheating." I didn't care if he was rich. I didn't need to cheat to win.

"I'm with Wylie. We play it straight, or not at all."

I could always count on Lamar.

Chase added, "Uh, yeah. We play it straight."

Cam's face was as red as his hair. He pushed Chase over into the dirt. "Don't be such a suck, Tracky."

I got up and grabbed my board. "Whatever man, we gotta go. First bell just rang." I hoisted my backpack onto my back, then reached my hand down to help Chase up, but Cam kicked him back down.

"Dude, seriously?" I got up in his face. "What is wrong with you today? You're being a douche." He wasn't usually this much of a dick to any of us.

"Uh, his step-dad probably, uh, kicked the crap out of him last night. N-nobody likes a red-headed stepchild." Chase taunted, lying on his back in the dirt.

"You little —" Cam lunged for Chase.

I held him back. "Tracky, shut up and get the hell out. Cam, stop." He pushed his chest against my hands. He may have outweighed me by 20-pounds, but I was pretty strong. "Lamar, get him out of here."

He helped Chase off the ground and they both scurried out towards the opening.

I kept my hands on Cam's chest. "Cam. Look at me. Stop."

He finally stopped pushing and stared at me. I could feel his heart pounding against my right hand.

I took a deep breath. "Chuck being a dick to you again?"

Cam nodded, jaw clenched. I had my own quasi-step-dad problems, but mine involved a crusade-like religious fanaticism rather than physical abuse. Sometimes, I wished they'd just hit me.

"Alright. Ok." I dropped my hands to my sides and reached into my pocket. "I snuck this from my mom's stash. Was saving it for the weekend but, seems like you need it more than me." I handed him an oblong, white pill—yet another thing Captain Grabby-hands failed to find on me.

"What's this?"

"Just a xannie. It'll chill you out. Just take it."

Cam popped the pill into his mouth and swallowed it as we headed out from under the bleachers and into the overcast morning. We both hopped on our boards and headed towards school. I loved the feeling of the wind rushing through my hair and the feel of my board "Aces" under my feet. I knew every crack and gap in the sidewalks in this whole town by heart. Every little jolt sent vibrations into my feet, through my legs, and up my spine. Each told a story of attempted escape from the home I call prison. Each bump represented more distance, more freedom, until ultimately, I would realize I had no way of supporting myself. On my return home, each bump signified defeat rather

12

than distance. I would fantasize about becoming a pro-skater and winning thousands of dollars. Then I could get out for good.

A few minutes later, Cam and I joined the rest of the stragglers running onto campus just as the second bell rang.

"Let's go folks. You've got two minutes to get to class. Get a move on!" Mrs. Sprag, the Vice-Principal, was out in front of the school, ushering in the last of us with the voice of a bullfrog and a look of disdain. I've never understood people who clearly hate kids, but spend their lives working with them.

"No skateboarding on campus! Don't make me confiscate those boards." Sprag's evil eye was trained on us as we cruised right by her. We hopped off for two steps—long enough for her to be satisfied we were doing what we were told before we hopped back on once her back was turned. Cam flipped her the bird. One of these days, his hand was going to freeze that way.

I left him alone in front of his English class and considered for a moment sneaking away to smoke another joint. This morning's bullshit still had me on edge.

"Masterson quit dawdling and get to class!" Sprag was directly behind me, ruining any chance I had to dart across the quad towards the PE field. "Off the board!"

Defeated, I picked up my board and jogged around the corner and into Computer Science 2, sliding into my seat just as the final bell rang.

The second-hand moved slowly around the dial of the plain-faced clock, massaging each number as it passed. The morning dragged on, unrelenting in its monotony. Computer Science… Environmental Science…English Lit…Algebra II. I solved for "x" for the last time that day and willed time to warp so that the bell would ring sooner.

I looked across the room over at the new kid, Alex. Yeah, he was in my Algebra II class. He just started here about a month ago. A skater—like me. Parents could obviously afford to buy him all the coolest gear. That's all I knew about him because he kept to himself all the time. He flipped his head so that his long, brown bangs swung out of his eyes as he put his pencil down, glanced at me and then up at the clock. I thought that perhaps with our combined brain power, we could alter time.

After several eternities, the shrill, mechanical bell released us from our morning of institutionalized learning. I jumped up from my seat at the back of the room, kicked my board up into my hands, and bolted out the door before Ms. Davidson could give us any last-minute reminders. I made a beeline to the back corner of the campus where the off-white portable classrooms were, stopping only for a moment at the soda machine to buy a Pepsi.

"Sweet board." A quiet voice emerged from behind me as I stooped down to fish out my bottle of caffeinated refreshment. I stood up and turned around. It was Alex.

"Thanks. I made it last year in wood shop."

"Can I see it?" He asked, holding his hand out.

I passed it over to him. His own board sat behind his back, cradled in the straps of his backpack. He turned mine over in his hands, examining the trucks I bought with two months of poker winnings and the lacquer job I spent three weeks per-fecting. The four playing cards hovering in the layers of resin. It was nothing fancy, but it was mine. And it was the coolest thing I'd ever made with my two hands. He stared at it like it was an antique—something to be revered. I felt pride welling up inside me.

"You're Wylie, right?" He returned the board to me, his eyes slowly moving from it to me.

"Yeah." I rested my board on top of the black high-top Vans I snagged from my brother two years ago.

"I'm Alex. Cameron said you'd show me where your game is." He flipped his bangs out of his eyes and looked down at me. He was just a few inches taller than me and almost as thin.

"Yeah. Come on." We rushed past the other students dutifully heading to the cafeteria. We were swimming upstream, but managed to make it to "The Pit" before the others, who all had PE fourth-period.

"So, you're new here." That's me, Captain Obvious, at your service.

"Uh, yeah."

"Where'd you come from?"

"San Francisco. My dad got transferred down here to manage a new division of his company, so I had to transfer here."

"You don't seem too happy about it."

"No. Not really." He looked directly at me, big brown eyes slightly obscured by his hair. I couldn't tell if he was pissed or forlorn.

"I don't blame you. This place is a shit hole."

Alex flashed a wry smile. I was starting to feel a little bad about leading him into the lion's den.

The rest of my crew finally arrived, joking around like they were best friends, which, they were, but after this morning, I figured things might be a little tense. Guess I was worried for nothing.

Cameron, playing the gracious host bowed to Alex. "Alex, nice of you to join us."

Alex just shrugged.

"Well, come on." He waved at us all to sit. We took our respective places in our daily circle. It was me, then Lamar, Chase, Alex, and Cam. Everyone's butt was on a board in the center of the space. Cameron whipped out the chips he nicked from Chuck, along with a deck of cards. Everyone put their $10 into the center of the circle. Cam swiped the bills and handed out the chips. Then he pulled out a white button that read "Skateboarding is not a crime" in black letters across it. This was to show who the dealer was at any point during our lunchtime tournaments. It also reminded me of my encounter with Shit Town PD this morning, which got me pissed off all over again.

As per our usual custom, high card was the dealer. Cam dealt five cards face up, conveniently dealing himself the highest card. If I didn't know better, I'd say he was dealing from the bottom of the deck. Wait, I did know better. I picked up the cards and handed them back to him with an unmistakable look of disapproval. He shrunk down a little. I was about ready to get up and walk away when he mumbled, "Sorry" under his breath.

"Just deal it straight." I hissed.

Cameron was the dealer, which meant I was the small blind and Lamar was the big blind. After Cam dealt two cards to each player, I put my fifty-cents into the pot and Lamar put his dollar into the pot to start the game. Cam then dealt The Flop - the first three community cards in the center of the circle. On the "table" was the 9 of Spades, 9 of Clubs and 2 of hearts. I had the 2 of spades and 2 of diamonds in my hand. Full House - not a bad first hand.

Chase looked at his cards, blew a puff of air out between pursed lips, and folded.

"That's right Tracky, let the big boys play." Cam taunted.

Alex raised $2.

"Somebody's proud of their hand." Lamar muttered.

Cam called, tapping his fingers on the top of the deck.

I stared at Alex, looking for any sign that he might be bluffing. I mean, could he have two nines? Is Cam that bad of dealer? I saw no tick though. No hint of a smile, nothing. Fine. I would draw him out.

"Raise $1." I then put $2.50 into the pot.

Lamar swore under his breath before folding.

Alex and Cam both called.

Cam dealt a 10 of Clubs. I was still looking at Alex. No change in his facial features. No foot or finger tapping. It was possible he could have four of a kind, which would beat my hand. But, I was feeling pretty good about my Full House.

"Raise $1." I dropped more chips into the pot.

"$2." Alex, stone-faced, dropped two dollar chips into the pot. I dropped another.

"Dammit." Cam threw his cards into the pot. He was out of the game.

"Uh, guess that means you're at the kids table with us now." Chase motioned at Lamar and himself.

Cam flipped him off.

There was just one more community card to deal - The River. Cam placed another 10 into play. I watched Alex for any sign of a reaction. Neither of us moved a single muscle. We didn't even blink.

"$5." I dropped my chips down, giddiness rising inside my belly. I looked Alex straight in the face.

"$10." He challenged, opening up his black leather wallet and pulling out more bills. I did the same.

"Beat that." I told Alex, as I flipped my cards over, Kool-Aid grin plastered across my face.

He flipped his own cards over. A Four of a Kind—9's. Shit! My stomach dropped like the ground just opened up and sucked me down into the depths of hell.

"You asshole!" I picked up my cards and flung them at Alex. My face flushed with anger and embarrassment. This is not how things usually go down.

"That was a bad beat man, but it happens." Alex shook his head and slid the contents of the pot towards himself, separating out the bills and stacking his chips.

"Awe, is wittle Willow gonna cry?" Cameron rubbed his eyes with his fists, pretending to cry. Chase mimicked him, laughing.

"Don't call me that, asshole. Gimme the cards. It's my deal."

"You can deal, but you can't play. You've got no chips." Cam handed me the deck. I grabbed my wallet, pulled out ten $1 bills and threw them at him. The last ten bucks I had left.

"Don't be a little bitch." Cam sneered, picking up my cash and sliding a stack of chips back over to me.

I shot Cam a look that I hoped conveyed that I was in no mood for his crap. I'd like to tell you that this hand turned things around for me, but I ended up folding the next two hands after losing almost all of my second buy-in. Alex was up. Way up.

By the last round, Chase and Cam were out of the game. I was broke. I mean, I didn't even have enough to cover the blinds, but I was determined that this would be my chance to win everything back. I couldn't start another week at zero again. I needed to build up my savings so I could get the hell out of here. I couldn't take another morning like today. With desperation expanding in my gut, I got up and grabbed my board.

"I'm all in." I set the board down in the middle of the circle before sitting back down on the concrete. My heart was pounding like there was someone beating on my chest from the inside—tiny fists trying to get my attention and save me from my own stupidity

"Fool, I haven't even dealt the cards yet." Lamar protested, though more out of concern for me than for game protocol.

"Then you better get on it." I snapped, sitting cross-legged on the ground, eyes on my handmade board. That board had been my escape, my confidante, for over a year. The thought of losing her turned my stomach.

Lamar dealt the cards.

With two aces in my hand, I was feeling a little better about things. But I still had this heavy feeling in the pit of my stomach as Lamar and Alex went through round after of round of betting. At that point, I was little more than a spectator. A spectator with everything on the line. They had increased the pot to more than we'd ever seen in a lunchtime tournament. If I won, this could be the start of my way out. If I lost, well, I'd be hoofing it into the foreseeable future. And I couldn't play until I saved up enough of my lunch money for the buy-in.

Anxiety had a firm grip on my guts as I watched them. Unless they were bluffing, I needed an ace in the River or I'd lose my board. Lamar threw down the last card. Both Alex and Lamar went all-in. We all flipped over our cards.

I didn't think my heart had the ability to shrink any more.

Lamar thought he had the game with 3-10's. Even that beat my two miserable aces. Alex thrashed both of us with a Flush, Kings high. Enraged, I jumped up, grabbed my bag and ran off in the direction of the soccer field to a chorus of jeers. I just caught Cameron mutter, "crazy dike" before I emerged from the alleyway between the portables.

The bell rang, beckoning us back to the drudgery. There was no way I could sit through AP World History today. I kept running, tears streaming down my face until I reached the fence on the far side of campus. There stood a big magnolia tree with a trunk just wide enough to hide me from anyone who might have been looking.

I threw my backpack on the ground and plopped down next to it. I wiped my eyes, cursing Alex and my so-called friends under my breath. And why was I crying so damn much lately? Reaching into the front pocket of my jeans, I found my last slightly crumpled joint and my lighter. I put the joint between my lips, lit it up and drew the smoke into my lungs, enough to feel them protest. I held my breath, feeling my heart rate decrease and a warmth spread through my chest. I exhaled, feeling that familiar dizziness that always proceeded the deep calm I sought. This was my spot. No one had ever caught me smoking here.

I could hear the cars rushing by on the freeway, less than a mile from here. The four of us sometimes liked to stand on the overpass and play "free vs. slave"—a game we made up to identify which cars held the commuters and which held people leaving this shit town for a better life. I wondered if I would ever get out of here. Away from Sybil, the mother figure, who was so obsessed with "appearances" that she was driving all of us to drugs, including herself. My older brothers thought it was funny, but they didn't get the full brunt of her and her boyfriend's extreme religiosity. Like, how is it that I always got hassled for wearing my brothers' clothes when it was perfectly fine for them to wear them? All of a sudden, it was a shameful sin that I wanted to look like a boy. Didn't everyone in biblical times wear robes? I doubt the women wore pink ones and men wore blue ones. Why the hell did Jesus care what kind of clothes I wore?

"Hey." Alex's voice interrupted my melancholy musings.

"What do you want?" I didn't even turn around. I wanted him to feel unwelcome, but I also didn't want him to see me crying.

"To see if you're okay." He came around to sit down in front of me. "And to give you this."

He put my board down between us, eyebrows raised underneath his unruly brown locks.

And look like a little bitch in front of my crew? No thanks. "No. You won it fair and square. Keep it."

I took another hit off my joint. But I didn't offer it to Alex. I just held my breath and stared at him.

"Look, I get it. You want to save face in front of your 'friends.'" He made little quote signs with his fingers. "Just... tell them you kicked my ass and took it back. I won't deny it."

He rolled the board in my direction. I exhaled in relief. Aces was a part of me. I considered his offer for a minute before reaching my foot out to slide my board closer to me. Maybe he's not such an asshole after all. I leaned forward, my arm outstretched to offer Alex a hit off my joint.

"Truce?" He asked, taking the small, white roll-up from me and taking a draw.

I shrugged. It's not like we were at war or anything. I stared at him as he exhaled. What was he playing at? Something inside me wanted to trust him—wanted him to be worthy of my trust. Mostly, I was just thankful to have my board back so I could escape from my life. Man I wish I'd stayed in bed today.

We sat in silence for some time before Alex spoke again. "Why did Cameron call you a dike?"

I didn't answer immediately. It's complicated. At least for me. I mean, yeah, I like chicks, especially Brianna, not that she'd ever look at me. I took another hit, considering whether I could trust him. I clearly couldn't trust Cam. That's for damn sure.

I studied Alex for a minute, then took the leap. "Cam thinks I'm a lesbian."

Alex looked confused. "I thought you were a guy."

I smiled inwardly. I worked hard to look like a dude. Not that it's that hard when you're flat-chested and almost skeleton-thin. My brothers' hand-me-down clothes were baggy enough to hide any minor curves I might have been developing. "Thanks."

"I'm sorry?" Alex seemed confused.

"No, seriously, thanks. I want to look like a guy." I wanted to be a guy, actually, but those prayers were never answered. So I stopped praying.

"Oh. So you're trans then?"

"Huh?"

"You're transgender. You were born a girl, but feel like a guy."

"Yeah..." I said slowly. "How do you know how I feel?"

"My mom's a psychiatrist therapist type. Specializes in gender stuff. Talks about it all the time. She's got trans friends. We hang out sometimes." He looked out over the field adjacent to campus. "At least, we did before we moved here." He trailed off as he reached over to take the joint from me. He took another hit, then released the smoke slowly from his mouth. "There's transgender people all over the place in San Francisco."

"I've never heard that word before. I didn't know other people felt like this." I was suddenly really glad I didn't kick his ass earlier.

"Yeah, it's a real thing. People go on hormones like testosterone to lower their voices and grow hair on their faces. There's even surgeries you can have."

"Seriously?" I couldn't believe something like this wasn't common knowledge. Or was I just some simpleton living in a backwards part of the world? My mind was racing a mile a minute. How many other people are like me?

"Oh yeah, there was a movie about a transgender guy out last year. Boys Don't Cry. You didn't see that?"

"Nah. Looked like a chick-flick."

Alex shrugged. "You should come over some time though. Talk to my mom. She's pretty cool—for a mom, that is." He gave me a sly smile. "Don't tell her I said that though. I'm trying to encourage her to embrace 'detachment theory' parenting."

I wanted to shout, 'yeah, let's go now' but I restrained myself. Alex handed me back the joint so I could finish it off, which I did. By the time the bell rang ending fifth period, all anger at losing everything I had to Alex at lunch was replaced by excitement over the reality that there are others like me. Maybe I wasn't such a freak. Did he mean I could actually be able to live my life as a guy?

I looked over at Alex and was hit with a pang of guilt. "You know, Cam only invited you to play today because he thought you'd be an easy mark."

He smiled. "I know."

"I didn't exactly try to stop him." I hung my head down. "Sorry."

"It's all good." He slapped me on the leg with the back of his hand. "You planning on going to 6th?"

I thought about it for a moment. Looking around the tree trunk, I could see kids milling around in the distance, making their way to the final class of the day. They felt a million miles away.

"Naw. You wanna skate?" I asked, eyeing my board.

"Hell yeah." Alex grinned and picked himself up off the ground.

We climbed over the chainlink fence behind school and ran

through the dirt field until we reached the road. We jumped on our boards, enjoying the rhythmic clunk of our wheels on the uneven pavement as we put more distance between us and campus.

2

Alex

It was hard to keep a straight face knowing I was sitting on a Flush. I felt a little bad, because Wylie seemed to be taking this pretty seriously. I mean, he even put his handmade board in the pot. It was hard to fully enjoy the moment when we all showed our cards because I could tell how bad he felt. I was about to tell him he could keep his board when he ran off. I probably should have expected that. But still, I was a little hurt. I didn't do anything mean. I just...won. So much for making friends. It had been a lonely month since I transferred down here from San Francisco.

The Inland Empire. That's what this place is called. I'm not sure who would have fought to conquer this "empire." A fool, no doubt. I had stopped calling it *The Evil Empire*. At least around my parents. They got tired fast about me complaining about the move all the time. About a week ago we had a bit of a blow-out about it. Well, by blow-out, I mean we had "a civil family meeting where everyone was encouraged to talk about their feelings and reach an understanding." So, me, my mom and my dad sat down and I told them how much this place sucked. Then they told me how much my attitude was sucking the light out the whole adventure. That was my mom's take on all this.

"Think of it as an *adventure*." She said. "While it may not be as 'cool' as San Francisco, there are opportunities for you here to meet different people. Experience different things."

I rolled my eyes at that. If that's the best thing you can say about this place is that there are "different people" and "different things"—that's pretty sad.

"Come on bud." My dad said. "No eye-rolling, we've talked about that. You're much too intelligent to resort to such base forms of communication."

He was right. I had been sulking ever since they told me about my dad's big promotion and that we would be moving. To be honest, I was getting a bit sick of myself.

"Fine." I stood up. "I'll give it a chance. Can I go play Legend of Zelda now?" While my parents weren't big on bribing me for good behavior, they did cave and buy me a PlayStation and a 36-inch TV for my room. I didn't want them to take *that* away just because I was being stubborn.

"Crazy dike." Cam muttered. "What have I told you guys about letting *that* one into our fold?"

Chase and Lamar just nodded. I was confused. And let down. Of all the guys in that group though, Wylie seemed like the nicest, even if he did call me an asshole for legit winning. I got up to follow him.

"Hey, where ya going?" Cam called out. "Yo, same time tomorrow."

I ignored him and made my way out of the portable classroom maze. I saw Wylie running out towards the back end of campus and duck behind a giant tree. The bell indicating 5th period rang out across the field. I stopped for a second, contemplating whether it was better to go to class or to make sure Wylie was ok. Language Arts could wait. A little voice inside told me I should talk to him. Now. I got a better grip on the two boards I was holding and headed out after him again.

As I approached the big tree, I got a strong whiff of weed. Well, at least he'd be calmer and wouldn't try to knock me down again. I saw him sitting at the base of the tree. It looked like he'd been crying.

"Hey." I said.

"What do *you* want?" He didn't even look at me. His tone said 'go away.'

"To see if you're okay." I sat down in front of him, a few feet away. "And to give you this." I put his board down between us.

He stared daggers at me. "No. You won it fair and square. Keep it."

I got it. Cam would give him crap about begging for his board back. I knew him well enough to figure that out. "Look, I get it—you want to save face in front of your friends." And I use the terms "friends" loosely. "Just...tell them you kicked my ass and took it back. I won't deny it." I've got nothing to prove to those jerks.

I rolled the board closer to him. I saw a flicker of something like hope or gratitude or something in his face. He stuck his foot out, still staring at me, and pulled his board closer. Then, he reached his arm out and offered me his joint. Yes! Look at me mom, making friends!

"Truce?" I felt my eyebrows raise as I took the joint. If this was a peace offering, how could I say no? I took a long draw and held my breath, waiting for him to say something. He didn't. I exhaled, wondering what to say next. Then I remembered Cam's snide comment when Wylie ran away. "Why did Cameron call you a dike?"

He looked down at his hands. After a while he said, "Cam thinks I'm a lesbian."

Wait, what? "I thought you were a guy."

I started scrutinizing his face and body, trying to find some sort of gender-determinant factor I could cling to so I could categorize and move on, like a good explorer in a foreign land.

Wylie smiled. It was the first time I'd seen him smile that day. "Thanks."

Shit. Was that a real 'thanks' or one of those sarcastic 'thanks' that actually means 'go fuck yourself?'

He must have been reading my mind because then he said, "No, seriously, thanks. I want to look like a guy."

Ahhhh. Now this, I think I understand. "Oh. So you're trans then?"

"Huh?"

"You're transgender. You were born a girl, but feel like a guy." How could he not know this?

Wylie cocked his head at me. It looked like something had clicked in his head too. "How do you know how I feel?"

I explained to him how my mom's a psychologist that specializes in gender issues and how sometimes, that's all she freaking talks about. It was interesting though. I mean, she had a bunch of friends that were transgender—guys and girls. I got to hang out with them in The City. They were cool people. I suddenly felt bad for trying so hard to assign a gender to him. I'd seen how much that can hurt.

Wylie shook his head. "I've never heard that word before. I didn't know other people felt like this."

That's because you probably grew up in this ass-backwards town where they probably only recently discovered fire. Ok wait, that was mean. I really had to stop dogging on this place so hard. I could feel Wylie's mood get a little better. I tried to imagine what it would be like to feel like I was a girl. It was hard for me to do.

"Yeah, it's a real thing. People go on hormones like testosterone to lower their voices and grow hair on their faces. There's even surgeries you can have." I remembered talking with Roger, a trans guy my mom knew. He was pretty open about his transition and talked to me a lot about what he went through to look and feel more like a guy.

Wylie smiled again. "Seriously?"

"Oh yeah, there was a movie about a transgender guy out last year. *Boys Don't Cry*. You didn't see that?" Oh fuck. Why did I mention that movie? The guy gets killed at the end *and* it's based on a true story. Smooth move Alex. I had a bad habit of speaking before thinking, as my mom liked to point out.

I told him he should come talk to my mom sometime. He seemed to be interested in doing that. My mom loved to help people. She had a big heart. I felt bad for giving her so much crap over this whole moving thing. I made a vow to myself to be better to her.

We finished off Wylie's joint as the 6th period bell rang. I was starting to feel a bit goofy. PE sounded like a bad idea. Why play kickball though, when you can skate?

"You planning on going to 6th?" I slapped him on the leg.

Reading my mind. "Naw. You wanna skate?"

We hopped the fence and made our way through the tall, brown weeds and out to the main road. Wylie led me to some run down neighborhood a few blocks away, to a house that looked like it was abandoned.

"Come on." He stepped off his board, popped it up and led me around the side of the house and through a gate.

I looked around to make sure no one saw us. The last thing I needed was to get arrested for trespassing. I'd lose my PlayStation for sure. We walked to the backyard where, in the ground, sat a dry, kidney-bean-shaped pool. Wylie turned and looked at me, shot me a big smile and dropped into the deep end of the pool, banking along the vertical walls and up the slope to the shallow end and back around again. I was impressed. I'd never skated in a pool before. Not many of those in SF. My mom's words echoed back at me— "Think of it as an *adventure...* Experience different things."

I smiled inwardly and dropped in to join my new friend. We showed off for each other for a little over an hour. He was really good. When I told him that, he said, "Thanks. I want to go pro. Get the hell out of this shit town."

I did an ollie up the incline towards the shallow end. "Do you compete?"

Wylie performed a perfect acid drop from the top step of the pool and raced past me in the other direction. He banked back and stopped next to me. "Only in the canal. Most comps are in LA or SD. Been trying to save up enough money for bus rides."

"Your mom won't take you?"

"Ah that's right, you haven't met my mom." He looked at his watch.

I felt a stab of guilt for taking all his cash off of him at lunch. I didn't think he would take it back if I offered. I didn't need it, but I didn't want to insult him. "You guys don't get along?"

Wylie shrugged. "Not really. It's prolly my fault. If I would just act the way she wants me to act—like her little princess, I have the feeling we'd get along just fine."

"What about your dad?"

He picked up a stick that had blown into the pool and threw it onto the sidewalk. "Not around."

I felt like he was getting bummed again. I didn't know what to do, other than to change the subject. "What's the canal?"

"I'll show you tomorrow." He headed towards the stairs. "I gotta go. My mom's prolly gonna be pissed I'm not home already." He turned to leave.

I ran up the stairs after him. "Hey, what's your number?"

Wylie hesitated then pulled a sharpie out of his backpack and grabbed my hand. Across my forearm he scrawled the numbers: 714-687-5999.

"Late." He capped the pen, grabbed his backpack and board and ran out the side gate.

"Hey mom, I'm home!" I called out as I slammed the front door.

"In the kitchen." Came her disembodied voice, along with sounds of chopping.

I tucked my board behind the couch and dropped my bag on the floor. In the hallway, I caught a glimpse of my sweaty self in the mirror. My hair was so wet I might as well have gone swimming in that pool. I ran my hand through it on the way to the kitchen to get it out of my face.

"Hi sweetie. How was your day?" My mom was chopping carrots—my favorite after-school snack.

I snagged one off of the cutting board and dunked it into the cup of Thousand Island dressing before snapping the thing in two with my teeth. I leaned up against the counter, chewing, while she finished chopping. I was starving, so I noshed another two before answering her question.

31

Between bites. "It was...interesting."

She raised an eyebrow. "Interesting? How?"

"I think I made a friend." I felt a smile spread across my face.

Pointing to my arm with her chopping knife. "Is that her number on your arm?"

I looked down and laughed. I forgot Wylie's number was there.

"Yeah. I mean, no." I stammered. "She's trans. No. He's trans." Sometimes I got the terminology confused.

She smiled. "So he was born with female sexual characteristics, but presents as a male?"

Yeah—what she said. I nodded my head, chewing on another orange stick.

"Well, that's fantastic news, sweetheart." She put the knife down and waved for me to sit down at the dining room table. "How did you two meet?"

I told her about Cam and the poker game and how Cam had called Wylie a dike. I didn't tell her about the joint, or about ditching two periods. Not that I really thought she'd have a real problem with one or the other, but both may be pushing it. My parents always encouraged me to experience all that I can, but to make good choices. I'm not sure if all of my choices were good today, but hey, I'm still alive.

"Well, I would love to meet Wylie. Why don't you invite him over after school tomorrow?"

"Yeah, maybe. We may stop and skate for a while first. Is that cool?"

"Of course. And, you'll be returning that money you took from him as well." She got up to get some iced tea.

"Mom, no."

"Alex, yes. I don't like the idea of you gambling and you don't need his money." She set a glass down for each of us.

"I know I don't need it, but if I give it back he'll be offended." Geez, did she want me to lose my first Evil Empire friend the first week I got one?

She looked at me for a long moment. "Invite him to dinner tomorrow."

Cool. That meant she wouldn't push it. I got up and gave her a hug. "Will you make bacon mac and cheese?"

She pushed me away. "Yes, and you'll have a salad too, mister. Now go take a shower. The neighbors can probably smell you."

"Don't carrots count as salad?" I smiled.

"Last time I checked, you needed at least two vegetables to call it a salad. And besides, you're going to turn orange one of these days."

I grabbed my stuff and headed upstairs to my room. I copied Wylie's number down into my notebook so I wouldn't lose it before jumping in the shower. As the water washed away the sweat of the afternoon, I debated whether I should call Wylie tonight and invite him over, or if I should just ask him tomorrow. He'd probably have to ask his mom for permission, so I should probably do it sooner rather than later. Once I got out and dried off, I dialed his number. A young, male voice answered.

"Um hi. Is Wylie there?"

"Willow!" The voice yelled out.

I pulled the phone away from my ear.

"Your boyfriend's on the phone!"

I heard scuffling in the background, then Wylie's voice - "Hello?"

We had a stilted, awkward conversation where I asked if he could come over for dinner tomorrow and meet my parents. He seemed reluctant, which confused me because earlier it seemed like he really wanted to meet my mom.

"Can I let you know tomorrow?" He asked.

"Oh, yeah. Of course." Then I remembered that his mom wasn't terribly cooperative. "My mom can bring you back home, if that's an issue."

Wylie was quiet for a minute. "Yeah, that would probably be a good idea."

"Yeah. Ok." I said. "I'll see you tomorrow."

I had barely gotten the words out before I heard the dial tone. I set the phone back in its cradle and laid back onto my bed, staring at the Star Trek Next Generation poster on my ceiling and wondering if maybe he had changed his mind about being friends. I hoped not. Today was the first really good day I'd had since I moved here.

The guy on the phone called him Willow. That must be what Cam meant earlier. When I talked to Cam yesterday, he referred to Wylie as his "best man." What a two-faced dick.

Speaking of dicks, my best-friend, Pete, still hadn't emailed me. We promised to do it everyday, but that didn't last more than a week. I called him last weekend and we talked for a few minutes, but he had friends over and was kinda distracted. It felt like he had already replaced me. I guess it was probably normal. Out of sight, out of mind. Didn't mean it hurt less.

3

Wylie

"Who was that on the phone dear?" My mom called from the couch where, as per usual, she spent the day watching lame soap operas and talk shows. Actually, she'd been sitting there when I got home. When I walked in 15 minutes late, she was mildly pissed, but left me alone the rest of the afternoon, which I was grateful for because I couldn't stop thinking about what Alex said today.

They could actually make me into a real guy. I tried to imagine myself with a mustache. No—a goatee. Nobody would ask me if I was a boy or a girl anymore. Not the kids at school. Not the cops. I pushed down the sick feeling I got when I thought about this morning's encounter. I could be a real guy. My voice could get deep like my older brother Mason's was. And surgeries? Did that mean I could have real…guy…junk?

"Willow! Who was on the phone?" Sybil's voice grated from my eardrums down my spine.

I turned and walked into the living room. "Just a friend."

"Which friend."

"You don't know him. He's new at school."

"And what is this new friend's name?" She turned the volume down on the TV so that the laugh track of whatever sitcom she was now watching sounded like it was reacting to our talk, and broke a piece of chocolate bar off in its wrapper before popping it into her mouth.

I summoned my "best daughter" attitude and sat down on the floor. Might as well have a convo about him. Maybe she'd let me go to his place for dinner. "His name's Alex. He moved here from San Francisco."

"San Francisco? His parents must be rich!"

I didn't understand what that had anything to do with anything. "I don't know. His mom's a psychologist and his dad—" I tried, but failed to remember if Alex told me. "I don't know what his dad does, but he just got a promotion and they had to move here."

"They sound rich." Another square of chocolate disappeared into her mouth. She didn't seem at all concerned that she's going to ruin her dinner. Oh wait, that's my job. Cue laugh track.

"How did you two meet? Is he cute?"

It took a herculean effort not to roll my eyes. She was always trying to get me interested in guys. Sorry, not gonna happen lady. "He's in my Algebra class. He's a skater, like me."

Her face fell. "He's just going to think you're one of the boys. Ladies do not skateboard. Why don't you try those roller blades I got for you at that yard sale?"

Hello? Earth to crazy bitch—when are you going to get it through your ammonia-soaked head that I AM NOT A LADY?!?!?

I took a deep breath. "He invited me to dinner with his parents tomorrow night. Can I go?"

She thought for a moment. "I don't know. That sounds like a date to me."

I was about to lose it. First, she practically pimps me out to any boy that is remotely good-looking, then she gets cold feet about me dating? It felt like my brain cells were short-circuiting. "Mom! It's not a date. He's new at school and has no one to hang out with. We're just friends. Plus, his parents would be there. What kind of date is that?" At that point, I wasn't sure whether it was better to argue that is was a date or that it wasn't a date. "Oh yeah, and his mom can bring me back home, so you don't have to worry about picking me up."

Whether it was the promise of parental supervision to ensure my virginity or that she wouldn't be inconvenienced, I don't know, but she agreed to let me go. I was so excited I did something completely uncharacteristic and jumped up and hugged her. Her face looked pleasantly shocked.

"I was thinking Hamburger Helper for dinner. What do you say?" She asked me as I was about to walk to my room.

I knew that was code for: make us Hamburger Helper for dinner. "Fine." I made a u-turn and headed for the kitchen. "Will Roy be joining us?" Roy was my mom's asshole boy-friend who took more from our table than he brought to it.

"Not tonight dear, he's watching the game at Friday's."

Fantastic. That means he won't eat half the food and expect the four of us to share what's left over.

I scrubbed last night's dinner from the big frying pan and set it on the flame to heat up. I grabbed a pound of hamburger meat from the fridge and threw it in. The whole time the beef was sizzling on the stove, I was imagining what it would be like talking to Alex's mom. Would she be able to tell me more about the whole transgender thing? I wondered if I might get to meet some of her trans friends. Would she be able to tell me why I am the way I am?

I was barely present through dinner and dreamed my way

through dishes. I couldn't get the thought out of my head that I wasn't alone in feeling like I did. When I fell asleep, I dreamed about graduating from high school—as a boy.

♠ ♥ ♣ ♦

I knew even before I got to the bleachers the next morning that no one would be there. Cam and Chase had always met me on Cam's street. Always. For two years. But on this day, I skated alone. I wanted to confront Cam about what he said about me yesterday. That's no way for a friend to act. Especially after all I'd done for him. I mean, I knew he was having a bad day yesterday because of his step-dad, but still—I think it would be safe to say *mine* was worse.

When I arrived to find our meeting spot empty, it left me with a hollow feeling inside. I just stood there trying to understand why all-of-a-sudden, I was out. This was my crew. We were a team. We had each others' backs. Or...maybe we didn't. Maybe I was stupid to think that they actually accepted me. Could I have been that blind?

The first bell rang out in the distance.

Screw them. I got on my board and headed in the direction of school filled with a strange mixture of anger at my crew and excitement about going to Alex's house tonight. I couldn't wait for fourth period so I could tell Alex my mom said 'yes.'

As I got closer to campus, I could see Cam's unmistakable red hair weaving in and out of the cars full of kids and their parents who just wanted to get out of the parking lot and get to work. Then I saw Lamar's afro behind him and, every once in a while, Chase's head would bob up in between the cars.

And then, my heart sank. Skating alongside Cam, was Alex. Seriously?

I couldn't believe they'd just up and replaced me with someone else. And Alex? He talked a good game, but obviously he couldn't be trusted either. I showed him my own secret skate spot and everything. I was going to take him to the canal today. That fucking traitor!

I was so pissed I started skating faster, dodging other students on the sidewalk. I would take the side entrance to avoid the whole-rotten-lot of them.

Then, I heard wheels behind me. "Looks like wittle Willow got her wittle skateboard back." I heard Cam yell as they closed in on me. "Did you go crying to Alex so he'd give it back?"

Chase was laughing along with Cam. Lamar gave me a sad look.

I stopped, kicked up my board and turned around. "What the fuck is it to *you* man?"

Cam stepped up and got in my face. "You watch how you talk to me, *Willow*."

I dropped my shit and pushed him as hard as I could. "I've told you before—don't fucking call me that, asshole."

I managed to knock him backwards a few steps, but he quickly recovered and stalked back over towards me and put his finger in my face. "I'll call you anything I damn well please, loser."

I slapped his hand away just as Alex rolled up. "Hey, what's going on?" He hopped off his board and walked over towards us.

"This doesn't concern you, Alex." Cam had his face inches from mine. His hands were clenched in fists by his sides.

"Yeah, piss off." I snarled at him.

Alex stopped and looked at me, confused. "Look, I think everyone just needs to calm down." He took a step closer to

Cam and I, who were still trying to kill each other with the invisible daggers we were shooting from our eyes. Having Alex here was confusing everything. I was mad, and even though I didn't want to admit it to myself, I was hurt. I could feel tears starting to well up in my eyes, which made me even more mad.

"No, I just need to teach this loser dike a lesson." Cam pushed me. Hard.

I fell backwards on my ass.

Alex stepped in between us. "Back off Cameron."

Cam looked at Alex. "You taking this loser's side?" He jutted his thumb in my direction. "You know, you're either with us, or against us."

"Then it looks like I'm against you." Alex shoved passed Cam. He held his hand out to me and helped me up off the ground, then helped me gather my things. Together, we walked towards the main quad.

"Whatever man. You can go be losers together." Cam yelled after us. "Alex, you could have had a spot with the winners. Remember that."

"Ignore him." Alex pulled me forward when I tried to go back after Cam.

I realized that a crowd had gathered, as they usually did when there was a fight starting. Some of them I knew, including Brianna, the girl I'd been crushing on all year. She turned away when she saw me looking at her and started talking with her friends. I felt the tears start again. This was too much. I pulled away from Alex and ran off so I could be alone.

"Wylie, wait!" I heard him yell, but I kept running.

After spending the past three years there, I knew the campus inside and out. I found one of my hiding places behind the math building and ducked down under a window AC unit. I sat there and cried. I cried through the two-minute warning bell. And the final bell. I wished that I could just melt into the dirt. Then I wouldn't have to face everyone. Then they would forget about me. I fished two small pills from my pocket—a double-dose of Xanax—their shapes distorted by my tears. I couldn't keep ditching classes. They'd call my mom. I'd never hear the end to how I 'shamed the family' and how mortified she is to be my mother. I popped the pills into my mouth and swallowed them. That action, something I could control, made the tears stop.

When I finally felt like I *was* actually melting, I got up and walked to class. I liked the way they made me feel— light and floaty. I felt like I was disintegrating. Invisible. I needed to be invisible today.

I slogged into Computer Science and sat down. My teacher was bent over someone else's shoulder with his back to the door, so he didn't see me sneak in. I booted up my iMac computer and stared at the screen while it woke up. Then, I fell asleep, only to be awakened by the girl sitting next to me who was apparently disturbed by the pool of drool expanding on my keyboard.

I floated through my next two classes, having only one minor run-in with Cam. He dropped a shoulder on me before 3rd period, nearly knocking me over. I was too dazed to do anything about it, so I just ignored him.

Alex looked relieved when he saw me walk through the door fourth period. He crossed the room to come talk to me before the final bell rang. "Hey." He sat down in the empty desk across from me. "You ok?"

"Yeah." I sighed. I didn't know what to think about Alex at the moment. I mean, he did stand up to Cam this morning. And he did take my side. But then again, Cam and the crew used to be on my side too. Everything was just so confusing. I couldn't think about it.

"You sure? You look a little drunk or something."

"I said I'm fine." I sat up straighter, but my body wouldn't cooperate. I slumped back down again.

Alex looked at me for a moment like he was about to say something when the bell rang. He closed his mouth and went back to his desk.

I dozed in and out during Algebra II, barely registering that the bell had rung, telling us to go to lunch. Alex came back over before I could get up.

"Come on." He picked up my board before I could and led me outside. I waited for him while he grabbed us something from the snack bar and we walked out to the field to "our spot" underneath the magnolia tree.

"What were you doing with Cam this morning?" I asked him once we'd sat down.

He handed me a cheese roll-up. "What do you mean?"

"This morning. I saw you guys skating together. And they didn't meet me like they alway do." I choked down a small bite of the congealed cheese wrapped in a tortilla.

"It was nothing. Wanted to make sure I was gonna join them for the lunch game." He looked me straight in the eyes. "I told them no."

I wanted to believe him. I also really wanted to lay down in the dirt and go to sleep.

"Forget about them Wylie." I think he could tell I wasn't convinced. "Did you ask your mom about tonight?"

I had totally forgotten about dinner. Should I go? I really wanted to talk to his mom. But what if Alex was just as two-faced as Cam? But then, he did stand up for me earlier. In front of everyone. That says something, I guess.

"Hello? Earth to Wylie?" Alex waved his hand in front of my face. "What are you on man?"

"Yeah, sorry." I guess I had been quiet for a while. "She said I could come if your mom brings me back home."

Alex smiled. "You wanna just come over after school?"

I nodded. That would make it easier. And it would keep my mom from dictating my clothing for the evening. Then I remembered I had promised to take Alex to the canal today. I wondered if Cam and the others would be there today. I hoped not.

We sat in silence for a while. I took a couple more bites of my cheese-wrap, but my eyes were so heavy, they kept closing and I would doze off in between chews.

"Dude, what are you on?" Alex pushed me slightly on the shoulder the second time it happened.

I looked around, confused for a minute. "Um, just a couple xannie." I shrugged. "No big deal."

Alex looked at me for a second, maybe trying to figure out what to say to me. He just shook his head and looked out at the field beyond the fence. I was too tired to care if he disapproved.

4

Alex

I looked at Wylie sitting slumped over next to the tree. I'd
seen plenty of people like that in The City. Mostly homeless people. It kinda scared me to see my friend like that. I
didn't know what else to do, so I just let him sleep for the
rest of lunch. I hoped he'd feel better tonight. I had a surprise
for him.

My mom brought up the poker money again last night. I
made her a deal that I would use the money to buy Wylie a
bus ticket to the LA skate competition coming up, since that
was what he was saving for anyway. She got that goofy look
on her face again, the one she gets when she's proud of me. It's
kind of embarrassing when she does it, but at least no one else
was around. I gave her the money and she promised to go by
the bus station today and pick up a round trip ticket so I could
give it to him tonight.

The first bell rang out across the field. Groups of students
got up from spots they had staked out months ago and began
filing into 5th period. Wylie didn't move.

"Hey man, wake up." I gave him a little shove.

Wylie stirred and opened his eyes. "Wha—?" He almost fell over.

I rolled my eyes and popped open a can of Pepsi then handed it to him. "Drink. All of it." Maybe the sugar rush would wake his ass up. I watched as he chugged the contents of the can, letting out a huge belch that seemed to echo across campus. We laughed.

"You awake now?" I heaved my backpack onto my back while Wylie picked himself up off the ground.

He smiled. "Awake enough to kick your ass."

"You'll have to catch me first." I took off running full-speed towards the classrooms on the other side of the school. I looked back and saw Wylie grab his board and start after me, but my lead was too great for him to catch up. We ran across the concrete basketball courts and into the main quad before slowing down to avoid the masses of students milling around. The second bell rang, warning us to get to class immediately.

Wylie caught up to me, breathless. "Meet me out front after school. I'll take you to the canal."

I nodded and made my way through the hallway to Computer Science class—my favorite one, by far. I managed to sneak a look at my email account, but still nothing from Pete. I wanted to talk to him about Wylie. Hell, about anything, really. Was he just not going to talk to me now that I don't live 5-minutes away? I sighed and logged out before I got caught. Student's weren't supposed to log into email or chat rooms on school computers. The administration was too frightened of viruses crashing the system. I suppose it's a valid fear, but I swear, they think we're all a bunch of hackers here.

I was too preoccupied thinking about Wylie and Pete to be productive in 5th. I even sucked at kickball during 6th period, even though I was actually pretty good at the game. I was starting to get mad at Pete. I know my mom said it's natural for friends to lose touch, but we were best friends. We did everything together. We even got to second base on the same day—at the same movie. That was the week before we moved down here. Could my parents have had worse timing? I mean, finally, I get some action going and they decide to move me 500 miles away. How's a guy expected to get to third base with that many miles between us? Not that the extra time would have really made much difference, since Mandy ended up breaking up with me for some guy named Matt three days later. But Liz was still there, in the wings. And I heard she went all the way with Nick last month. She was a sure-thing.

Thinking about Liz and the prospect of advancing my position on the great field of sexual exploration was getting me hard—not the kind of thing I liked to happen in the locker room. I made myself think about something else: brussels sprouts, Roseanne Barr, anything I could. That seemed to do the trick. I slid on my jeans, hoping nobody had seen me. As the last bell of the day rang out, I grabbed my stuff and bolted out the door to meet Wylie.

I saw him standing in the grass off the main sidewalk. Well, that was a good sign—at least he was able to stand, which means he was not as drugged up as he was at lunch. I knew I needed to talk to him about taking Xanax. I just didn't really know how to do it.

"Hey man, you ready?" Wylie flipped his hair out of his eyes, which seemed more alive than they were before, and started walking towards the street.

We dropped our boards down and hopped on. I followed him about a half-mile to a street that looked like it was separated by a bunch of large bushes. As we turned down that street, I noticed a small clearing in the bushes and a chain-link fence. Wylie led me towards the clearing. I followed him as he spread the broken links apart and squeezed his body through. On the other side was the canal—a big concrete indentation in the ground that looked like it could contain a raging river if necessary. About 10 or so skaters were already there, showing off for each other by doing more complex tricks than the person before them. From the outside, you wouldn't even know that anyone was here.

A guy I'd never seen before rolled up and performed an elaborate handshake with Wylie. "What up Y-dog?"

"Nada, Z." They ended their handshake with their thumb and forefingers up to their lips like they were smoking a joint. I wondered if that was an official 'secret handshake' for the canal. I hoped not. That seemed lame.

"Who's that?" The skater known as 'Z' cocked his head in my direction.

"Alex. He's cool." Wylie motioned for me to come over.

"X-man. Sweet." Z motioned like he was tipping a top-hat on his head before dropping down into the canal to join the others. Wylie smiled at me, then disappeared after him.

I watched them for a minute before dropping my backpack and dropping in—launching myself up the other side to do a front-side 5-0 at the top before coming back down. Wylie and I took turns challenging each other to more and more difficult moves and combos. It was so rad—nothing like the scene up north. Once in a while, someone else would drop in and propose a new combo and we'd follow along or counter with another, even more sick combination that sometimes ended with someone skidding on their ass down the side of the canal. Someone showed up with a boom-box blaring Damian Marley's *Welcome to Jamrock*. All-in-all, it was a good vibe.

48

Then, Cam showed up. Shit got real. Fast.

"What are you losers doing here?" Cam announced as he surveyed the scene. "This is a loser-free zone."

"Yeah, this is a loser-free zone, losers." Chase cackled next to Cam.

I knew they were talking about me and Wylie, who stopped dead in his tracks when he saw them. Could they get less original?

"Come on Cam, give it a rest." I hopped off my board and kicked it up into my hand. Before I could blink, Cam dropped down into the canal straight towards me, tackling me. We slammed to the ground. I felt a stabbing pain in my ass as I hit the pavement. Cam's weight knocked the wind out of me. I gasped for air, finding none. My heart raced.

Cam landed a punch right in my stomach, keeping me from getting a breath. "You don't talk to me, loser. You understand?" He raised his fist and was about to bring it down on my face when all of a sudden, someone rolled in hard and fast. Wylie launched himself onto Cam, knocking him off of my body.

I could hear yelling all around me as I struggled to breathe. Finally, I was able to take a couple of deep breaths. I wiped the uninvited tears from my face and sat up to find Wylie on top of Cam, fists flying at his face. Chase was screaming for Cam to get up and kick Wylie's ass. Cam, blood pouring from his nose, managed to fling Wylie off of his chest. Wylie toppled over Cam's head.

Cam stood up, his face bright red. "I'm gonna kill you motherfucker." He kicked Wylie hard in the stomach and was about to punch him in the face when Z tackled Cam from behind.

I'm guessing Z was in high school because he was a lot

bigger than the rest of us. He sat on Cam's chest, his hand around Cam's throat. His voice was calm. "Are you done?"

Cam didn't move. Everyone was silent and dead-still.

"Nod your head to tell me that you're done." Z kept his hand squarely around Cam's neck.

Cam's face was purple. The nod of his head was almost imperceptible, but Z must have felt it because he released his grip. Cam started coughing.

"I'm going to get up." Z explained to Cam. "And you are going to leave. Understand?"

Cam held his throat and nodded, his face fading from purple to red.

"Good." Z got up off of Cam's chest. "Take your weasel friend with you."

Cam got up and looked like he was about to say something to Wylie.

"Nope." Z held up his hand. "No talking. Leave." Z pointed to the exit.

Cam and Chase made their way out of the canal. Relieved, I walked over to Wylie and offered him my hand. "You ok?"

Wylie had his arm around his stomach, but reached up for my hand. He nodded, wiping his dirt and tear-stained face before turning to Z. "Thanks for stepping in man."

"All good Y-dog."

The three of us climbed up the wall of the canal. The others took up their boards and started skating again—the screech of rubber wheels and the grind of wooden boards once again filled the air. Z offered us a sip from a Big Gulp sitting by his stuff. Wylie took a long swallow before handing it to me. The ice-cold Mountain Dew felt good going down my throat. Wylie reached into his front pocket. I expected to see a bag of weed or a joint. Instead, Wylie's hand came up to his mouth. He was going to take something again.

I reached my hand out and stopped him. "What's that?" My voice was hoarse.

Wylie looked annoyed. I didn't care.

"Just a Xanax. Don't worry about it." He tried to get out of my grip.

"Dude, no." I gripped his wrist harder. "That shit messes with your brain. You don't need it."

"There a problem?" Z stepped up next to us. He looked at me. "I can ban your ass too."

I looked at Wylie, willing him to just stop. "Come on man, let's just go to my house. My mom will have snacks. It'll be ok."

Wylie stared me down, then relaxed and put the tablet back in his pocket.

Wylie looked up at Z. "Naw man, it's all good." He handed Z back the drink. "I think we're gonna bounce."

Z shrugged. "Later dudes."

Wylie grabbed his stuff and motioned for me to exit. I heard him holler "Late" over his shoulder as he followed me out.

5

Wylie

When we finally rolled up to Alex's house, I was still shaking from the fight with Cam. The more I replayed the scene in my mind, the more pleased I was with the outcome. I mean, don't get me wrong, I was still supremely pissed that Cam turned on me. But the fact that he went after Alex proves that Alex wasn't lying to me about being friends with Cam. And the fact that I actually got some solid contact with that asshole's face pleased me to no end. I was glad that Z stepped in though, otherwise, my advantage probably wouldn't have lasted long.

I looked up at the house Alex stopped in front of, his board scraping across the surface of the sidewalk. It was nice. Nicer than mine, anyway. But it didn't scream "we're rich!" by any stretch of the imagination. I didn't think my mom would be impressed. We kicked up our boards and walked up the narrow path flanked on both sides with red brick and deep-green grass. Alex turned the silver nob on one of the orange double-doors. It opened with a groan. We both dropped our bags and boards behind the couch near the door, startling a black and white cat that darted into the next room.

"Whoops. Sorry, Oreo." Alex called after the cat. "Mom, we're home!"

There was no answer from anywhere in the house. Alex shrugged and led us into the kitchen where a giant plate of chocolate chunk cookies sat on the center of the counter.

"Score!" Alex snagged one from the top before opening the fridge and pulling out a gallon of milk.

I took a cookie and shoved half of it in my mouth, not realizing until that moment just how hungry I was. Aside from that cheese roll-up at lunch, I hadn't eaten anything all day. Alex, his mouth full of cookie, motioned with his head for me to sit down at the dining room table. He set down two tall glasses and filled each one to the top, then grabbed two more cookies and set them down on the glass table top between us. He fell back into the chair across from me, a big smile on his face. I gulped down half the glass of milk when Alex's mom walked in, cordless phone in her hand.

"Sorry boys, I was on the phone with a client." She put the phone back in its cradle and looked from Alex to me. "This must be Wylie?" She raised an eyebrow.

I stood up. "Hi, Mrs. Keen." I walked over and shook her hand. She seemed a little shocked. My mom was big on manners when it came to interacting with other people, so I guess that kind of thing was ingrained in me. I was nervous, but also really excited to finally be able to talk to someone who knew more about me than I did.

"It's nice to meet you Wylie. We're very pleased that you're here." Her hand was warm around mine. She seemed genuinely glad to see me. I liked her immediately. "And please, call me Reyna."

I nodded and sat back down, not sure of what to do next.

Reyna went to the fridge and brought out a plate of cut up

vegetables and a bowl of Thousand Island dressing and set them down on the table. "How about a little nutrition before more cookies, huh?"

Alex ducked his head and smiled before snatching a carrot from the mound of veggies in front of us. I was glad to have anything to eat that I didn't have to cook or fight for a share with four other people. We munched in silence for a few minutes while Reyna got some things ready for dinner. Then she poured herself some iced tea and sat down at the table with us.

Reyna looked at Alex more closely this time. "You are absolutely filthy. Did you roll down a hill on your way home from school?" She ruffled his hair, more to get a twig out than anything else, I think. She looked at me. I looked at my hands. They were red from punching Cam in the face repeatedly. I put them in my lap, hoping she didn't notice.

"Wylie showed me a local skate hangout." Alex offered. "Met some of his friends."

Reyna raised her right eyebrow.

"We *may* have had a minor run in with that guy Cam I told you about." Alex hedged. It was like she knew he was keeping something from her. I can't believe he told her. I worried that she would be mad and take me home right away and I would never get a chance to talk to her for real.

"Anything I should be concerned about?" Reyna asked, not seeming mad at all.

Alex shook his head. "I don't think he'll bother us again."

I held my breath.

Reyna nodded, but didn't say anything more about it. Then she turned to me. "Well, Wylie. Alex tells me that you may be transgender."

I exhaled and nodded. Grateful that she wasn't going to send me home. Grateful I didn't have to bring it up myself.

"You want to talk about it?" She took a sip of her drink, as if this were the most natural thing in the world for us to be talking about at the dining room table.

I nodded again, somehow unable to summon my voice. My eyes dropped to my hands again, at my left forefinger running over the emerging bruises on my right knuckles.

Reyna tilted her head down to catch my gaze. "Is it ok if Alex is here with us? Or would you like to talk with me alone?"

I looked over at Alex. I decided it would be more uncomfortable to talk about this without him there. Besides, he was the one who told me about transgender people in the first place. "Naw, he can stay."

Alex smiled back at me and popped the rest of a carrot into his mouth, biting down with an enthusiastic crunch.

Reyna smiled at me. "Very well. Tell me about yourself." She reclined into her high-backed chair and tossed her hair behind her shoulder. I could see Alex in her.

I didn't know where to start. What exactly did she want to know? I started to panic. Maybe I would say the wrong thing. Maybe she would tell me that I'm not transgender, but that I'm mentally ill and a freak and there was nothing she could do for me.

"I know this can be an overwhelming thing to talk about." It was like she could read my mind. "It's ok to feel whatever it is you're feeling right now. You are safe here."

No one had ever told me I was safe—anywhere. But something inside me wanted to believe her.

"Maybe you could tell me how it feels to be called a girl?" She asked.

Well, that was easy. "It feels wrong." I told her.

"Can you tell me more about that?" She asked.

I thought about it for a moment, then looked at Alex.

"Like, when people call me 'she' or 'Willow,' it's like maybe how you'd feel if I called you 'Reyna' all the time." That was the best I could explain it. I felt like Alex understood what that would feel like, to be called his mom's name. I saw him nodding his head.

"That's a really great way to explain that feeling Wylie." Reyna smiled at me. "How long have you felt this way?"

It seemed like forever, honestly. But then I remembered a time when it really started to bother me. "I think when I was like three or four. My brothers had started calling me Wylie, after the coyote in *The Roadrunner* show. It was my favorite cartoon. I would stand a foot in front of the TV whenever it was on and laugh my head off every time the coyote got knocked on the head with an anvil." I looked up at Reyna, feeling kind of silly talking about this. I took a deep breath and kept going. "I loved it. It was like they were saying 'I love you' every time they called me Wylie. From then on, whenever my mom called me Willow, it made me really mad. Sometimes she'd play along, but definitely not in public. Then I would cry whenever she made me wear anything that I thought was too girly. I mostly wore my brothers' hand me down clothes at home. Whenever we had to leave the house, it would end up in a fight over what I was going to wear." Geez, it seems like my whole life has been one long fight.

Reyna nodded and motioned at my clothes. "It looks like she's let up a bit now though, huh?"

I shook my head. "I change out of the clothes she makes me wear as soon as I leave the house."

"I see." She took another sip of her drink. "Have you been able to talk to her about your feelings at all?"

A thought occurred to me and I started to panic again. "You aren't going to tell her, are you?"

She looked shocked. "No Wylie, I won't say a word to her about this." My face must not have convinced her that I believed her because she added— "this is your life, Wylie. It's not anyone's place to tell you how you should live it. Some people live 'out' from a very early age. Others take their time in coming out to their family and friends. Some people never do. There is no shame in any choice that you make." She hesitated, then put her hand on my knee. "And it's certainly not my place to tell anyone that you are transgender."

I breathed a sigh of relief—both because she promised not to tell my mom and because she thought I was trans and not some mental case. "Alex had mentioned that some people like me can use testosterone to look more masculine?"

Reyna sat back and nodded. "Yes, that's true." She hesitated. "Teens are usually put on puberty blockers until they turn 17 or 18, then they can take testosterone or estrogen, depending on what they want to achieve."

"Cool. How do I do that?" I was getting giddy. The thought of not developing breasts like the rest of the girls my age was a huge relief.

"Well, that's going to be a tricky thing for you, since it doesn't seem like your mom is onboard." She sighed, as if taking personal offense to my mom's position. "But, you could be surprised. With a little education, she could come around."

Doubtful, I thought to myself. "Is there any way that you could just talk to the doctors and tell them what's wrong with me?"

"Oh sweetie, there's nothing wrong with you. Remember that, ok?" She looked like she wanted to hug me or something. "And you can certainly talk with your doctor, the worst they could do is say 'no' right now, right? It's just the law that they need to have your parents' consent."

I felt deflated. I wished I had been born into this family, instead of the one I was in.

"Hey." She said, gently. "I will be here for you in whatever way I can. If there comes a time when you're ready to talk to your mom and you want me to help, I'll do everything I can."

I nodded, head down, hands folded. The next words out of my mouth came out barely a whisper. "Why am I like this?"

This time, Reyna *did* hug me. She leaned forward, put her arms around me and squeezed me tight. Normally, I didn't like it when adults hugged me. But I liked the way it felt to be accepted by her.

"I don't know." She sighed. "You're not alone though. There are thousands of other kids just like you out there." She released me. "Just because so many people don't understand what it means to be transgender, doesn't mean it's not a perfectly normal part of nature."

I wiped the tears from my face. I felt like all I've done these past two days is cry. Alex must think I'm a total cry-baby. I looked up at him, but he seemed more concerned than anything else.

"I have the feeling you're going to get everything you want out of this life, Wylie." Reyna said, with confidence and a sympathetic smile. "It may not feel like it right now. Just keep being who you are."

She handed me a cookie. "Chocolate makes everything better. At least for a little while."

I took it. "Thanks. For everything, I mean."

"Oooh that reminds me." She walked out into the living room and came back with an envelope in her hand. "Sweetheart, do you want to give it to him?"

Alex reached out for the envelope. I couldn't imagine what it could be.

"You know that skate competition in LA next weekend?" He asked, holding the envelope out to me. "This should get you there and back."

I took the envelope from him and opened it. Inside was a bus ticket to downtown LA and back. I couldn't believe it. "Why?"

"Why not?" Alex retorted. "My mom said she'd take you herself, but we're going up to SF to visit some friends for the weekend."

"Alex tells me you're a very talented skate boarder." Reyna added. "We would love to help out in any way we can."

"Yeah." Alex echoed. "And I felt bad for taking your money the other day, so...here you go."

I didn't know what to say. Alex suggested we go up to his room to play *Tony Hawk's Pro Skater.* I agreed, still staring at the bus ticket in disbelief. This is it. I can actually start competing. I've been dreaming about this for two years and now finally, I could join the ranks of my skateboarding heroes, win some cash, and get the hell out of this town.

We settled in on some bean bags in Alex's room and he popped the Tony Hawk game cartridge into the console. After it booted up, we started playing. My mind wasn't really into the game though. Alex was trouncing me.

"Hey man, thanks for bus ticket." I'd have to do a lot better in real life than I was on screen, but this was only the second time I'd ever played the game. "I'll pay you back when I win."

Alex paused the game. "Man, I bought that with *your* money. Don't worry about it." He was silent for a moment. "Actually, you can thank me by promising not to steal your mom's pills anymore."

"Why?" I didn't understand what the big deal was.

Sometimes I just needed something to numb the pain. "It's just like weed. Not a big deal."

"But it's *not* like weed. It's a chemical. And it does crazy shit to people. I've seen it." He looked at me with an intensity I'd never seen in him. "You were scary out-of-it today."

I didn't remember much about today. Sometimes life is better when you don't know it's happening.

"Please, just promise me that. Ok?"

I hesitated for a moment. I really wasn't sure I could actually keep that promise. How could he understand anyway? His family was perfect. His life was perfect. But, I didn't want to seem ungrateful. "Fine. I promise." I told myself I would keep the promise. Whether I believed myself was another story.

On the car ride back home, Alex and I agreed to meet the next morning at the canal. I was so excited at the prospect of competing next weekend that I barely registered anything my mom said to me when I got home. After she tried to grill me about where they lived and their cars and crap, she gave up when I came up blank on what kind of furniture they had.

"I don't know mom, they had a white couch. And some tables. Who cares?" I shrugged, feeling constricted in the low rise jeans and tight t-shirt I had changed back into in the garage after Alex's mom dropped me off. "Can I go to bed now?"

She gave me a long look and shook her head. "After dishes."

I threw up my hands. "I didn't even eat here. Why can't Mason or Jared ever do dishes?" Or you? I thought to myself, not wanting to push my luck. This was so freaking typical.

"Mason had a date and Jared had a baseball game." She turned the volume back up on the television. "Just do as I say."

I knew that line. It always signaled the end of the discussion—any discussion. I growled under my breath, resisting the urge to swear, knowing that would likely get me grounded.

I couldn't risk that. I needed to practice for next weekend's competition. I stalked into the kitchen. An entire days-worth of dishes filled the sink and the adjacent counter. Dark, ominous music filtered into the kitchen from the TV, lending an eerie soundtrack to the flies darting around the oatmeal-encrusted bowls from this morning, the hardened taco meet from my mom and Roy's lunch, and the congealed pasta sauce pan from dinner. The only thing that kept me from stomping back out was the image of that bus ticket in my hand. It may only have been a ticket to LA, but to me, it was the door to ultimate freedom. I had to be careful.

After an hour of scrubbing and drying, I snuck back to my room, closed the door and pulled the bus ticket from my backpack. Sitting down on my bed, I took it out of its envelope and turned it over and over in my hands. I closed my eyes and imagined what it would be like to stand on the podiums like they did in the X-Games. Tony Hawk. Bob Burnquist. Andy McDonald. These were my heroes. I'd watched them on TV for years as they pushed the bounds of the possible. I fell asleep thinking about the combos I'd hit next weekend.

I woke up early Saturday morning, before anyone else did, threw on my clothes and dashed out the door before anyone could see me. It was the weekend, so I generally wasn't hassled about what I wore, but I didn't want anyone killing my mood. Today was going be a great day.

The wind rushed through my hair as I barreled down the hill towards California and Jackson. There wasn't much traffic, so I did a fair amount of curb grinding to fakies, alternating with some ollies on the way down. Skating almost everyday for the past two years, I felt pretty much one with my board. It was a natural extension of my body—as if I was meant to be born with wheels. I guess that wasn't the only equipment I was missing. I'd find a way to fix that. Somehow.

Alex and I met at the canal entrance just after 8:00. He rolled up with a half-eaten banana hanging from his mouth. Without getting off his board, he reached into his back pocket and pulled out another one and handed it to me as he passed by. We goofed around for a while on the street, finishing our fruit and falling into a figure-8 pattern together. Z rolled up about 5 minutes later and entered the canal first.

I heard his Keanu-Reeves-like voice through the bushes. "Whoa."

Alex and I looked at each other, hopped off our boards and went in to see what was up. When we emerged through the hole in the fence, I immediately saw what Z was talking about. There, on the opposite wall of the canal entrance, was fresh pink graffiti that read:

Wylie = Willow = Loser Dike

Alongside the words were some rudimentary stick figures that I could only guess were me and Alex. The stick figure meant to be Alex had a huge boner aimed at the triangle-dress-clad stick figure meant to be me.

"What the —?" Alex cropped up beside me and saw it.

"Fucking Cam." I spat the words out. I wanted to find him and kick his ass for real this time. But first, I needed to get that graffiti covered up. It was embarrassing as hell. Plus, no one else here knew me as Willow. I had wanted to keep it that way.

Z looked at me, then back at the paint-covered wall. His face looked like he was trying to work out a multifactorial equation. I didn't know what to say to him. I was afraid he'd ban me. Or start treating me different.

Finally, he turned back to me. "Are you a —?"

Figured it out, have you genius? "Yeah, so?" Fear and anger had me ready for a fight. But none came.

"All good, Y-dog." He held up his hands, as if in surrender. "Got some paint at the house. Hang out."

Z exited through the bushes leaving me and Alex alone. I heard a rustle in the leaves of the oleander bushes that surrounded the canal, but it was only the breeze. I hoped none of the other guys would show up. Some of them were in high school. I wanted to make a fresh start next year at a new school. If too many people knew me as Willow that would be impossible. My stomach turned. Yet another reason I needed to get out of this town.

"Wylie?" Alex's voice brought me back to the present.

I looked at him. Then back at the near-life-sized stick figures. I wanted to sink into the ground. Then, the familiar sound of Chase's cackling laughter broke through the morning air. It was joined almost immediately by Cam's. Alex and I looked around to see if we could see where they were hiding. After a few seconds, they burst out of the bushes just above the graffiti, laughing and pointing at me, chanting "dike" over and over. They had purposely waited until Z left before showing themselves. Cowards. I dropped my board and charged after them, but they took off in opposite directions—Chase towards school, Cam towards the beach. I was determined to follow him the 30 or so miles to Newport just so I could drown his ass.

"Wylie!" Alex's voice yelled from behind me. I stopped. There was little point in me following either of them, but I really just wanted to punch Cam in his freckled face a couple dozen times. Resigned, I skated back to where Alex was standing.

"Come on. Let's hit up your secret spot." He tugged on my

shirt to get me to follow him. I followed him as he ducked down through the bushes and chain link and out onto the street.

"Which way?" Alex looked back at me.

I pointed up the street. We got on our boards and rode in silence through the sleepy neighborhoods. It was late spring and the lawns were starting to yellow already. I led him through the suburban maze until we reached the abandoned house with the empty pool. We didn't speak until we passed through the splintery gate, its' hinges creaking in protest, and crossed into the weed-covered backyard.

"That was shitty, man. You ok?"

I shrugged and sat down on the first step of the pool. I kind of wanted to be alone. But not totally. I just didn't know what to say or how to be around anyone at that moment. I snatched up a fallen stick and flung it across the pool to the other side. This was all my teachers' faults. Most of them insisted on calling me Willow, even when I told them everyday to call me Wylie. Even "W" would have been better than calling me Willow.

Everyone but Ms. Davidson, my Algebra II teacher and Mr. Kaplan, my World History teacher, insisted on calling me by my "official" name. That's why everyone at school thinks I'm a lesbian. That's why Brianna wouldn't talk to me. I tried to talk to her at the beginning of school, and she actually did, for a while, because we had History together and Mr. Kaplan was cool about my name. She liked me. I know she did. She touched my hand once, on accident. We were working on a project together in class. I felt all tingly from my hand all the way to my stomach. Then she pretended to "accidentally" touch me again, and just left her hand next to mine. My insides got all quivery. Then, after people started to figure it out, someone told Brianna. From that point on, she actively avoided me. I should've hated her. But for some reason, I didn't. I thought she was the most adorable creature to ever walk the earth. Even if she wouldn't talk to me. Sometimes I thought I was crazy for liking her so much. As Alex ultimately pointed out later, she didn't deserve my affection. I don't think my heart and my brain were on speaking terms that whole year.

Alex sat down next to me. "You have a strategy for the comp next weekend?"

I sighed. I was grateful to get off the subject of Cam's cruel street art. We talked for a while about possible combinations that would knock the socks off of the judges and earn me a place on the podium.

Alex stood and tugged his pants up. "Well, let's see what you got then."

I made my way off the lip and down into the pool, hearing Alex let out low whistles as I alternated 180s and 360s with kick flips and burntwists with some one-footed 5-0 thumpin grinds, heel flips to blunt slides, primo grinds to 540 flips and down to one-footed nosegrinds. Every time I fell down, Alex would suggest a change in trick order or a slightly different stance to keep my balance into the next move. I kept at it for three hours until I could do it flawlessly.

Then, every day that week, I would spend an hour before school and two hours after school at my secret spot practicing my moves. Sometimes Alex would join me, but a lot of the time, he let me practice alone. I stayed away from the canal and kept my distance from Cam and the others at school. I heard an occasional snide remark from Cam during class a couple times, but I mostly ignored him. I was focused as hell— determined to win. So determined, I had no problem keeping my promise to Alex to stay away from my mom's pills. I felt clearer than I had in a long time.

It was still pitch-black when I woke up that Saturday morning. I slipped into my brother's old jeans and a faded black Metallica t-shirt. My stomach growled as I made my way through the house in the dark. I grabbed a chewy granola bar and an over-ripe banana and shoved them into my backpack before heading out into the cold morning air. I told my mom I was working on a project with Alex all day, so she wouldn't freak out if I didn't make an appearance that day. I usually left the house early Saturdays anyway to skate, so it wasn't a big deal that I wasn't there.

The bus station was a few miles away, so I munched on my breakfast while I skated through the quiet, empty streets. The only sounds I heard were my wheels rolling across the concrete and the occasional dog bark — probably in response to my presence. I kept going over my moves in my head over and over. Every flip. Every twist. Every grind. I was going to win.

I kept to the streets when I got downtown, in order to avoid the tarp-covered bums sleeping on the sidewalks. I had learned the hard way that the sidewalks were occupied late one night when I snuck out of the house. I was intent on running away from home for good and I wasn't paying particular attention to anything. But, when I ran straight into a sleeping mass, I was launched head-first over top of the person and skidded on my stomach across the urine-soaked pavement. A hulking street-person grabbed me by the back of the shirt and screamed at me for waking them up and for killing their dog (there was no dog) and for burning the cake (there was no cake). Terrified,

I squirmed out of my shirt, grabbed my board and ran as fast as I could in the other direction. From then on, I let sleeping lumps lie and skated on the streets exclusively.

Light was creeping up the eastern horizon when I entered the bus station. I tucked my board between my body and my backpack, using the straps as a sling, and headed over to the attendant. I pulled the ticket out of my pocket and handed it to the woman behind the gray countertop. She took it and pointed at a bus behind me and just outside the door.

She glanced at the clock. "Leaves in 5."

"Thanks." I took my ticket from her, walked outside and onto the large, blue and gray RTA bus that would take me to LA. I took a seat next to the window near the front of the bus. There were about 10 other people scattered throughout the place. I hoped I would have a row to myself. After stowing my bag and board under the light blue seat, I leaned back and closed my eyes, visualizing my combos over and over. I vaguely heard the driver make some announcement over the intercom, but I was so focused, I didn't really register what she said. Then, I felt the bus lurch forward and the air brakes release. We were moving. I had no idea what these other people were traveling towards, but I knew I was traveling towards freedom.

6

Alex

The plane dropped below the cloud line, revealing the orange span of the Golden Gate Bridge against the deep, blue Pacific, filling my entire window with vibrant color. I felt a warmth spread through my body at the sight. This was home. Not the brown, smoggy concrete jungle of the Evil Empire. I could almost smell the moist, salt air and feel it on my skin. *Bro Hymn*, by Pennywise, was playing on my portable CD player when my dad lifted my headphones off my head.

"Are you excited?" A Kool-Aid-worthy smile parted his bearded face.

It was hard not to smile back. I nodded and put my headphones around my neck, pressed the Stop button and watched the silver disc slowly spin itself to a stop. "Breakfast at Joe's?" I asked, hopeful.

"You better believe it." He leaned back into his seat and grabbed my mom's hand.

Joe's was our favorite breakfast spot in North Beach. We used to go every Saturday morning. It was the only place we ever got dessert with breakfast, well, brunch really—Italian jelly donuts. I felt a twinge in my gut. I missed our tradition. We hadn't established a new one, partly because we haven't found anywhere as good as Joe's for breakfast and partly because my dad had been traveling a lot for work.

My ears started aching, so I knew we would land soon. I tried yawning to clear them as I watched the familiar buildings of The City pass by beneath us. Coit Tower. Transamerica Pyramid. Palace of Fine Arts. That was probably my favorite place to go and just think. Sometimes I would skate around inside the domed structure, getting lost in my thoughts. In the spring, we would spread a blanket out on the enormous green lawn and have picnics. Sometimes we'd invite friends and make it a party. Sometimes it just turned into a party on its own. That's where I met Mandy, actually. Not at one of the picnics though. It was one of the times in November when I went there to be alone. After I found out we were moving...

Dammit. I was starting to get depressed. I put my headphones back on and pressed Play. Angsty guitar riffs formed the soundtrack to our bumpy, aggressive landing.

The plush, red booths at Joe's were a welcome change from the cramped, smoke-filled cab we arrived in. The waiter was filling our glasses with ice when Kevin arrived. Kevin's arrivals were always extravagant—almost as extravagant as the clothes he wore. Today was an if-Bollywood-made-Saturday-Night-Fever kind of day for Kevin, who wore brown, low-rise polyester tight pants, little brown bejeweled slippers, and a shiny, lime-green, shirt with a butterfly collar, topped only as Kevin can, by a purple feather boa and over-sized white sunglasses.

"Reyna, darling! Kevin sauntered into the restaurant with his arms spread wide. "So good to see you." They kissed each others' cheeks like in foreign films. "And I see you've brought me a treat!" He turned and put his hand in front of my dad like he was the pope presenting his ring.

My dad, always the good sport, took Kevin's hand and kissed it.

"You know I love you dear, but hands off my man!" My mom sat down and scooted over towards me to make room for Kevin, but he sat down next to my dad, practically on his lap. I slid over towards my mom so my dad could eat breakfast without Kevin laying on him.

"Where's Jordan?" My mom asked, placing her napkin in her lap.

Kevin took off his sunglasses and gave her a pouty face. "He's volunteering at the community center today. I pleaded with him to join us. I mean, how often are we blessed with your presence anymore?" He waved his hand in the air like it was hopeless. "But you know him—when he gets into something, he goes all the way." His hand found its way to my dad's knee and gave it a squeeze.

I couldn't help but laugh. My dad's face was candy-apple-red. Kevin was always flirting with my dad, so this was nothing new. I think my dad was actually flattered by it. I suddenly wondered if he ever—

"Well, his commitment to the community is admirable. We can't fault him for that." My dad reached for his water glass. "But we'll see him tonight, right?"

"Yes, you must come to Roger's." My mom interjected.

Kevin picked up his menu. "I'll drag his skinny butt to Roger's kicking and screaming if I have to. Don't. You. Worry. Honey." He ran his finger down the offerings. "Ooo, waffles!"

He dropped the menu, clapped his hands and then turned to me. "Young man, how are you enjoying your imprisonment in the uncultured valley of the red neck?"

I chuckled. I liked Kevin. I liked most of my mom's friends. They never patronized me. "It's alright." I shrugged. "I mean, it totally sucked at first, but I finally met someone cool, so —"

"Ah, young love." Kevin folded his hands in front of his chest. "Tell me all about him." He leaned across my dad as if he didn't exist, giving him a nose full of purple feathers.

"It's not—" I managed to get out before the waiter arrived.

"Will you be joined by anyone else?" The waiter pointed at the empty place setting next to my mom.

"No." My mom said. "It'll just be us."

The waiter motioned to a busser across the room, who came and cleared the cutlery and glassware.

"Can I interest you in—"

"A carafe of mimosas, why yes!" Kevin interrupted.

The waiter took the rest of our orders and hurried away, returning moments later with three champagne glasses and a carafe.

Kevin put a hand on top of the waiter's. "Sweetheart, we'll need another champagne glass."

The waiter looked at me, but before he could say anything, Kevin added, "I'm a two-fisted drinker—always have been—since I was a wee one." All of sudden Kevin had an Irish accent.

It worked. Another glass appeared and I got to experience my first mimosa. I swished the sweet, fizzy liquid around before swallowing it. I could almost feel it bubbling in my stomach. My mom made a motion with her hand indicating I should slow down, so I put the glass down and sat back in the booth.

Kevin had apparently forgotten about his line of questions about my alleged love life, and was listening intently as my

72

mom talked about some art installation she and my dad had gone to in San Diego, which was fine. I kind of wanted to just chill. Honestly, I was feeling anxious about seeing Pete later. And I wondered how Wylie was doing in LA. Don't get me wrong, I thought he had a good chance of winning, but, I don't know, I just worried about him. What if someone else hassled him about his name or how he looked? Or what if something happened to him during the competition? I doubt he told his mom he was going. I took another drink of my mimosa.

I looked over at my dad. Like, really looked at him. I tried to see him like Kevin saw him. He was a good looking guy. And he was so comfortable with Kevin and his constant flirting. He spoke now with an excitement I didn't often see in him. He fit in just as well with my mom's colorful crowd as he did with the stuffy businessmen he worked with. I tried to imagine him kissing Kevin. Could he ever? I mean in the past? I wondered if there was a part of my dad that I had no idea about. Could he be bi-? Would he have told my mom?

I tried to imagine kissing Pete. I suppose I could, but it didn't really make me feel the same way as thinking about kissing Mandy. Her lips were so soft. Would Pete's be as soft? My mind wandered to the last time we made out. Then Pete's face replaced Mandy's.

"Alex?" It was my dad's voice.

I opened my eyes. I didn't know I had closed them. Everyone was looking at me. My face was hot. "Yeah?"

"You ok, pal?"

"Yeah. Good." I starred at the stack of pancakes in front me, topped with bananas and pecans. "Just...meditating."

"Meditating?" My mom cocked her head and looked at me.

"What? Let's eat." I picked up my fork and dove into my pancakes trying to push the thought of lips intertwined out of my mind. Mine. Mandy's. Pete's. Kevin's. My dad's. My mom's. Something foreign opened up inside me and I wondered if I even knew my parents at all. Or myself.

♠ ♥ ♣ ♦

"Alex!" Pete's voice echoed across Baker Beach. "Over here." He was surrounded by five or so other people over by the bluff, the Golden Gate forming the backdrop.

I made my way down the sandy steps, the wind harsh against my face. I could hear music wafting across the beach from someone's boom box. Pearl Jam. *Evenflow*. I stopped at the last step and removed my shoes and socks. One more step and my feet sunk into the cool sand. I dropped my shoes and jogged over to the group. It was Pete, Jake, Liz, Rachel, Nick, some other guy I didn't know, and...Mandy. My heart sped up when I saw her brown eyes look me up and down. I wondered if she and Matt were still a thing.

"Hey, man." I gave Pete a hug. "What's going on?"

"Not a thing, man." Pete pounded me on the back before releasing me. He had gotten bigger since I left. Must be working out hard with the lacrosse team. He sat back down in the sand and leaned against a giant tree trunk. Rachel passed a joint to him before sliding down next to him. Pete took a hit as Rachel laid her head down in his lap. I couldn't help feeling a little out of place. Is this how it's going to be then? I try to keep the friendship going and he just gets more aloof?

Nick and Jake were busy stacking wood into a pile to start a bonfire. Liz and Mandy sat together on the other end of the tree trunk from Pete and Rachel. I knew all of them from my old school, although they're older than me and Pete. Nick and

74

Jake were in 11th and had convinced Pete to take up lacrosse with them. Liz and Mandy were in 10th and were practically inseparable. I made my way over towards them.

"Hey, Alex." Their voices rang out in unison. "Come sit with us."

Well, at least someone wanted to see me. I sat down between them.

"We've missed you." Mandy said, over the crash of the surf.

"Yeah?" I looked at her. Her eyes dropped to the log as she traced a finger over the knarled, dry wood.

"*I've* missed you the most." Liz threaded her fingers through mine. This was new. And not entirely unwelcome.

"Not true." Mandy grabbed my other hand. "I've missed you more than *her*."

This was either getting really weird or really good. I couldn't decide, though a not-so-small part of me was trying its hardest to influence the vote.

"Mandy!" Nick appeared in front of us. "What the hell?"

Mandy let go of my hand. I guess she and Matt are no longer a thing.

"I was just saying 'hi' to my old friend." Mandy stood up and kissed Nick on the cheek. "Don't be mad at me."

"How about you keep your hands to yourself." He grabbed her hand and put it on his crotch. "Or myself." He grinned at me and dragged Mandy towards the water.

Jake started squirting lighter fluid over the pile of wood as the other guy flicked lit matches into it. A few seconds later there was a "whomp" and a giant flame emerged. A wave of heat hit us straight in the face, a welcome change from the cold wind that was blowing off of the ocean.

Liz leaned over and whispered in my ear, "Have you met Matt?"

I turned and looked at her. She nodded her head in the other guy's direction.

So that's Matt. "Haven't had the pleasure."

"I have." She stood up, let go of my hand and walked down the beach to where Mandy and Nick were chasing each other in the fading light.

I shook my head. Today was just too freaking weird. I was really looking forward to being home again, but it was like everything was just—*off*.

I got up and walked back over to where Pete and Rachel were sitting. They had been joined by another group of people that just arrived. From the looks of things, they were all friends of Matt.

"Hey man, I've missed you." I sat down next to Pete.

"Yeah?" Pete drawled, his fingers twirling in Rachel's hair. He was high.

I was getting mad. "Yeah. Obviously *you* haven't missed me at all. I thought we were friends."

"We are." He was starring off at the water, flames flickering in his eyes.

"How can you say that? We barely talk anymore."

"We talk."

I threw up my hands. "We talk? When?"

"Dude." He finally looked in my direction, but his eyes wouldn't focus. "I invited you here didn't I?"

Just then, Matt put a Miller Light in Pete's face and dropped a bag of Doritos in his lap.

"Awe man, yes!" Pete shoved his hand into the bag and crammed two chips into his mouth at once, forgetting our conversation.

Matt slapped him on the back, walked back to one of the new girls that had arrived and slid his arm around her waist.

Rachel sat up and looked at me. "Just relax. Have a good time." She took a sip from the beer Matt brought over. "Liz has been talking about you for weeks. She's totally into you. Go have fun while you're still young."

"Yeah man, go have fun. Get laid." He finally looked me in the eyes. "I *highly* recommend it." Then, he turned towards Rachel and stuck his tongue in her mouth.

So that's it. He's made it to home base and is camped out there.

Hurt and honestly, a bit jealous, I got up and walked towards the water. I rolled up my pant legs and let the freezing cold water cover my feet. Cold was better than lonely. My mom was right. Pete was drifting away and there was nothing I could do about it. I considered leaving. Going back to Roger's. Anything would be better than this.

I walked along the waterline towards the stairs that would lead up to the road, when I heard footsteps pounding behind me.

"Where you going?" It was Liz.

"I don't know." I kept walking.

"Can I join you?"

"I don't care."

"Hey." She grabbed my hand and turned me towards her. "What's wrong?"

"I don't know." I sighed. "I guess I just—shit. I don't know. I don't belong here."

"Walk with me?" Liz pulled me forward.

I followed her. I didn't expect her to understand. It was like home wasn't home anymore. I had all these expectations about how it was going to be and none of them have worked out. I felt like if I could just get Pete to talk to me, things would be better again. But he doesn't want to talk. He's obviously replaced me with his new friends.

Liz led me to a little cove out of the reach of the waves, where the full moon illuminated blanket-clad couples dotting the sand. She sat down, leaned up against the rock wall and patted the sand in front of her. "Sit."

"Fine." I plopped down in front of her, legs crossed. I couldn't believe she wasn't freezing in those little denim shorts.

She held her hands out. "Give me your hands."

I obeyed, thinking I should just get up now and find a cab.

She took my hands and faced my palms up, then traced the lines with her fingers like she was reading my palm. It was incredibly relaxing. I let my eyes close, feeling the rumbling of the earth underneath me as the waves crashed on the shore. All of the confusing thoughts faded from my mind, replaced only by the feel of her fingers on my hands, the cold sand beneath me, the wind on the back of my neck and the sounds of the beach. I unclenched my jaw and let my shoulders soften.

"There." I heard Liz's soft voice. "Better?"

I nodded.

She let go of my hands. I could hear her stand up and shake the sand from her body.

I opened my eyes to find her standing above me. With her feet on either side of my legs, she sat down in my lap.

"You belong right here." She wrapped her arms around my shoulders and brought her face close to mine.

Her blue eyes looked like silvery pools in the moonlight before she closed them, licked her lips and placed them on mine. They were soft and wet and massaged my lips, like she had done with my hands. She slipped the tip of her tongue into my mouth. My entire body was electrified. All thoughts of leaving were gone. All I wanted was to explore every part of Liz. My tongue found hers, yet my focus was on the friction of the hot denim between her legs running back and forth over the biggest erection I'd ever had. I reached up and found her bare breasts under her hoodie. They were soft and heavy. Her breath was coming faster now. She knotted her hands in my hair and the pace of her grinding increased. The heat of her crotch radiated through my jeans. All I could think about was peeling off those shorts and, well, you know.

I was about to lose it. But before I could even think about removing anyone's clothes, I wrapped my arms around her and pulled her hard against me. She stiffened and cried out before burying her face in my neck. A few seconds later, I blew the load of my life inside my boxers.

She rested her forehead on mine as our breathing returned to normal. Did this count as getting laid? Or was penetration a requirement? I wasn't sure. Regardless—this was a close second.

Liz sighed.

"You ok?" I asked.

"Hmmm." She released her grip on my hair and wrapped her arms around me again. "Mandy said you were a good kisser."

"Did she?" I felt a smile spread across my lips.

"Mmmm." She sighed again. "We like to share guys. Compare notes. She said you were a 7. But I think you're a solid 9."

I felt my smile fade. The cold of the ground started to creep up my spine. Was it the cold, really? Or was that just kind of screwed up? I mean, it wasn't like I was in love with her or anything, but that just sounded a little…I don't know. Creepy?

Dammit. This whole night has been one big—

"I gotta go." I lifted her off of my lap so I could extricate myself from her legs.

She looked up at me with a confused look on her face. "What's wrong?"

I looked down at her. "Like I said—I don't belong here." I turned around and jogged back towards the stairs, feeling that cold spot on my boxers sticking to my body and the taste of disgust rising in my throat.

I stepped out of the cab and realized that the party had spilled out of Roger's place and into the street. Fifteen or so people stood talking, sometimes shouting, and drinking on the sidewalk and part of the actual roadway. Roger's place was a townhouse right in the center of the Castro. He had some sort of really successful dot-com business, which was why he was able to afford such a swanky place. He's the one that got me into computers and programming and stuff. His party was to celebrate his company going public. Anyway, apparently everyone in The City was here, crammed into every spare corner even the two small balconies out front.

Just what I needed—a house full of happy people. I trudged inside, avoiding getting smacked with the extreme hand gestures that seemed the hallmark of the drunk and fabulous. Aretha Franklin's voice streamed from the enormous speakers of Roger's stereo, demanding R-E-S-P-E-C-T over the din of the party. I spotted my mom in the dining room talking with Jordan, Kevin's boyfriend, and some woman I didn't know. She waved at me, then went on talking. I weaved my way through the living room, realizing suddenly that my dad was on the bottom of a pile of men on the couch—a stunt instigated by Kevin, of course. Everyone, including my dad, was in hysterics. He had to be drunk. He was normally pretty buttoned down. My mom said he was an introvert. Well, at least someone was having a good time.

"Did you have a good time at the beach sweetheart?" I mom ran her hands through my hair.

I pulled my head away and shrugged. "Yeah, it was alright." It felt weird to have her hands in my hair when just an hour ago Liz had her fingers wound through it.

"Just alright?" She had her concerned face on now. Shit. I didn't want to get into it tonight.

"No, it was good." I tried to smile. "I'm just tired. Gonna go to bed."

"You sure? Roger is around here somewhere. I know he'd love to see you. I told him about Wiley." She stood on her toes and craned her neck to try and find him.

"I'll see him tomorrow mom. I just want to go to bed." It was hard to hide my irritation. I turned and headed upstairs, swimming against the tide to get up to the guest room. It was a miracle someone wasn't in there. I closed the door, which did little to drown out the party. I threw myself facedown onto the bed as a Rolling Stones song boomed up through the floor. According to Mick Jagger, I can't always get what I want.

What *did* I want?

Duh.

I wanted my friend not to be such a douchebag.

I wanted to get laid, without feeling weird about it. I thought about Liz. Why was I so creeped out about what she said?

My questions were interrupted by a tap on the door.

"Alex?"

Ugh, go away.

"Yeah?" I strained to make myself heard over the party.

"It's Jordan, can I come in?"

I sat up and peeled my boxers away from my skin to get them un-stuck. The night hasn't gone right so far, why should I get what I want now? "Yeah, sure."

Jordan cracked the door just enough to get himself through, then closed it softly behind him. I wasn't sure who he was trying to be quiet for, because the house was throbbing with activity.

"Hey guy, how's it going?" Jordan sat down in the reading chair next to the bed and crossed his legs. I thought it was strange how different he and Kevin were — at least as far as clothing went. Kevin looked like he strutted off the jacket of a 70's record album. Jordan looked like he stepped out of a J-Crew catalogue.

"You here to give me free therapy?"

"Do you need therapy?" He brought his fingertips together in front of his mouth and then grinned. "You may be able to fool your mom, but I know bad-date-face when I see it. Spill."

I laughed. I'd known Jordan since I was like 10-years-old. He and my mom worked at the same mental health clinic before we moved. "I don't know man. It's been a weird night. I was supposed to hang out with Pete at his place, but then at the last minute he told me to meet him at the beach. Then there were all these other people there. And he was high and being kind of an ass. I mean, he's pretty much not interested in being my friend. Instead he's hanging out with all these lacrosse ass-holes and turning into a d-bag." I took a breath. "So, then I'm trying to leave and this chick comes up and —"

I sighed. "Then shit just got weirder."

Jordan's eyebrow raised. I don't know if he got that from my mom or my mom got it from him. "Define weirder."

"I don't know. I mean, I actually kind of liked her. We started fooling around." I felt my face getting hot. I looked down at my pants and saw a crusty spot along my zipper from where Liz was grinding on me. I ignored the tingle that sprouted in my boxers. "I mean, it was good…but, then after, she made this comment about sharing guys with her best friend and they rate us and, it just felt…weird."

"Did you get a bad rating? Slobbery kisser? Tooth banger? That kind of thing?"

We both busted up.

"No. Nothing like that." I shook my head. "Is that *normal* behavior though?"

"Comparing lovers? 'fraid so. Sometimes it can be the downfall of all relationships."

"Yeah, but—they made it sound like a game."

"And you were the pawn."

And I was the pawn. Yeah. That's basically it—I felt used.

"Nobody likes to have their emotions toyed with. We men like to have other things toyed with, but not our emotions." He winked at me. "You're a sensitive guy Alex, and that's a *good* thing."

I rolled my eyes. Sometimes it felt like I just cared too much.

"And, I'm sure I don't need to tell you this, but, be sure to protect yourself. Condoms are your friend. Especially if you're dealing with partners who have had lots of other partners."

"I know." I didn't want to admit that I hadn't yet done the deed. But, I was glad I didn't actually do it with Liz. Then I remembered how I had marked her as an easy target to get to third base with. Then I felt like a hypocrite. I flung myself back on the bed and groaned.

"What?" Jordan asked.

"Nothing." I didn't want to admit being a hypocrite to myself. I certainly didn't want to admit it to Jordan.

Based on the sounds coming from the floor below us, it was karaoke time. Shouting and catcalls competed for airtime with two men singing *I've Got You Babe* by Sonny and Cher. I listened for a few seconds. I think one of those men was my dad.

"Hey, Jordan?"

"Yeah?"

I didn't know why, but I had to ask. "Do you think my dad's bi?"

"Why do you ask?"

"I don't know. He just...well, you know how Kevin is always flirting with him..."

"Ah yes, Kevin loves himself a man with a beard."

"Ok, but, I mean, my dad seems like maybe he enjoys it?"

"Do you think this is something maybe you should ask your dad about?"

"C'mon man—would you have that conversation with *your* dad?"

"Good point." Jordan cleared his throat.

"So you're not going to answer me then?" My mom would say this is classic deflection. He must know.

"Would it make a difference to you if he was?"

I thought about it for a moment. I'm not sure why it mattered so much to me to know. I guess I would just want him to be happy. But I would hate it if he left my mom because he wanted to be with someone else. "I don't know. I guess not."

"Most people don't want to admit it, but I think sexuality can be pretty fluid."

"What do you mean?"

"Well, I mean sometimes a person can go their entire lives liking men and then suddenly find themselves attracted to women. And vice versa. I don't think it's as black and white as society wants to make it out to be."

That kind of made sense. I mean, I suppose if I met some guy that I just fell in love with, I wouldn't fight that. "Have you ever been with a woman?"

"Gross, no!" Jordan faked like he was gagging himself with his finger down his throat. Then he got serious. "Kidding. Yes. I tried dating girls when I was your age, but it just didn't feel right to me."

"What about you? Have you ever been with a guy?"

I sat up again. "Me? No. I've barely been with a girl."

"Well, there's hope for you yet." He smacked me on the knee and stood up. "I'll let you try and get some sleep."

"Thanks Jordan." I got up to get my backpack from the corner of the room. "Hey, why don't you have a beard? I mean, if Kevin likes bearded men so much—"

He stopped, his hand on the doorknob. "A chia-pet can grow a better beard than I can. Trust me. It is not a pretty sight."

I chuckled as Jordan closed the door, feeling a little better than I did before. And strangely grateful that I hadn't gone all the way with Liz. Not that I had any illusions of a "perfect first time" but, I don't know, I think I'd rather be in a good mood after—not creeped out.

7

Wylie

I was weightless. My feet traced the arc of my board across the blank canvas of the hot afternoon sky. The pump and rush of blood through my veins was the only thing I heard. Not the pounding punk rock music. Not the announcers. Not the roar of the crowd. I was executing the most perfect set of my life. The arc terminated as my board landed back on the smooth wooden surface where it accelerated beneath my feet—across the flat—launching me up the other side of the ramp until my wheels touched nothing but air. My right hand grabbed the rail for a one-arm headstand, the other grabbed my board for an instant before arcing again down the ramp before the buzzer sounded—ending my heat.

Only then did the outside world re-materialize in my reality.

"A strong showing by newcomer Wylie Masterson."

I listened for my score as I slowed down at the base of the ramp.

"And the judges are giving Wylie an 85, putting him in 3rd place overall in the 13-17 vert division."

I couldn't believe it. The whole day was like an out-of-body experience. I had dreamed of this day for so long and now—I got a podium finish at my first competition!

Unlike many of the other skaters, I didn't have a group of family or friends cheering me on. And honestly, that was ok with me. All I could think about was my prize: $250 in cold, hard cash.

I exited the competition area to a chorus of cheers and back-claps from people I'd never met, and probably would never see again. As I made my way through the sweaty, boisterous crowd, I thought about my dad. I don't do that too often any-more. It struck me that I wished he had seen me skate. That little kid part of me imagined that he would be there when I stood on that podium. I'd be lying if I said I didn't scan the crowd once I was up there, just in case he was.

Not to spoil the ending or anything, but he didn't show.

You know who did though? Tony. Freaking. Hawk.

Nobody knew he was coming. At least, it wasn't public. He was just standing there when we came off the podium. Then, he shook the guys' hand in front of me and said something to him, but I couldn't hear anything above the music. Then, I was standing in front of him—the Skate God himself. Holy crap!

He looked at me and smiled, putting his fist out for me to bump it. "Nice job out there."

My knees almost gave out beneath me. I just fist-bumped Tony Hawk. Did he actually see me skate? Did he really think I did a good job?

"Yeah?" I asked, barely able to feel my tongue.

Tony nodded his head. "Keep that up and you'll be spon-sored in no time."

I was elated. It didn't matter if my knees gave out, because I was floating. And I wasn't coming down.

"Dude. Sponsored?" Alex's eyes were wide, his mouth agape. "Tony Hawk said you could be sponsored?" He shook his head. "That's incredible, man. Congratulations!" He shuffled the cards so we could play another round of Texas Hold 'Em on the way to San Clemente Beach.

"Thanks." I was still high from Saturday's competition. The steady hum of the Keen's RV's tires was interrupted with a series of clacks of the metal grates dividing the pavement of the bridge we crossed over. I still couldn't believe I was here. I looked over at Alex sitting across the table from me. As if reading my mind— "Dude, I can't believe your mom let you come with us to San Clemente for Spring Break!"

"I know, right? They should give your mom a medal or something for being able to persuade Sybil to let me out of her sight for a week, let alone spend it with a boy." I'm guessing my mom figured he's my boyfriend now, so she could stop worrying that I'm a lesbian. I hadn't had the courage to tell her about the whole transgender thing. Alex's mom has been really supportive, but I think my mom's head would explode if I told her the truth.

"Wylie, Alex, are you hungry?" Alex's mom called from the front of the RV.

We looked at each other. "No." We burst into almost silent laughter. The truth was, we'd been sneaking Oreos and Doritos for the past hour. I felt a little sick to my stomach.

"Ok, we'll be there in about 45 minutes. We'll barbecue once we get settled." She looked at us through the rearview mirror thing that runs across the top of the windshield.

Alex dealt the cards. "Yeah, you're mom's a real piece of work. She actually told my mom that we couldn't be alone together after dark."

I shook my head. The kind of rules this woman got in her

head—I would never understand. Why could she sleep with her boyfriend without getting struck by lightning but I couldn't be around a guy at night without subjecting my soul to eternal damnation? It's not like I wanted to screw Alex. I wasn't even into guys.

"Whatever, man. All I know is that for the next week, we're going to show those coasties how it's done in the valley." Both me and Alex had our skateboards under our feet at the table, rolling them back and forth across the linoleum flooring. I could barely wait to get to the campground and head over to the San Clemente Skate Park. It was my sole intention to win first place at the Skate Fest next weekend.

Alex flipped over the first three cards on the table to start our game. It wasn't as much fun with only two people, but, since my crew mutinied on me and tried to kick our asses, it has kinda just been the two of us for a while. It was cool though—we planned to win some bills from the locals in SC while we were there. We spent the rest of the journey trying to out-bluff each other at poker, but the fact was, we were so freaking excited, we weren't exactly at the top of our games. Alex put the cards back in their box and tucked it into his back pocket. As he stood up, his board rolled across the small space when his dad steered the massive vehicle into the camp site.

"John, watch the curb." Reyna warned Alex's dad, just as he curb-surfed the RV. We got bounced around a bit as the vehicle righted itself.

"Sorry sweetheart." John sneaked a peak in the rearview to make sure we were alive and unharmed. "Everyone ok back there?"

Alex and I looked at each other and laughed.

"All good Mr. K." I retrieved my board, which shot off into the kitchen cabinets when we jumped the curb.

Alex shook his head. "Geez dad, next time let mom drive."

Alex's dad wove his way through the camp ground until we found our assigned spot. Once the RV was parked, Alex and I darted out the door and headed for the beach.

"Be back in an hour for dinner!" Reyna called out to us.

We kept running up a small, sandy hill. Once we hit the top, we were met with a 180-degree view of the Pacific Ocean. The sun sat low on the horizon, like a giant, orange Oreo being dipped into the sea. Hundreds of seagulls swarmed the shore, shrieking "mine...mine...mine" like a playground full of two-year-olds. We kicked off our shoes, which had already filled with sand, and shoved our socks into them. The sand was cold between my toes as I dug my feet down into the soft grains.

Alex tore off his black *Rancid* shirt and threw it on top of his shoes before sprinting down the hill towards the water. "Come on!"

I hesitated for a moment before doing the same. I had longed to do this since I was told not to as a young child. I never understood why my brothers could do it but suddenly I couldn't. But there was no one here to chastise me for running around without a shirt. Nobody knew me as a girl here. Well, no one but Alex and his family. I silenced the voice of my mother in my head telling me to act like a proper young lady and tore down after Alex. Feeling the cool air on my bare skin, I almost cried. I felt—free.

As Alex stormed the shore, he scared the birds who took flight amidst a dissonant clamor. My arrival dispersed any brave stragglers. I looked at him. At his body. We didn't look that different, really. All muscles and bones. Well, mostly bones for me. He turned and motioned for me to join him closer to the water. I was a little self-conscious, but Alex treated me as if me not wearing a shirt was the most normal thing on earth. Was this the feeling I imagined, when I left home on my board, each time, "for good" only to find myself right back home hours later? This feeling that I was free to be who I am, without judgment?

I pulled up my jeans, which had inched their way down my non-existent hips despite my belt, before plopping down onto the sand. Alex dropped down next to me.

"Well, what do you think?" He spread his arms to encompass the whole of the ocean.

"So cool!" Nothing like the lakes I'd been to growing up.

We sat in silence, staring at the waves as they approached us. At the sun in the distance, about to disappear into the sea. The ground shook with the force of the surf, which sounded a lot like thunder when it hit the shore. The wind coming off the water was cold, but I loved the feel of the heavy air as it played over me, tickling the invisible hairs on my arms, neck and torso. Goosebumps rose all over my body and my nipples hardened. I felt a shiver run through my body. I wasn't sure if it was from the cold, or if I was getting a little turned on by all of the sensations.

"What do you think high school will be like?" I buried my feet into the sand, which had retained some of the sun's warmth. What I really wanted to ask was if he thought there would be tons of cute girls there that would want to go out with me. I had spent most of 9th grade crushing on Brianna, but she would never give me the time of day because she knew I was a girl. No, thought I was a girl. I remembered what Reyna had said about me being a boy, just not exactly how our society had defined them. It was still confusing for me, even though I had felt like a boy my whole life.

"I don't know." He took a handful of sand and let it go over his knee like a broken hourglass. "Probably better than junior high school. Harder classes. More to do. I don't know." He shrugged.

"Do you think we'll get girlfriends?" I didn't look at him. I didn't want to see the look on his face that might suggest that no girl would want to go out with me. And that I was foolish to even think of such a thing.

"Duh. We're going to have access to more tits than we know what to do with." He created two gigantic mounts with his hands in front of his chest, implying that all the girls at Riverview High were bound to be DDs.

I shoved him in the shoulder and he toppled over into the sand. We both laughed.

Alex picked himself up off the ground. "Don't worry Wylie. If that asshole Cameron can get to second base, you're guaranteed to get some lovin' next semester." He reached down to grab my hand and pulled me up.

He had a point. I'm way better looking than Cam. But still. Things are so—complicated.

Alex read my mind, as he so often did. "Stop worrying about high school chicks. We've got a week here at the beach. You're gonna dominate at the Skate Fest—which means local honeys will be begging to hang out with us."

That thought kept me warm and happy as we walked back up the berm to retrieve our shirts and shoes, opting to carry them back to the campsite, rather than cram our sandy feet into our shoes. We both tucked the tails of our shirts into the back waistband of our jeans so that they hung down behind us and waved as we walked. The farther away from the beach we got, the warmer it was. My goosebumps subsided and I vowed to spend the entire week here without a shirt on.

We rounded the corner and found Alex's mom barbecuing and his dad setting the picnic table next to the RV. The smell of sizzling ground beef greeted us. My stomach growled—evidently over the afternoon's Oreo-induced nausea.

Reyna spotted us and waved. "Perfect timing. You boys wash up and grab a plate."

I loved it when she called us "you boys."

Alex and I fought over the kitchen sink inside, making a mess in the process. The RV rocked back and forth as we jostled for a position under the faucet. We finished washing our hands and patted them dry on our jeans on our way back outside. The sky was a hazy gray with blue and pink streaks. Mr. Keen lit a citronella candle on the picnic table, citing the threat of mosquitos and West Nile virus. I think he was a bit of a hypochondriac. I'd never had an encounter with him where he didn't talk about some rare disease or another.

"I think you've already scared all the mosquitos away with your terrible music selection." Alex thought his dad was a hypochondriac too. My stomach tightened. I would never get away with saying something like that to my mom. I'd heard Alex and his dad exchange these kinds of taunts before, but it still made me nervous—like one day he's going to go too far and his parents would get really mad.

"Son, watch your manners. You don't need to show off for Wylie." Mr. Keen set the last of the condiments on the table. "And for the record, Chuck Mangione is a legend in the jazz realm."

Alex rolled his eyes. "Jazz is for old people. You don't want to be old, do you dad?" He grabbed a plate and handed it to me, then picked one up for himself and pushed me over to the BBQ. Mrs. Keen handed me a bun off the grill and then put a beef patty on top if it, cheese melting down the sides.

Mr. Keen picked up a plate of his own and bopped Alex on

the top of the head with it. "Don't be manipulative. I was just starting to like you."

I watched their interaction and was struck by how different things were in their family than in my own. John and Reyna treated Alex almost as if he was an equal. I don't think my mom's ever said she liked me and she sure didn't treat me like her equal. I mean, Alex's parents still demanded respect, but they also seem to respect Alex as a person. I was treated more like a servant.

Later that night, Alex and I laid in the giant hammock his dad set up next to the RV, our heads at opposite ends of the netted sling. I could hear the crackle of campfires from multiple camps layered on top of the waves breaking on the shore. It was late, but the occasional sounds of our neighbor's conversations creeped through the brush that separated the campsites.

"Hey, you never told me how your trip up north went." My eyes followed the track of a commercial plane in the distance.

I felt Alex shrug. "Kinda ok. Kinda lame."

"What was the 'kinda ok' part?" I propped myself up on my elbows, which would have slipped right through the holes in the hammock, were it not for the blanket.

Alex sat up, a smile spreading across his lips. "I *may* have gotten a little action."

"A little?" I raised my eyebrow. Since I had basically zero experience in the realm of love, I needed—"Details."

"Well, there's this chick that I was kind of interested in before we left. We got together at the beach." His voice was hushed. His parents were inside the RV, but I could see a light glowing in the bedroom window.

I lowered my voice too. "Like *got together* got together?"

"Naw, not quite, but almost." Alex trailed off and plopped back down.

I didn't get why he seemed so sad about almost scoring. "Well?" The suspense was killing me. "What happened?"

He sighed. "Ok, so before we moved here, I was going out with this girl, Mandy. She was really—" He paused, staring up at the stars. "Open."

"Open?" I didn't understand.

"Open, like, you know—open to doing stuff. Like, not just kissing."

"Is that why you went out with her?"

"No. I didn't know her before we went out. She just kissed me at the Palace of Fine Arts one day. My friend Pete told me later that she had gone all the way with her last boyfriend. So yeah, I was hoping that she would be *the one*, you know?" Alex shifted in the hammock, causing it to sway a bit. "Anyway, we ended up getting to second base before she broke up with me."

"So you guys got back together?"

"No, she's with this other guy, Nick, who used to be with Liz, the girl I ended up with."

"Sounds like Liz gets around." Not that I really cared. In fact, I regretted saying it. It was such a freaking double-standard that guys were praised for getting laid and girls were dubbed "whores." I vowed to try not to add to that conversation anymore.

Alex sat up to look at me. "I know, right?" Then he looked down. "I had been counting on that before we moved. I figured, 'Hey, she's done the deed with someone else, so she's a sure thing.' Right? So anyway, I was about to leave the beach because Pete was being a dick. Liz catches up to me and tries to get me to relax. So, you know, we end up making out. So I'm sitting on the beach and she's sitting on top of me grinding away—" Alex moved his arms like he was holding Liz in his lap. "And we both ended up...you know." He cupped his hand by his crotch and made an outward motion, spreading his fingers like water coming from a firehose.

I tried to imagine myself in that situation. Tried to imagine my mouth on Brianna's. My fingers in her hair. I felt a tingling in my crotch. Brianna would feel the same, but she would have nothing to grind on. My lap would be missing one crucial element—the fire hose. I closed my eyes and slumped back on the hammock, frustrated.

"That sounds amazing. Why are you bummed?"

"Yeah, it was amazing, but get this. She tells me that she and Mandy share guys and rate them."

I opened my eyes. "What?" I was shocked. I couldn't imagine being so—I didn't even have a word for it.

"Exactly." Alex's eyes were wide again. "I got creeped out and left. Then I started feeling guilty because I realized I wanted to get with her because I knew it would be easy to get into her pants." He flopped back down. "Which makes me an asshole."

I sat up again, hammock rocking. "You're not an asshole. This is what we're supposed to be doing now. Getting laid." Even as I was saying it, I knew I wouldn't be getting laid any time soon. How would I even go about it? And besides, I hated taking off my underwear. It always reminded me that I wasn't 'anatomically correct.' I had to admit—I envied Alex.

"I don't know." Alex sighed again. A car sped by our site too fast, a Top 40 love song blaring from its open windows.

I wasn't sure what he was so upset about. Isn't everyone our age just trying to pair off and get off?

"How far have you gotten?" Alex asked.

I heard the RV creaking next to us and saw the light go out.

97

John and Reyna must be going to bed. I laid back down again. I was a little embarrassed and glad for the darkness. "The closest thing I've come to action was getting felt up by a cop a few weeks ago."

"What?" Alex's voice carried through the air, almost as jarring as the Top 40 serenade. "Wait, what happened?"

I could feel the heat of Alex's body next to mine. I'd never been this close to anyone that I wasn't related to by blood. It felt foreign, but somehow comforting. I felt safe here. I took a deep breath. Reluctantly, I told him about my encounter with the cops on the way to school a while back. To be honest, I was just trying to be glib about the whole thing. I didn't expect to have to elaborate. I felt that sickness creeping into my stomach all over again.

"Did you report them?"

"No." I wasn't planning on telling Alex, much less let others bear witness to my humiliation.

"Why not?"

"Because it doesn't matter."

"How can it not matter?" His voice got louder. They committed a crime."

"Shhh." I was starting to regret telling him. "Just leave it."

"Wylie, you can't just leave it. You have to tell someone." His voice was getting louder—more insistent.

I was getting mad. "Don't you understand? It's embarrassing. I don't want to talk about it." My voice cracked. I could feel the tears welling up in my eyes. Why was I crying so much lately? Shit, get a grip Wylie.

Not wanting to spill even more tears in front of Alex, I struggled out of the hammock and rushed down the path that led towards the beach. My eyes burned, not just from tears, but from the heavy campfire smoke that hung low and lazy beneath the heavy marine air. I wiped my eyes with the back of my arm.

"Hey, watch it!" A female voice cried out in the darkness. In my haste, I didn't realize I had wandered onto the concrete bike path that ran parallel to the beach. I managed to jump out of the way, watching in embarrassment as a girl glided by me on a longboard—her blonde hair flowing behind her. It was the most graceful site I think I'd ever seen.

"Sorry!" I called out, almost as an afterthought. I was mesmerized by the slow sine-wave curves of her board across the cement. Everything about her flowed—from the motion across the path to the thin material of her short sun-dress. Something in my gut stirred. I ran a few yards after her before I realized it was no use. I watched her silhouette until she disappeared into the night, kicking myself for not having my board with me. My distress forgotten, I vowed to find her tomorrow.

That familiar vibration ran up my legs as my board glided along the smooth concrete boardwalk, interrupted every now and then by a small rumble as our wheels encountered a small crack or patch of sand. The wind rushed by my ears and across every hair on my torso. I could feel the heat of the morning sun seeping into my chest as Alex and I skated towards the skate park. Back and forth across the path we weaved, repeating the pattern that the mystery chick made last night as she skated away from me. I hoped she'd be there, at the park. I hadn't told Alex about her. I'm not sure why. I was still a little upset about last night, even though he apologized. Despite the cool breeze and warmth on my chest, I felt heavy—lethargic even. I definitely wasn't feeling myself.

"Dude, why're you lagging?" Alex called over his shoulder.

I didn't realize I was so far behind. I pumped the ground a few times with my right leg, in an attempt to catch up with him. I felt a sharp pain in my stomach with each stroke. What the hell is wrong with me today? I tried to shake it off and pumped some more, eventually catching up to Alex as he neared the park.

I could hear the sounds of trucks grinding on concrete and decks slamming onto the ground. There was already about 15 or so other kids there. It reminded me of the canal back home. At least I wouldn't run into Cam here. We stopped just short of the giant concrete indentation in the ground, meant to mimic a large built-in pool, but with multiple lobes to accommodate more skaters. Someone had brought a portable CD player and was blasting Social Distortion's version of *Ring of Fire*. Skaters of varying levels of talent glided through the bowl and up the sides, some sticking their landing, others sliding back down the side after up-turned boards. On the opposite side of the pool area was a set of concrete steps. A few kids were doing tricks off of these, but there were maybe 8 or so people hanging out, watching the action. My gaze moved up to the top of the steps, where *she* stood atop her board, tracing a lazy figure 8 along the sidewalk.

At that moment, I felt sick and exhilarated—at the same time. I stood there, like an idiot, staring at her until Alex traced my line of sight and spotted her too.

"Oh man." He gasped. "She's gorgeous."

She's mine. A voice inside me growled, but all I could say was, "yeah."

I snatched my t-shirt from my waistband and shrugged into it, then grabbed my board and jogged over to the pool. I dropped in, trying to time it so that when she was facing me, she would

100

catch me doing a one-handed headstand on the rim of the pool. I don't know if it worked or not, but I pulled off the trick perfectly. As I came back down the wall, I noticed Alex bombing towards me, doing his own headstand before following me back down and doing it again on the other side. Ohhhhh, so *this* is how it's gonna be. It was on. Every trick I did, Alex did too, and then some. We tried for over an hour to out-skate each other. I honestly don't know if either of us succeeded, but by the end, we were laughing too hard at each other to care.

Afterwards, I bombed down one wall and up the other side—landing on a large patch of concrete that ended in grass. I hopped off my board and rolled down, letting the cool green blades tickle my arms as I stared up at the sky. I closed my eyes, feeling the wind blowing across my sweaty body as my heart rate returned to some semblance of normal. I heard the rumble of rubber wheels on concrete and figured it was Alex coming to join me.

A shadow intruded on the brightness streaming down on my closed eyelids. "You know, your legs are blocking the path." A female voice sounded right above me. I knew it was her before I opened my eyes.

It looked like she was wearing the same dress she wore last night when she almost crashed into me. She was close enough that I could see little braids intermixed in her hair, but she was backlit, so I couldn't see the details of her face.

I tried to think of something witty to say. All I came up with was, "Of course—how else was I to get your attention?" My heart started racing again. Did I just say that? Was that witty? Or creepy?

"Oh." She practically floated down to sit next to me. "I thought you were trying to get my attention with those fancy skate tricks."

Calling me out on my own game? I liked that. "Oh, I didn't know you were watching." I sat up.

She wrinkled up her freckle-clad nose."I'm not sure you noticed this, but everyone was watching you and your boyfriend out there dancing like it was prom or something."

My guts froze. Did she really think Alex was my boyfriend? Was she put-off by my little show? Dammit, why do I suck so bad at this?

"I'm Wylie." I stuck my hand out. "And he's not my boyfriend."

Skater chick looked at my hand, then out at the skate scene in front of us. Alex was grinding across the rim before he disappeared down into the pit. "Duh. That much is obvious. He *is* your friend though, right? But I mean, really, what kind of friend tries to impress a girl his friend is obviously in love with."

I put my hand down. "I'm in love with you?"

"Obviously." She kept starring straight ahead.

I stared at her profile. Her nose was small and rounded with a thin silver ring through her nostril. More silver rings rimmed her ear. I wondered how old she was. She had to be way older than me. With those piercings and all that...*confidence*. And the fact that she could *see* so much and be so right about things. Her confidence was a turn on, for sure. But I also felt a little weird about her calling Alex out. I didn't really think he was trying to get her attention too. We were just skating. Right?

"Don't think about it too hard, genius. You might hurt yourself."

I liked her snark. "You know, usually that type of introduction is followed by a reciprocal introduction."

She looked at me sideways and smirked. "*Reciprocal introduction*? Alright, captain manners. I'm Desiree. Everyone calls me Dez."

I didn't want to be *everyone*. I wanted to be the one to call her, "Desiree."

She looked at me and flung her hair over her shoulder. "Watch yourself lover-boy."

I could have floated off the ground. She doesn't think I'm a girl! I was trying to think of something to say next, when Alex came up and flopped down on the other side of Desiree. He looked at me behind her back, raised his eyebrows and mouthed '*Oh my god!*'

"This is Alex."

She flipped her head back to look at Alex. "Charmed." Then she turned back to me, "Wylie, buy me an ice cream?"

Just as quickly as she sat down, she hopped back up and grabbed my hand, pulling me off the ground.

"Oookay?" I scooped up my board and followed after her. I turned briefly to catch Alex shaking his head while he waved goodbye.

Desiree led me down a winding path to the snack bar. My hand tingled from her touch. I'd never held anyone's hand before. And she was so…perfect. As we stood in line behind three chatty, bikini-clad teens, I stared up at the menu, trying to think of something to say. There were only two thoughts running through my head— 'why are you paying attention to me?' and 'holy shit, you're holding my hand.' Neither seemed cool to say out loud though.

When it was our turn to order, Desiree ordered an ice cream cone. And a hot dog. And an order of fries. Was that all for her? Or was she ordering for me, too? I played it safe by ordering another ice cream cone as I pulled my wallet from my pocket. Dropping $20 on snack bar food wasn't exactly how I planned to spend my skate winnings, but to be honest, I would have bought her the world, if I could afford it.

She ate all the food I bought, except the extra cone. But I didn't care. We spent the entire day together, talking about life, music, and skateboarding, walking, sitting in the sand. I learned that she was only 15 and that she was spending the summer with her dad in San Clemente. She loved to skate and take pictures. She had a three-legged black cat named Jinx and she wanted to be an artist and live someplace cool, like Chile or Tahiti.

I told her about Alex and how we met, how I was going to be a big time skate sensation and escape from my crappy hometown too. I shared a little about my crazy family. About how my oldest brother, Mason, is probably the coolest of all of them. I think he understands me the best. I didn't tell her why though. I liked that she saw me as a guy. And I remembered how Brianna stopped talking to me when someone told her my real name. I wanted to have a chance at my first romantic experience and I wasn't sure how Desiree would react if I told her the truth. Everything felt right with her. I didn't feel like I had to keep my guard up about how I sat or how my voice sometimes got high when I got excited about something.

The sun dipped low on the horizon. My mind kept creeping back to Alex. Would he be mad that I ditched him all day? I mean, isn't it like guy code or something that when you meet a hot girl, you get a free pass from hanging out? I wasn't sure. And I didn't want to be one of those people that ditched their friends when a girl came around.

"Hey, I think we should head back." I was about to stand when Desiree reached her hand up to my face and kissed me. It was such a surprise it took me a second to realize what was happening. Her lips were soft on mine. I closed my eyes. She opened her mouth and stuck her tongue in mine. It felt foreign, but also incredibly great. Those same tingly feelings that

I felt in my hand earlier were now shooting through my entire body. I let my tongue feel hers and I started copying the things she was doing. I couldn't believe this was finally happening to me! I brought my hand up to her shoulder and ran it down the soft skin of her arm to her hand. She twined her fingers in mine and placed my hand on her chest. I started getting hot all over. I was getting seriously turned on! I'd gotten to first *and* second base all at one time. Wait 'til I tell Alex about this. Suddenly, my stomach started to hurt again and I felt the creep of wetness between my legs. I pulled away, ending the kiss, but Desiree wanted more. She pulled my head back towards her.

"I don't—" I stammered. "I gotta go." I stood up, grabbed my board and started for the path that would lead me back to the campsite.

"Wylie, wait." Desiree got up and followed me. "Don't you like me?"

I stopped and turned, trying not to double over from the pain in my stomach. "Of course I like you. It's just—" I thought I would throw up. "—I… I don't feel so good."

"I think I can make you feel better." She put her hand on my chest and started moving it slowly down my body.

I wanted to stay. But I really thought I was going to throw up. "I'll see you tomorrow." I pushed her hand away. "I'm sorry." I started walking as fast as I could towards the campsite, turning back for a second to flash a feeble wave in her direction. I didn't want her to think I didn't like her, but I didn't want to rolf all over her flowy summer dress either.

By the time I reached the Keen's RV, I was sweating all over and my stomach was in knots. I mumbled "Hi" to Alex's dad, who was sitting in a camp chair reading a book, and burst into the RV almost knocking Reyna over.

"Wylie!" Reyna jumped back, startled. "Are you ok?"

"Yeah." I mumbled as I pushed past her in my haste to get to the bathroom. Once inside, I wasn't sure whether I needed to crap or puke. I decided to drop trow and sit down. Nothing happened. Then I saw it. The blood soaking the crotch of my pale blue boxers.

No no no no no! This can't be happening. Hot tears threatened to spill down my face. No, not yet! Not now! I was going to get on puberty blockers. I wasn't supposed to *ever* get my period. Reyna was going to help me. This wasn't fair! This wasn't supposed to happen. Was I going to start looking more like a girl now? The tears poured down my face and onto my lap, leaving dark spots on the non-soiled parts of my boxers.

"No. This can't happen." I heard myself say. Wadding up some toilet paper, I tried to clean myself up. It was so wet and sticky at the same time. There was so much blood. Bright and red and mocking. My stomach boiled. I lurched up and twisted around just in time to launch my lunch into the pink water of the toilet. I heaved until my sides cramped up and there was nothing left in my stomach. I felt like a hollow shell of who I was.

Reyna knocked lightly on the door. "Wylie, are you ok?"

I grabbed more toilet paper and wiped my mouth, then tossed the soiled tissue in the trash. I sat back down on the toilet, staring at the drying blood that betrayed who I was.

"Wylie?" Reyna sounded worried.

"Yeah?" My voice was weak. I didn't know what to say. I'd been so happy earlier. The happiest I'd ever been. Everything was going right. Desiree saw me as a guy. She even kissed me. My first kiss! I was passing as a guy. Everything should be amazing, but it felt like my life was over. Desiree probably thought I was a weirdo, which, I probably was. I kicked off my shoes and ripped off my jeans, tore off my boxers and shoved them in the trash.

"Wylie, I'd like to come in." She paused, waiting for me to answer.

Half-dressed, I stared at the door. I could see her figure through the frosted glass centerpiece less than a foot from my face. It's an RV bathroom—where did she think she was going to go?

"No." I started pulling my jeans back on. "I'm ok. Be out in a second." I watched as Reyna hesitated, then backed away. Sighing, I buckled my belt, washed my hands, and flushed the toilet. It might as well have been me in that watery vortex— my life creeping down the dark hole, amongst the blood and chunks of french fries.

When I finally emerged from the bathroom, the sun had set, casting an orange-pink light into the RV. Reyna sat on the couch, her face illuminated by the lamplight.

"Come sit." She patted the couch cushion next to her with that look of concern that only moms get.

I looked at that cream-colored cushion and shook my head. I wanted to leave a mark on the world, but not necessarily on their couch. My gaze dropped to the floor.

"Wylie, I want to help you, but if you don't talk to me, I can't."

That name—*Wylie*. I felt like an imposter. Who was I kidding, anyway? I watched those stupid health class movies. I was going to grow boobs and hips and everybody would think that I was a girl, just because of my body. I looked down at Reyna. She had been so cool to me. Understanding and supportive. There was nothing she could do about this.

Just then, the screen door squeaked open and Alex's dad walked in, book in hand.

"I just—" I looked over at Mr. Keen, then back at the floor. "I just ate something bad, I think."

"You know, I've been feeling a little queazy as well." Mr. Keen put his hand on his stomach. "Maybe it was breakfast?"

The disaster that was my life was even making Alex's dad sick. "I'm just gonna go lay down." I turned and headed for the room Alex and I shared at the back of the RV. As soon as the door closed, I rolled into the bottom bunk and curled into a ball to try and stop the cramping feeling in my gut, wishing I had brought some xannie with me. My body felt heavy. It wasn't long before I drifted off to sleep.

I woke up to the sound of laughter and the smell of barbecued chicken. Inside my room, it was pitch black. I pushed the button on the side of my watch to illuminate the time. 7:36. I slid open the curtain covering the small window by my bed. John and Reyna sat across the picnic table from Alex and—Desiree? What was *she* doing here? Alex glopped a giant scoop of what looked like potato salad onto Desiree's plate as she chewed on a half piece of corn on the cob. She stopped to lick the butter from her fingers. I remembered the feel of that tongue on mine. I felt a pleasant quiver in my stomach as I escaped from my current hell for a memory of an afternoon in the sun with the most beautiful girl I had ever met.

"Should we wake Wylie so he can jon us?" Mr. Keen asked.

Reyna turned and looked towards the RV. I let the curtain fall back into place. I couldn't go out there. Not now. I could sprout boobs and an hourglass figure at any minute. Everyone was going to know.

"I don't know. Maybe we should just let him sleep." I heard Reyna's voice over Desiree's unmistakable giggle, a sound I had nearly drowned in earlier that day. What was so goddamn funny? And why was she hanging out with Alex now?

I laid there on my back, staring up at the wood-paneled bottom of the top bunk, not seeing anything by my life dissolving before my eyes. I stayed there until the voices faded. I stayed there until the last plastic dish was washed and dried. I stayed there until the rocking motion of the RV stopped, indicating the Keens had settled into their own bed for the night. Where was Alex? I strained to listen to the sounds outside. I could hear muffled conversations in the distance, but nothing nearby. I rolled back out of bed and felt something warm gush out into the crotch of my jeans. Dammit! Was I going to bleed to death here?

I eased the bedroom door open and was met with more darkness. I took a minute to clean up in the bathroom before sneaking outside. I needed something to calm my nerves. Weed, xannie, I didn't care, as long as it took me away from this new hell that was my life. My board was propped up against the front tire of the RV. I scooped it up and walked down a little ways before hopping on. I didn't want to wake the Keens.

The cool air felt good on my face as I made my way towards the skate park. There had to be someone there selling. I wove my way down the winding path, enjoying the solitude and the occasional sound of the surf crashing on the shore. The glow of the skate park lights cast a dome of light in the distance, pushing away the darkness. As I made my way up and over the gentle slope, the whole park came into view. Maybe ten or so skaters ran through the courses, with an equal amount of onlookers. I coasted down the grass-flanked path towards the park and the familiar sounds of rubber wheels skidding on cement and wooden decks grinding on metal bars. I skimmed the cement steps where the onlookers chatted, half looking for Alex, half looking for anyone that looked like they might party. Beyond the skate course, bodies stood silhouetted under street lamps—non-skaters at a skatepark could mean dealers. I headed in that direction, passing a couple making out in the shadows on the grass.

Then I heard it—that same giggle I had heard at dinner. The same one that I had fallen for this afternoon. I slowly rolled past the couple sprawled out on the ground. Alex lay on the grass with Desiree above him, her body laying against his, one bare leg over one of his. His head rested on one hand, while the other ran down her back. Her long, blonde hair hung down, shielding their faces from the world as her hand disappeared beneath the buckle of his belt.

Then, all I saw was red. The red flames of rage rose behind my eyes. The red stain on my boxers. The red "F" branded hot on my forehead.

F—for female.

F—for failure to be a man.

F—for fool to believe anyone would be my friend.

I stopped my board, my shadow falling on their bodies. I wanted to hurt them. I wanted both of them to feel the pain that I felt—the pain of betrayal.

Desiree flicked her hair back as she turned to see who was intruding on their private make-out session. Alex opened his eyes, which got twice as wide when he saw me standing there.

"Fuck you." I whispered, and skated back into the darkness.

8

Alex

"Wylie, wait!" I yelled after him. Desiree's hand was still down my pants. I am such an asshole. I grabbed her arm and slid her hand out of my clothes.

"Oh, baby, just let her go." Desiree pouted.

I instantly regretted letting it slip that Wylie was trans. She didn't get it. I had no business talking about it anyway. And now, Wylie's going to hate me for life. But she was so—*disarming.* When she came back to the park we just started talking and she was so easy to talk to. And so gorgeous. And so, just—easy.

How do I keep getting myself into these situations?

I am such an asshole.

Desiree was still half-laying across my body. I rolled her off of me. "Don't call him that."

"What? *Her?*" She sneered the word. "That's what she is, isn't she?"

I got up. "Look, you don't know what you're talking about. And clearly, you're not so open-minded as you think you are."

Desiree looked hurt. "Why are we fighting over this? Let's

just go down to the beach and continue where we left off?" She reached up to grab my hand. I pulled it away. I had to go check on Wylie. I had to make sure he was ok.

"Just do me a favor and leave us both alone." I flipped my board over from the grass to the cement path and hopped on, kicking off with my left foot. Desiree yelled something after me that I couldn't quite make out. *Asshole,* probably. And she would be right. I didn't look back.

When I reached the RV, all the lights were on. I was about to open the door when Wylie burst out, backpack on his shoulder. He looked at me before pushing past me on his way to our Jeep we towed behind the RV.

"Wylie, wait." I followed him. "Look, I'm an asshole. I know that."

He kept walking, ignoring me.

"Wylie, I'm sorry." I pleaded. "Please. Let's just talk about it."

Without looking at me, he jerked open the passenger door and climbed in. The door slammed shut before I could get there.

"Alex, come in here please." It was my dad.

I stood outside the jeep, looking up at Wylie's face. His jaw was clenched. His eyes raw.

"Wylie please. I'm sorry. You have to know how sorry I am."

He kept starring straight ahead.

"Alex." My dad repeated.

I sighed and turned back towards the RV. The phrase *I'm an asshole,* repeated like a snare drum with each footfall on my way back.

"Alex, what happened?" My mom met me at the door.

I hung my head. "What did he tell you?"

"Nothing." She threw her hands up. "He burst in here, in

tears, and demanded that I take him home. Did something happen between the two of you?"

"Yeah." I sighed and looked up at her. "Remember that girl, Desiree?"

"Yes, Alex, she was here for dinner less than three hours ago. I am not so old that my memory deteriorates that quickly." She had her hands on her hips. That was a bad sign.

"Right. Well, Wylie kinda likes her and, well, he kinda found us together tonight." I suddenly became very interested in some grime underneath my middle finger and worked to scrape it out. I couldn't look at her.

"He found you doing what?" My dad asked.

I really didn't want to tell them. Not that I thought they would have a problem with me making out with someone, but I didn't want them to see me as I saw myself right then. I deserved it though, didn't I? I did a crappy thing to my best friend and I deserved to be seen for the asshole that I was.

"We were making out. Desiree and me." I admitted.

"Oh, Alex." My mom said, clearly disappointed. "Are you really that influenced by your penis that you were willing to break your best friend's heart?"

I didn't have anything to say to that. It was worse, really. I betrayed his trust and told Desiree things I had no business saying. I didn't want to admit that to them, my mom especially.

"You need to apologize to him." My dad interjected.

"Dad, I know. I tried. He won't even look at me." I ran my hands through my hair, damp with sweat.

"Wylie's been going through a really tough time in his life. He needs you to be the person I know you to be." My mom had entered therapist-mode. "And, I'm a little ashamed to admit it, but I overheard you two talking last night, about Wylie being sexually harassed by the police."

113

Crap, what else had she heard?

"Alex, do you believe that he was telling the truth?" My dad asked.

"What? Yes, of course. Why would he lie about something like that?"

"Some people tell stories to get attention." My mom cut in. "But it didn't sound to me like a story."

"No, he really didn't want to talk about it." I remembered how angry he got when I told him he should tell someone.

"Yes, I heard. The thing is, I'm a mandatory reporter. I have to tell the authorities."

"Mom no! He's going to think I told on him." I started to panic. "He already probably hates me—this will only make it worse. You can't!"

"If he hates you, which, I doubt he does, it is because of your own insensitive actions. You can't blame me for this." She turned towards the door.

"Where are you taking him?"

"Back home." She snapped. "See you in five hours." The door squeaked open and slammed shut. Her footsteps sounded angry in the gravel leading towards the car.

I felt terrible. I starred at the door, hoping they would come back in. Hoping my mom could somehow explain to Wylie that I'm not so bad. I just made a bad decision. We could move past this. But the door didn't open. The roar of the Jeep's engine broke the calm silence of the night, fading away until there was nothing but the cold silence between me and my dad. I hated the way he was looking at me. That look of disappointment was worse than any words he could say.

"Dad." My voice was a whisper. "What do I do?"

"The only thing you can right now." He said, gently. "Give him time."

9

Wylie

"Why are the police in my living room asking to talk to you?" My mom's figure loomed large in the doorway of my bedroom. I hadn't left my room since Alex's mom dropped me off from San Clemente, except, of course, to go to the bathroom to sop up the never-ending stream of blood oozing from my body. When was this hell going to end?

"Haven't the foggiest." I muttered from my bed before turning over to face the wall.

"For Pete's sake, Willow, get up!" She was suddenly standing over my bed, throwing off the covers. "Oh dear lord!"

I could only imagine she was referring to the blood stained sheets and the smell that emanated from my body.

"Just leave me alone!" I grabbed the blanket and pulled it back over my head.

"Willow, sweetie, you got your period." She sat down on the side of the bed.

You don't say. I was hoping I was just bleeding to death.

"You're a woman now, sweetie." Her voice and her words

made me want to vomit. I didn't want to be a woman. I didn't want any of this.

"Go away." I groaned, wrapping my pillow around my head.

She sighed. "Willow, get up. Go to the bathroom and get a maxi pad from under the sink. Take off those smelly boxers and put on some proper panties and something presentable." She smacked me on the butt, as if that would get me moving. "Then meet me in the living room so we can get this police business straightened out." I felt her weight leave my bed.

"NOW." She yelled, when I made no move to get up.

"Fine." I kicked the covers off and rolled out of bed. "Would you get out of my room please?"

When she was gone, I did my duty and found 'presentable clothes' to wear for my date with the police. And by present-able, I mean my brother's jeans and a wrinkled black t-shirt, which had become baggier since I had stopped eating days ago. I couldn't imagine why they were here. I hadn't done anything wrong. Bypassing the bathroom, I trudged into the living room and found two cops standing just inside the door. The shorter one was a female with big brown eyes and long, dark hair that hung in a long braid down her back. The taller one was male, a much more friendly-looking fellow than the two that stopped me months ago. Oh shit. Is that why they're here? Did Alex fucking tell someone what I told him?

"Ah, here she is." My mom was shuffling about the room, straightening up stacks of newspapers and picking up trash and dirty dishes. That was new. Maybe I should refuse to come out of my room more often.

"Willow, I'm Officer Sheldon, and this is my partner, Officer Craig." The female cop motioned towards the tall, friendly-looking one with sandy blond hair.

"Ok." I muttered. Despite their friendly appearances, I could feel my pulse racing. I balled my hands into fists to keep them from shaking.

"Willow, we got a report concerning you and a couple of other officers. An incident that happened some time late February?" Officer Craig stood there, his face expectant. I offered him nothing.

"Do you recall encountering Sergeant Orell and Sergeant Northrup near the 7-11 on California Street on the morning of February 28th?"

"Names' don't ring a bell." My voice was barely above a whisper. I could feel my body start to shake.

"Why don't we sit down." Officer Sheldon suggested, now that there was actually somewhere to sit. She motioned towards the couch.

I sat cross-legged in the farthest corner of the couch, my hands clenched in my lap. My mom took a seat on the worn-out ottoman near the TV. Officer Sheldon kneeled in front of me on one knee, but Officer Craig remained standing a few steps behind her.

"Willow." She started.

I wish she'd stop calling me that.

"I have a feeling this is pretty hard for you." She continued. "We got a report that these two police officers harassed you and touched you in an inappropriate manner." She paused. "Is that true?"

"Oh my lord." My mom put her hand to her mouth. "Willow, why did the police stop you? What did you do? What did *they* do?" Her voice started getting shrill as she sat there, rocking back and forth. Officer Craig shot her an annoyed look.

I couldn't deal with this anymore. All I wanted to do was

forget it ever happened. All I wanted was for everyone to leave me alone.

"Willow?" Officer Sheldon tilted her head, the way adults do when they want you to know, 'you can trust me.'

But I knew better. I couldn't trust her. Just like I couldn't trust my crew. Just like I couldn't trust Brianna, or Desiree, or that traitor, Alex.

"Can you tell us what happened?" Her voice was soft.

"No." I whispered.

"No, you can't tell us?" She prodded.

"No." I said, louder. "It didn't happen." I looked her straight in the eyes and I lied.

Her face hardened a bit. "It didn't happen?"

I shook my head.

"The person making the report seemed pretty convinced that it did. Where they lying?" She raised her eyebrows.

"Who made this report?" My mom demanded, rising from her perch. "Willow, what is going on?"

I'd had enough. "I lied, ok? I made the whole story up. Nothing happened." I shouted, as I leaped up. I ran past Officer Craig and down the hall, back to my room. I slammed the door and locked it. Even over my ragged breath, I could hear them coming down the hall. I slid my feet into an old pair of vans and grabbed my backpack and board. I slid the window over my bed open and pushed the screen out before hopping down into the dirt. The last thing I heard was the knocking on my door and the shouts to open up before I ran down the driveway, hucked my board in front of me and hopped on.

This was it. The last time I would see my neighborhood. The last time I would bomb down this hill towards the canal. The last time I would step foot into this shit town. I would head for LA. Take the canals towards the beach and make my way to the city. Start my life over. I knew I could make money skating—if I could actually get sponsored. And maybe I could find that doctor that Reyna talked about, the one who was working on hormone therapy for transgender people. For several miles, I skated, past the familiar strip malls and dilapidated neighborhoods, past my old elementary school. The wind felt good in my greasy hair. I tried to remember the last time I took a shower. Maybe a week ago? I'll take one when I get to the beach. They have showers at the beach.

Once I reached the entrance to the canals, I slid between the sheets of chain link that had been cut years ago, probably by Z. When I made it through the oleander bushes, I could see the remnants of Cam's artwork, painted over in Rasta colors, also by Z. He was a man who treated words like diamonds, but his actions were what mattered, and his were always in support of me. That realization made me feel good. Like there was at least one person in the world I could count on. I dropped down into the canal, which was completely dry by now, and followed it towards my new home. Wherever *that* was.

It was well-past dark when I rolled into the smelly homeless encampment under the bridge the next day. Clouds had rolled in that afternoon threatening "April showers." A few black figures milled around in the shadows of what looked like a trash dump, some talking to themselves, some talking to each other. Men, women, young, old—they all had the same look about them. Eyes sunken. Some mouths sunken. Skin tanned a dark brown. Worn out. Filthy. Given my current state, I fit right in. A fire crackled in a barrel off to my left, surrounded by a group of men. It sounded like they were arguing about something. Overhead was a freeway—I don't know which one. Between the rush of the cars overhead and the multiple conversations going on around me, I could barely think.

I picked up my board and slid it behind my back so that it was cradled by the straps. I'd been skating for too many hours and my whole body was sore. My right quad was cramped. All I wanted to do was lie down. Nervous, I made my way through the camp. This was seeming less and less like a good idea. Suddenly, my foot slid out from under me, but I managed to keep from falling down. The smell that wafted up from my feet indicated shit. Dog? Human? I didn't want to know. My sudden movements garnered me some looks from some of the people around me. I kept moving, twisting my foot around with each step, trying to get the crap off. The trash dump that I had seen earlier was actually a camp with makeshift shelters constructed of whatever these people could scrounge up. I tightened my backpack onto my shoulders and kept my eyes focused on the ground. I climbed up the side of the concrete incline that lead to the underside of the road and sat down, alone.

What are you doing? A familiar voice asked from the dark recesses of my brain.

Getting the hell away from the people who hurt me. I'm not going back. Not this time. This time, I'm serious. I'm making my own way. And I don't need anybody's help to do it.

The only thing you don't need help doing is getting yourself killed.

Shut up. Nobody asked you.

"Oh no no no. I'm going crazy." I rubbed my hands together to warm them up. Sometime during my conversation with myself, it had begun to rain. Of course. It rains like 5

120

days a year here and today had to be one of them? At least I was far enough under the bridge that I didn't think I'd get wet. Bringing my knees up to my chest, I wrapped my arms around them to try and conserve my body heat, which seemed to be evaporating rapidly. All I had on was jeans and a t-shirt. I had no other clothes with me.

Nice planning on your part, genius. It was Alex, of course. What the hell? Why did he have to be the voice of my own, personal conscience?

Dude, shut up!

I tried to think of a song to drown out the doubt. The winning song - Metallica's *Trapped Under Ice*. A great song, but hardly helpful in distracting me from the cold sinking into my bones. I thought about the beach. About running shirtless with—Agghhh! I can't get away from the guy. I shook my head and looked down at the scene below me. One guy in particular caught my eye over by the fire barrel—mostly because I seem to have caught his eye. He just kept staring at me. Not like the staring people do at school, where they look away as soon as they see you look at them. This guy was blatantly staring me down. I looked away and tried to find something else to look at, but my gaze kept going back to him. His was fixed on me.

The sky opened up and water streamed in sheets down the sides of the bridge. Every now and then, I heard the screech of tires as the cars above tried to navigate in the rain. It seemed like the temperature dropped another 5 degrees. At least I was dry. I thought about my bed and how, just hours ago, I was warm and comfortably alone in my misery. No! You're not going back there. Geez, you're such a freaking baby. Every time you try to leave, you get spooked and run back home to mommy. And why? She doesn't even like you! I felt my fingers gripping my hair. I was truly going nuts.

Out of nowhere, black boots appeared in front of me. *Shit. Shit. Shit. Be cool.* I looked up. It was the guy with the staring problem. Up close, I could tell he was younger than some of the rest around here. His face wasn't as tan as some of the others and his face stubble indicated maybe he had shaved in the last few days. His hair was shoulder-length and scraggly under a dirty red beanie. When he opened his mouth, his teeth were brown and crooked.

"You're in my spot." He grunted.

"Sorry." I blurted out as I jumped up, grabbed my bag and moved over 10 steps closer to the edge of the bridge.

"That's my spot too." He said, louder, his black eyes boring into me.

Could he sense my growing terror? I walked a few more steps and set my stuff down. I was nearly in the rain.

"Keep movin' little man." He made a motion with his hands as if to say, "shoo."

I looked at him. Deflated. Then I looked at the rain. I didn't want to be out in that. And who knows where the next bridge was? Who the hell did he think he was anyway? He didn't need all that space. And how was I supposed to start a new life—the new, powerful Wylie Masterson, if I kept letting people push me around? Screw that and screw him!

"This is *my* spot now." I sat down, arms crossed around my knees, staring *him* down.

The guy laughed. "I was jus' messing with you, little man." He motioned for me to come back. "C'mon, I've got somethin' that'll keep us both warm." He brought out a baggie of what looked to be weed.

Now we're talking.

"Come on little puppy. I won't bite." He plopped down, brought out some papers and started rolling a joint, watching me walk his direction the whole time. He was still creepy, but weed was weed and I could use some escape.

"That's it." He licked the side of the paper to make the joint stick as I sat down next to him. "I'm Doc." He put the finished joint in his mouth, fished out a lighter from the inside of his oversized canvas jacket, and lit the thing, inhaling deeply. He held his breath and passed it to me.

I took a hit. The hot smoke warmed me instantly. I held my breath until I got dizzy, then exhaled.

"Yeah, that's it. You got a name, little man?" His voice sounded like he had swallowed gravel and he had this weird way of swaying when he spoke—like he had some ethereal music going on in his own head. I guess maybe we all have a soundtrack we live by. I didn't really trust this guy, but hey, I had vowed not to trust anyone ever again. Doesn't mean I can't be neighborly, especially with someone bearing gifts. Besides, it's not like it's my *legal* name anyway.

"Wylie." I took another hit.

"Wylie, you a young pup, eh? Those *cajones* ain't yet dropped." He took the joint from me and inhaled.

I laughed, then I started coughing. If only he *knew*. Maybe that's what all the blood was about. My balls were trying to drop, they were just making a mess of it.

"Easy there." He reached into another pocket of his jacket and brought out a clear bottle of brown liquid, unscrewed the cap and offered it to me. "Drink."

I drank. And drank. It burned going down and warmed me to the core. I felt like I was falling into oblivion. I wanted the fall.

Doc had to pull the bottle away from me. "Yo save some for me little man. Where your manners?"

"Wolves don't have manners." I heard myself say. Where did *that* come from?

123

"Oh I see, so now you a *wolf pup*?" Doc took a drink, keeping an eye on me like I was some specimen he's studying. "You a *lone* wolf, Wylie?" He handed me back the bottle.

I took it. "You know it." I gulped down more of the stuff.

He nodded. "I hear ya there." He took a hit, exhaling slowly. "Other people ain't nothin' but pain."

"That's what I'm talking about." I raised the bottle as a toast to his wisdom.

"Yeah, I see you hurtin' wolf pup." He shifted over so we were sitting closer together. "Luckily, ole Doc here has the remedy for the pain." His hand disappeared into yet another pocket, and came out with a baggy containing what looked like a syringe, a spoon and some yellow powder. He handed me the joint. "You just keep that company and make sure no one else comes over here. This medicine is just for you and your friend, Doc. You hear?"

I nodded and took another hit. I felt good, finally. I was floating above the world. Above the people who's faces were blurring together in a swirl of blacks and grays. I could hear the rain pouring down all around me, but I wasn't wet and I wasn't cold. Nobody could hurt me here. I took another drink, vaguely aware of what Doc was doing next to me.

I was laughing when he put the needle into my arm. Then I was crying when the stuff burned through my veins. I think Doc was crying with me. Then his arms were around me. And then, blackness.

10

Alex

The mid-day air hung heavy from yesterday's rain as I knocked on the Masterson's door. It felt like forever before she opened the door, her face swollen, red from crying. Shit. What was I interrupting?

"Is Wylie home?" I managed to ask, wishing I had called first. But I knew he wouldn't answer, just as he hadn't answered for the past week.

"Who are you?" The woman in the doorway demanded.

"I—I'm Alex." I stammered. Hadn't we met once? This *was* Wylie's mom, right?

"You have some nerve showing up here. After you broke my poor Willow's heart! It's *your* fault she's gone!" The velocity of the slamming door could have killed a grown man.

Gone? What did she mean gone?

I knocked on the door again. And again. Finally, she opened the door, a wad of tissue in her hand.

"What do you want?" She blew her nose.

"What do you mean she—" I shook my head, "I mean, he's gone?"

She looked at me and cocked her head, as if trying to figure out why I had eight arms. "Willow ran away after you broke up with her! *She's* been gone for three days!"

Slaaaammmm. I was starring at the door again. Ran away? I broke up with her? Geez, she's as crazy as Wiley described her. I thought about knocking again, but figured nothing else would come of it. If Wylie's been gone for three days, why wasn't she out looking for him? This made no sense. He had to be in there. She was just trying to keep me from him.

"WYLIE!" I shouted at the house. "WYLIE! I'm sorry I hurt you. PLEASE come out and talk to me! WYLIE!"

The door swung open. Wylie's mom looked like a bull ready to charge. "I told you, *Willow* has run away! If you were any kind of man, you would go find her!"

This time she slammed the door so hard, the top of the wrought iron porch light fell off, landing with a clatter on the ground.

I stared at the twisted piece of metal. Wylie's gone. For three days? My stomach felt like it was full of angry eels. This was my fault. I had to do something.

I grabbed my board and raced home to tell my parents. My mom immediately got on the phone to call Wylie's mom. It was so frustrating sitting there listening to my mom say things like "and then what" and "they did?" and "hmmm." I wanted to scream at them to get off the phone and find my friend. I sat there, my elbows on my knees, hands gripping fistfuls of hair, waiting for some form of information we could use to find Wylie.

"Hey bud." I felt my dad's hand rubbing my back, which was sticky with sweat. He had gotten up to sit next to me. "They'll find him. Don't worry."

I jumped up. "You can't tell me not to worry! They're not

even looking for him!" I screamed. "And it's my fault he's gone!"

"Ok...right...uh-huh...alright...got it." My mom hung up the phone.

My heart was pounding so hard I could feel it in my head. I needed to do something. No one was doing anything to find Wylie. Did they really not care what happened to him? I had to go find him. I headed for the door.

"Alex." My mom called from the dining room. "Wait a minute hon."

I stopped, but I didn't look back at her.

"Come sit."

"No. I have to go find him." I started for the door again.

"Alex stop." Her voice louder this time. "I fully appreciate that you want to find Wylie and I will do everything in my power to help, but we need a plan first. Come sit down so we can talk."

"Yeah, come on bud." My dad patted the couch next to him.

I turned back towards the both of them. "If you want to help, then let's get in the car and go find him." I threw my hands in the air.

"I think it would be more productive if you talked to the police. You know him best. Maybe there's some information you could give them that might help them find Wylie." She took a deep breath and let it out in a slow hiss. She looked tired. "You know where he likes to hang out. What his mindset has been. Let me call the police, then we'll all go out and look. Ok?"

It felt like every second I didn't spend looking for him, the chance for us to find him got smaller and smaller. She was probably right, I mean, I am pretty much the only person he's been hanging out with lately. But why couldn't we just go out to his secret spots and find him ourselves? My head was starting to hurt.

"Fine." I spat, stomping back to the couch and flopping down on the farthest side from both of them. I laid my head back and closed my eyes as my mom picked up the phone and dialed a number. Her voice faded into the background. All I could see was Wylie's shadow skating off into the night and the sound of his voice saying, "Fuck you." I got that same feeling in my stomach, like someone reached inside me, grabbed hold of any organ they could find, and twisted. I wanted to throw up. How could I have been such a jerk? And now I might never see Wylie again. He might be lying dead in a ditch right now and it would be my fault. The pounding in my head got louder, the pain more intense.

"Alex, come here." My mom held the phone on her shoulder.

I opened my eyes and pried myself off the couch and plodded over towards her.

She held out the phone to me. "This is Officer Sheldon. She has some questions for you."

I took the phone from her hand and listened as Officer Sheldon introduced herself and thanked me for answering the questions she hadn't yet asked. When she did, I answered as best I could, even the part about the last time I saw Wylie. She kept calling him *Willow* even though I corrected her every time. The questions seemed to go on forever and I was getting impatient. All of this talk wasn't doing Wylie any good. Finally, the officer thanked me again and I heard myself saying goodbye. I put the phone back in its cradle to charge, my right ear hot and sweaty from the pressure of the plastic receiver.

"Ok, can we go now?" I started for the front door again.

I could see my mom was about to protest, but my dad stood up and held up his hand. "I'll take him." He grabbed his keys from the bowl of marbles on the side table and followed me out.

"I'd feel better if you had some lunch in your stomachs."

"Mom!" I shouted, exasperated. Why was she making this so difficult?

"Fine. Fine." She grabbed a couple of Clif Bars from a wooden bowl on the kitchen counter and tossed them to us. "At least take these with you."

I caught the bars and shoved them in my pockets, grateful to be taking some sort of action.

The hazy afternoon sun just sat there, lazy, acting like everything was good in the world. My dad backed the Jeep down the driveway, but stopped abruptly when he say my mom come running out of the front door and across the lawn, waving her arms.

Seriously, what now?

My dad lowered his window as she reached us.

"I just got a call. Mason found Wylie. They're at the hospital." There were tears rolling down her face.

A wave of relief came over me, but it was temporary. "Hospital? Is he ok?"

My mom came around and opened my door. "I don't know sweetie. Let's just get down there."

I crawled into the back so my mom could get in the front seat. My dad drove faster than I've ever seen him drive before. He even honked at some old man who looked like he should be in one of those old-people scooters on the sidewalk, instead of behind the wheel weaving all over the road. I think we were all anxious to see how Wylie was doing.

The emergency parking lot was full, so we had to weave our way around the hospital parking maze before finding something in the farthest reaches of the campus. My mom was complaining the whole time that my dad should have dropped her off at the emergency entrance so she could go in and see what was what. It was kind of funny, considering she kept me waiting so long before letting me go look for Wylie. We practically ran to the hospital entrance. Once inside, my mom led us over to the Info station and asked where Wylie was. Of course, there was no record of any Wylie Masterson. I could tell it pained my mom to ask where Willow Masterson was.

The old man behind the desk handed us all Visitor badges and directed us to the emergency room. We passed through beige hall after beige hall, all smelling of that hospital disinfectant, navigating around gurneys and wheelchairs, until we finally reached the ER waiting room. There were only a few people scattered around the room, slouched down in plastic chairs. One woman with dirty-blonde hair sticking out everywhere held a kidney-bean shaped bowl they give out if you have to puke. A middle-aged man across the room had a greasy looking rag wrapped around one hand and held a beer in the other. I wondered for a moment how sterile that could be. A few chairs down from him were two teenage boys that vaguely looked like Wiley sitting in the corner. The older one's left foot tapped with a nervous energy. Were they his brothers?

My mom motioned us to sit as she headed to the intake window. We sat down across the room from the boys. A bored-looking nurse sitting behind a thick glass window asked my mom what her issue was.

"We're here to see Wiley—" She shook her head, "Willow Masterson."

The boys looked up. Yep, brothers.

"Are you family?" She sat up straighter and adjusted the pink scrub top with every manner of puppy on it. The top seemed incongruous with her personality.

"I'm his psychiatrist." My mom said, without hesitation. "Dr. Reyna Keen."

The bored nurse didn't know what to do with that. "One moment." She got up and went to another room.

A young man in black scrubs came out of the double doors with what looked like a red and grey toolbox. It had the biohazard sticker on it, so I guessed it contained blood, and not tools. He walked through the waiting room and out another set of doors and into one of the ubiquitous beige hallways. I considered sneaking into the ER through those doors while the nurse was out of sight. I wondered what I would find on the other side. Was Wylie beat up? Did he get hit by a car? I couldn't stand not knowing.

A mechanical voice came through the intercom calling a code blue. I'd watched enough TV to know what that meant—someone was dying and needed resuscitation. Was it Wylie? My heart jumped into my throat and thudded hard. My eyes went back to those double doors. My friend was behind those doors. He might be dying. I needed to see him. I looked over at the empty window beyond my mom's tall figure. Still gone. I jumped up and ran for the double doors. I heard my dad yell my name, but I didn't care. My hands grasped the metal bars that ran parallel with the ground, they gave way under the pressure and the doors parted. I ran through them, looking left and right to find the bed that Wylie was laying in.

He was there, at the end of the row, partially surrounded by a blue-green curtain that ran along a track on the ceiling. I stopped just outside the curtain. His eyes were closed and there was an oxygen mask strapped to his face, but no one seemed to be panicking, so he wasn't the one they called the code for. He looked emaciated, though. His mom was sitting there next to him, crying, as a nurse injected something into an IV going into to his arm.

"What's wrong with him?" I asked, willing him to open his eyes.

The nurse removed the syringe from the IV and looked up at me. "You're not authorized to be here."

I felt a hand on my shoulder. "Alex go back out to the waiting room." It was my mom.

"Is he going to be ok?" I stared at Wylie just lying there, not moving.

Then, my mom's face was right in front of mine. She grasped me by both arms. "Wylie is going to be fine. I need you to go out there and sit down. I will be out shortly."

I stared at her, not really understanding the words coming out of her mouth.

"Alex. Go." She turned me around and gave me a little push towards the doors I had broken through just a minute ago.

When I returned to the waiting room, my dad was talking with Wylie's brothers.

"And she was just lying there, next to this creeper guy who just kept saying, 'I'm sorry' over and over." The older one, Mason, was explaining to my dad. "She looked dead." He paused. "I pushed the guy over and started beating the crap out of his face. He didn't fight back though. He just kept crying." He cracked his knuckles. "So I went to see if Will—Wylie had a pulse and, and s-she did, so I picked her up and took her to the car and drove her here."

My dad put a hand on Mason's knee. "That was a very brave thing to do."

"You should have killed that creeper." Jared interjected, his arms crossed and his jaw set. "I would have killed him."

"Shut up, you weren't there." Mason retorted.

"Did he hurt Wylie?" I interrupted what could have become another fist fight by the looks on both their faces.

"I don't know." Mason shrugged. "She was passed out with one of those rubber things around her arm. I saw a syringe, so he probably shot her up with drugs." He put his face in his hands. "God, there was trash everywhere. And the guy stunk so bad."

"It's good that you got to him in time then." My dad's voice was soft, comforting. "Was Wiley...clothed when you found him?"

"Yeah, she had our old clothes on." Mason nodded at Jared, then he looked up at my dad. "Do you think he—?" He jumped up. "I will kill him now."

"Mason, calm down. It's unlikely he would have gone through the trouble of putting Wylie's clothes back on. It sounds more like Wylie overdosed and the man thought he was dead. That's all."

"That's all?" Mason was getting angrier. I didn't blame him. "She might have died! Oh my god, she could have hepatitis—or AIDS!"

"Man, stop calling him *she*!" I yelled. "Wylie's a guy." It made me mad that they kept misgendering him. I owed it to Wylie to stand up for him.

"What are you talking about?" Jared asked. "She's *our* sister."

Just then, my mom came out and sat down next to me. "Wylie is starting to wake up. The doctor's believe he overdosed on heroine, so they gave him a medication to counteract the effects of the drug."

"Can we see her?" Mason asked, still standing.

"They're asking Wylie some questions right now, but they said they would call you back when they're ready." She looked at Jared, sulking across from me and Mason, who seemed ready to bust through the doors like I did earlier. "Hey, are you boys hungry? John, why don't you take everyone down to the cafeteria and get some food."

My dad stood up. "Good idea. Let's go find some grub and give Wylie some time to wake up."

Mason looked at my mom. Glared, really, then nudged Jared on the shoulder and said, "Come on."

They all started walking towards the door, when my dad turned and motioned me to come.

"But mom, I want to see Wylie. I have to tell him I'm sorry. See how he's doing."

"Sweetheart, I know." She sighed. "But there are a lot of things that need to happen right now to make sure Wylie gets the care he needs. You need to take care of yourself, then you can be a good friend. So go. Eat something. Get to know Wylie's brothers."

"Fine." I grumbled, then followed the rest of them out of the waiting room. As we left, a woman in a gray suit passed us on her way into the waiting room. I saw her make a beeline for my mom, who stood and shook her hand. I wanted to stay and see what that was all about, but my dad pulled my shirtsleeve so I'd follow.

11

Wylie

"Willow." A voice called from somewhere far in the distance.

"Willow, I want you to open your eyes." The voice was closer.

I didn't want to open my eyes.

"Willow, wake up hon. I need you to open your eyes for me." Suddenly one of my eyes was forced open. A bright yellow light bore a hole into my optic nerve. The light went away, only to appear in my other one.

"Gah—stop it!" I tried to push the hand away, but my limbs were lead pipes. My mouth was dry and rough like the top of my skateboard. And what was this thing stuck to my face?

"Ah, there she is." The voice, a man's voice, was coming from above me. There was a dark blob associated with the words, but my eyes couldn't focus. I heard beeping noises in the background. And the unmistakable sound of my mom sobbing.

"Ah fuck—" was all I could get out before I puked up a quart of brownish-yellow sludge and passed out again.

135

♠ ♥ ♣ ♦

"Where am I?" I asked no one in particular. The room was dark, but I could see light coming in through a doorway that seemed miles away. Beyond the door, a faint beeping sound echoed through the otherwise quiet hall.

"Wylie, you're in the hospital." It was Reyna's voice. "How do you feel?"

Like that slug my brother poured salt on last month—dry and squashed. "Thirsty." I managed.

I heard a rustling as she looked for a light. With a click, a soft light came on over the bed and I could see my surroundings. Reyna poured some ice water from a pink plastic jug into a styrofoam cup with a yellow bendy-straw. She placed it on my lips and I drank as much as I could, swishing the cold fluid around in my parched mouth.

"More?" She asked, when the straw made a slurping sound.

I shook my head. Something on my arm started buzzing. A blood pressure cuff inflated, nearly cutting off the circulation to my hand. I handed her back the empty cup with my other hand, which was tethered to yet another piece of equipment via a vein in my wrist. "Where's my mom?" My voice was scratchy.

"I told her to go home and take care of your brothers. They're pretty traumatized by what happened." She stood next to the bed, a look of concern on her face.

I started to cry. Then I couldn't stop crying. I was so mad. And so scared. And so confused. Reyna just put her arms around me and let me cry. I felt bad for scaring my brothers. They've always been nice to me. But, I didn't want to be here anymore. Not in that house. Not in this town. Reyna ran her hand down my head and told me it would be ok. But, when was it ever ok? Yeah, maybe for half a second, then the world just crashes down around you

136

again. How do people live? It's so hard! Does everyone just trip from one bad decision to another their whole lives?

"What do you remember about…?" She trailed off.

I thought about it for a minute. It seemed like a dream. "I don't know." I wasn't even sure what day it was. How long had I been asleep?

"I remember skating. Trying to get to LA. It was raining. I stopped under a bridge. There was this guy named Doc."

"Doc?" Reyna asked.

I remembered the weed, and the booze, and the needle. Then I remembered the pain, and then, the nothingness. "He gave me drugs." It was all I could say. I was embarrassed. Reyna always treated me like I was worth something—worth caring about. But really, I was just a screwed up kid.

"Do you know what kind of drugs?" She asked.

I shook my head. "Weed, some kind of alcohol. Something in a syringe." I could feel the burning in my arm where he injected me. I heard his laughter. Remembered his crooked brown teeth. I shuddered.

"Yes, the doctors found an astonishing amount of opiates in your system. It's a wonder you didn't die out there."

I kinda wished I had. Now I'm back here again. Doomed to be *Willow* for the rest of my life. I felt the pressure of tears building behind my eyes again. I couldn't stop it. This time, my sobs were loud. I wanted to scream out the frustration I felt. I was trapped. I literally had no options.

"Is everything ok in here?" A nurse poked her head in around the curtain that separated my bed from the empty one next to me. I wiped my eyes and nose on my sheet, trying to hide that I'd been crying, but, who was I kidding?

Reyna turned to her. "Yes. Could you do me a favor and call for Ms. Candlewick?"

"Yes doctor, of course." The nurse turned to leave.

"And perhaps 5 mg of Ativan, IV."

"I'll put in the order." She called over her shoulder as she left.

Reyna turned back towards me. "Can you share with me why you ran away?"

I laid there, watching the movie of my life play out behind my closed eyes. What the hell?

I told her everything. My mom. My dad. Alex. The cops. Desiree. My period. My fear of being seen as female for the rest of my life. It was like someone unscrewed a bottle of Pepsi after shaking it. I don't know how long I'd been talking before the nurse came in and injected the Ativan into my IV tube. As the clear fluid made its way into my vein, a tall, thin woman hovered outside the doorway.

"Oh, Evonne, come on in." Reyna motioned for the woman to come in.

"Hi, Reyna." She entered, her back ramrod-straight. Her steps purposeful. She shook Reyna's hand before turning to me. "Wylie, is it?"

I nodded.

"I'm Evonne. Evonne Candlewick. I'm a social worker assigned to your case. Do you mind if we have a little chat?" She tucked a strand of brown hair behind her ear.

I looked over at Reyna, confused. "My case?" I asked.

Evonne sat down in one of the two plastic chairs in the room. "Yes, Wylie. I've spoken with Dr. Keen—" She nodded in Reyna's direction. "—about your situation. I had some questions, if you don't mind?" She looked up at me, as if asking permission to ask me questions.

"I don't understand. Why do I need a social worker?" I propped myself up in the bed, panicked.

"We just want to make sure you have the resources you need to be healthy, Wylie." Reyna said.

My heart started to race. "What do you—"

Ms. Candlewick barged on ahead. "Wylie, can you tell me about your home life?"

What life? I thought. "What do you want to know?"

She leaned back, smoothing her gray pin-striped skirt across her legs. "Let's start with your family." She suggested. "You have two brothers, yes?"

"Yeah."

"And what about your father, is he in the home?"

I leaned back down into the bed, pressing my head into the pillow. "No." I closed my eyes and answered her barrage of questions.

How do you feel you are treated by your brothers? By your mother? By your mother's boyfriend — Roy, is it? What kind of food do you have in your home? Do you feel you get enough to eat? Does anyone in your family use drugs? Do you use drugs? How are you doing in school? Will you tell me about your name? Why do you feel you are male? Do you feel that your family understands you? What made you run away from home? A seemingly endless stream of: Who? What? When? Why? How? Feel. Feel. Feel. Feel. This woman just wouldn't stop. I didn't want to feel anymore. I just wanted to go back to sleep and wake up...never. I was exhausted. That familiar Xanax wave washed over me and I felt myself drifting farther and farther away from reality.

"Wylie?"

I opened my eyes. A sliver of sunlight cut through the

depressing dimness of the small room. Ms. Candlewick was gone, but I could see a figure lurking by the door. It was Alex.

"Go away." I said, before turning to face the wall. I didn't want anything to do with Alex. Or anyone else for that matter. Why couldn't everyone just leave me the hell alone?

"Wylie, I'm so sorry." His footsteps approaching my bed. "Please, I know I was a complete and total asshole and I totally don't deserve your friendship."

Well, at least he's figured that out.

Silence stretched between us, the space filled in by the rapid swish of booty-clad clogs along the linoleum out in the hall and layered voices at the nurse's station.

"Look man, I know I screwed up and...I just..." He inhaled deeply, "I just hope you can forgive me."

I didn't answer. I just stared out through the part in the curtains, watching a crow in the sparse branch outside my window. As it cocked its head back and forth, I wondered if birds felt betrayal. As its head turned to the left, its right eye stared back at me. Did it see me through that invisible barrier? If it did, what did it see? A sad little girl? A scrawny boy trying to be a man? As if in answer, the crow cocked its head down, its' gaze more intense. Yeah, I know. Who was I kidding? I wasn't trying to be a man. I was childishly giving my best friend the silent treatment. The crow spread its wings and gave them a flap before taking flight, as if to say, 'my work here is finished.'

When I turned over, Alex was gone. I was alone. Thirsty, I pushed myself up in the bed and grabbed the cup on the table next to me and drank the lukewarm water. While I slept, breakfast had been delivered. I slid the plastic cover off the plate to find a mound of scrambled eggs sitting atop a slice of what looked to be sausage, but more resembled the plastic meat patty from the kitchen set I had when I was little—my mom's attempt to indoctrinate me into the ways of the domestic female.

Drops of condensation rained down onto the plate as I contemplated whether I could stomach the meal. I opted for the cup of orange Jell-O and dropped the cover back down on the plate. I popped open the lid and threw it back on the tray just as Reyna returned, this time with a man I'd never met.

"Wylie, this is a colleague of mine, Dr. Atley Springall. I think I mentioned him to you before. He's the—"

"Transgender Specialist, hormone cocktail creator, and general pain-in-the-ass to the powers-that-be who are determined to keep us all locked up in proper little boxes." Dr. Springall's tall, lanky figure sprung across the small room, hand outstretched.

I stuck the spoon of Jell-O into my mouth and shook his hand while the smooth, sweet blob soothed my throat as it went down.

"Right." He pulled up a plastic chair and sat down next to my bed. "So Reyna has told me a lot about you. I thought we might have a little chat."

Reyna rolled the tray away from the bed and into the corner so she could sit down next to me, opposite Dr. Springall.

I scooped another spoonful of Jell-O into my mouth and swallowed. "Chat about what?" I didn't want my voice to betray the excitement that was building inside me. Was my wish going to finally come true?

"Well, Wylie, I run an inpatient gender counseling program in Los Angeles. It's a place where you can interact with other transgender individuals, get the support you need, and be assessed for medical interventions."

"Seriously?" I looked over at Reyna. She smiled. This was even better than meeting Tony Hawk.

"Seriously." He straightened his white coat over his gray dress shirt. "I run a 6-week program where you would see a gender therapist three times a week, get a full physical work up to make sure your body will respond well to treatments, and you'll get to meet other young people who don't fit the gender binary."

Gender binary? I'd never heard that term before. But it made sense—two distinct opposites—male and female, like 0 and 1 in computer language. Oh man! This was too good to be true. I wanted to go so bad I could taste it.

"Well, it looks like I'm late to the party." It was my mom, swooping in like a celebrity or something. "Well, hello Reyna."

My heart sank. She would never be ok with this. I slumped back into the bed and closed my eyes. The vision of me graduating from high school with a goatee slowly fading away.

"Sweetheart, how are you feeling today?" She didn't wait for an answer, but instead, turned to Dr. Springall and stuck her hand in his face. "I'm Sybil Masterson, and you are?"

His chair scraped against the floor as he got up to shake her hand. "Right, you must be the mother of young Wylie. I'm Dr. Springall." "Oh, only his brothers call her that. Please, call her Willow."

Dr. Springall cleared his throat. "Well, that's something we were just discussing Ms. Masterson. You see, Wiley is what we call, transgender —"

"I'm sorry, trans-*what*?" She shifted her purse back up on her shoulder.

Reyna stood up and walked around my bed. "Sybil, Wylie identifies as male, even though he was assigned female at birth. Transgender is the medical term for that."

142

"My lord, this is nonsense. It's just a phase. She'll grow out of it. She's just spent too much time around her brothers. She...she just got her period—"

"Mom!" I sat up in bed. The blood pressure cuff came to life and I ripped it off my arm. "I'm not a *her*! I'm a *him*! Stop calling me Willow. I've been trying to tell you this all my life, but you just wouldn't listen. Why do you think I change clothes every morning after I leave the house? Why do you think that I hang out with guys all the time, doing guy-stuff? Why do you think I keep telling people my name is Wylie?"

I took a deep breath and let it out slowly. I'd never stood up to her before. I was afraid she'd be mad, but, she looked— scared. I actually felt kinda sorry for her.

"I'm sorry I couldn't be your sweet little girl who wears pink and dreams of barbies or whatever. I'm just...not that person."

"Ms. Masterson, Wylie is not alone in his feelings. There are tens of thousands of transgender individuals in America, and that's only those we *know* about. I've worked with hundreds of them in my years as a physician, and for the majority, this is not a phase." He reached into a pocket inside his coat, brought out a pamphlet and tried to hand it to my mom. "I run a clinic for people like Wylie. I'd like to invite him to stay with us for a few weeks to get the treatment he needs."

She brought her hands up in windshield-wiper mode, shaking her head. "No. No. No. God does not make mistakes. Willow, I know you've been spending a lot of time with Alex's family, but I think that has to come to an end." She turned to Reyna and glared at her. "Reyna, I would like you to leave right now and stop filling my daughter's head with your—"

"I want to go." I shouted.

My mom looked at me. "Yes, let's get you home darling."

143

She moved towards me, almost shoving Dr. Springall out of the way.

"No, mom. I want to go to the clinic. I want to transition." There. I'd said the words. She couldn't deny me the ability to be who I really was. She always said she wanted me to be happy.

"Absolutely not." She shook her head so hard it could have spun off like a top.

I couldn't understand her violent rejection of my deepest wish. Why was it so hard to understand that I needed this like a diabetic needed insulin? I had hoped she would understand. I had hoped she would see what this meant to me. I was beginning to understand what my decision to transition was going to mean for me and my family. Again I wished that Mason hadn't found me. If I was dead, it would hurt people, but not like this seemed to be hurting my mom. I was so tired of fighting.

"Sybil," Reyna came around and touched my mom on the shoulder, "why do you think Wylie ran away? And resorts to drugs to get through the day?"

"My daughter is not on drugs!" She thundered at them. "And she ran away because your son broke her heart."

I flopped back down. This was hopeless. The woman was completely unhinged.

Then, Reyna nutted up on her. "You have absolutely no idea what is going on with your own child! Do you know how many times I've fed this half-starved little waif? He's just as hungry for love and understanding as he is for food. Instead of validation, you render judgment and dismiss his deepest needs. Is it no wonder he uses drugs on a daily basis? *You* are the reason he ran away, only to be preyed upon again and nearly sexually assaulted!"

144

I'd never seen Reyna that upset. Even in the dim light, I could see her face was flushed.

"Hey, is everything alright in here?" A man in black scrubs appeared in the doorway, nearly filling the thing up.

"Everything's fine." Reyna's answer was terse. She was still glaring at my mom, who started crying.

"Perhaps you'd like to continue your discussion outside the ward?" It seemed like more of a demand than a request, but nobody moved.

Finally, Dr. Springall spoke up, "No, our apologies for the disruption. We will maintain low tones moving forward." He looked at Reyna above his round wire-rimmed glasses.

The man in the scrubs left, letting the light from the hall stream back into the room to mingle with the light coming in through the curtains. Reyna moved back into the shadow of the corner. My mom, her monstrous purse still clutched at her shoulder, stood in the center of the room and wept.

I felt terrible. My heart hurt—worse than when I found Alex with Desiree. I didn't want to cause anyone pain, much less the woman who brought me into this world. Why couldn't I just be who she wanted me to be? Why was I this way? I didn't know the answers to those questions, but I did know one thing—I could not live my life as a girl.

"Mom. I want to go get treatment. Please. Please…just let me be who I know I am."

My mom turned and looked at me. Mascara ran from her eyes like she was weeping black tears. After a long while that filled me with hope, she said, "I'll find you treatment. I'll talk to the church and find someone to help get these demons out of you."

"That's it!" Reyna threw her hands up. "I didn't want it to come to this." She advanced on my mom and, for a moment,

I really thought she would hit her. "I am prepared to seek guardianship over Wylie so he can get the treatment that he needs from a trained medical professional that specializes in the field of transgender medicine—not some religious quack who is more likely to cause more damage than good."

My mom's face was six inches from Reyna's. "You have no grounds to take my daughter away from me."

Without looking away from my mom, Reyna said, "Atley, would you be so kind as to page Ms. Candlewick please? I believe she has some paperwork for me."

"Right. Why don't we all just take a moment? Perhaps step outside and let young Wylie rest while we sort these things out?"

Dr. Springall ushered Reyna and my mom out and I was left alone again—wondering what the future would hold for me.

12

Alex

"Yo, where's your friend been?" Lamar stood backlit next to the tree that Wylie usually sat under at lunch. I didn't think anyone knew I hung out here. "Did he move or something?"

I finished chewing what the school felt was a decent representation of a burrito and washed it down with a swig of Pepsi. We'd been back from spring break for over three weeks now. "Didn't know you cared." I looked around to see if Cam and Chase were around. The three of them were usually inseparable, but today, they were nowhere to be seen.

Lamar sat down in Wylie's spot. "Don't worry, I'm alone."

"Card game get shut down?" Why was he here? I had grown accustomed to my solo lunches.

"Nah, I haven't been hanging with those fools for a while. Cam's been gettin' meaner and dumber. I kinda understand why his stepdad knocks him around." He stretched his legs out in front of himself and crossed them. "So, where's Wylie?"

Wylie was at that treatment center in LA. I hadn't seen him since that day in the hospital. "He's doing off-campus study for a while." That's the line my mom told me to give anyone that asked. Until today, only his teachers had. Oh, and that one girl—Brianna. That was weird. I thought she didn't want anything to do with Wylie. She accepted the line without question.

Lamar, not so easy. "Yo, that's usually code for rehab. Wylie getting clean?"

From what my mom said, it sounded like he would actually be counseled on his substance use in this place, but again, that's not the story I was supposed to tell. And I would never betray Wylie's secrets again. That is, if he ever shares them with me again.

"Dude, he's not in rehab. His family just had to go out of town for a while." I hoped that would satisfy him. "I think his grandma died."

Lamar just stared at me for a few seconds, as if trying to discern whether I was lying. "My gramma died last year, ain't nobody pulled me out of school. But hey, if it means maybe I get a shot at being valedictorian, then 'thank you' to Wylie's dead gramma."

Vale-what? How could these two be in the running for valedictorian? I mean, I know Wylie's smart, but, damn, with all the shit he's gone through and all the drugs he likes to do? I'd never even seen him study. And I didn't really know anything about Lamar. I just assumed he was like most skaters I'd met— not exactly the nose-in-a-book type.

"Wylie's valedictorian?" I shook my head. "Really?"

"What, he didn't tell you about how he's got this photographic memory and shit? That fool sees something once and remembers it forever. Makes it harder than hell to beat him." Lamar slapped his leg. "Maybe I just have a chance now."

I nodded, absently. It was going to be another few weeks before Wylie would return. I wondered if he could keep his standing. I gave my mom all of his books and stuff to take to him. I hoped to see him this weekend, but it depended on some report my mom was talking about. I wondered if he knew Lamar was his competition. I never really aspired to valedictorian, but then again, the school system here was all weird. I'd been a freshman in an actual high school in San Francisco. Now I was in this weird junior-high school that ends at 9th grade. I didn't know I was supposed to be aspiring to some goal this early. Not that I got bad grades or anything, but honestly, I hadn't really been trying that hard this semester—partly because I was pissed about the move and partly because I'd screwed things up so bad with Wylie. I guess I've been in a funk for a while.

"Alex." Lamar was waving his hand in front of my face, a joint pinched between his thumb and forefinger. "You want?"

What the hell? I wasn't going to be head of the class this year. Might as well have some fun. I reached for the joint. "Thanks."

Lamar nodded. "You up for some cards?" He pulled a deck out of his back pocket. "I don't want my skills gettin' rusty."

I held my breath as the smoke burned deep inside my lungs. "I don't know man." The words came out, strung along by a stream of smoke. It felt like maybe I was being hustled again.

Lamar ignored me and started dealing. "Not for money fool, just for fun."

I took another hit and watched him deal the cards. It felt kinda good not being alone for once. I starred at the two cards in front of me for a minute before peaking a look. Nothing worth playing.

"So what's your story Lamar?"

"My story?" He looked at his cards, then threw them on top of the upturned cards between us. "Fold."

I handed Lamar the joint, collected the cards and shuffled them. I was curious about who he was and why he'd hang out with Cam and Chase. And why he didn't stick up for Wylie when Cam was bullying him. "Yeah. Like, what is a valedictorian-in-the-running doing hanging out with people like Cam?"

"Awe, he wasn't always like that. I've known him since 4th grade. His dad died when he was in 5th grade. They were really close." He took a hit. "His mom was the stay-at-home type, so she had to find some way to work. They lost their house and had to move into some crappy apartments downtown. He was always alone. Then Chuck came into the picture. I swear, that fool hates kids. Cam just got dealt a bad set of cards and he doesn't know how to play them."

I suddenly felt really sorry for Cam. It was so easy when he was just that asshole bully. But his story—it was so similar to Wylie's. No wonder they were friends. I dealt the next round. "What about your family?"

"What are you? Writing an after-school special?" He passed me the joint and looked at his cards.

"Fine. Ask me a question." I took the last draw off the joint and crushed it into the grass next to me.

"Call." He crossed his legs and leaned forward. "You got brothers or sisters?"

"Nope. Raise $5." I flipped another card up between us. "You?"

"One pain-in-the-ass older sister. In college. Raise $2."

"Why's she a pain-in-the-ass?" I slid another card into the center. "Call."

"She's a pain-in-my-ass because she was head of her class all through school and now she's on her way to becoming an ACLU lawyer like my mom and everyone expects me to do the same." He slapped his cards down. "Four of a Kind."

I had nothing. I tossed the cards over to Lamar and regarded him, perhaps for the first time for real, realizing the preconceived notions I had made about him. "So, what do you want to be?"

"Doesn't matter." He put the cards back in their box as the first bell rung out across the field.

I stood up. "What do you mean? Of course it matters."

"Because it's all planned out for me, fool. Graduate from high school. Valedictorian. On to Morehouse College in DC. Then law school at UCLA." Lamar stood up and brushed off his jeans. "My story's written."

When I got home from school, there was a thick white envelope sitting on the kitchen counter. The envelope was addressed to me. The yellow sticky note on it was also addressed to me. "There are carrots in the fridge for you. Be home late. ♥Mom."

I grabbed the carrots and Thousand Island dressing from the fridge, along with a Cherry Pepsi and sat down at the breakfast bar. I dunked my carrot into the cup of dressing and shoved it in my mouth as I contemplated the large envelope. The return address was Stanford Robotics Lab, featuring the unmistakable crimson logo. I spit out the carrot and tore the thing open.

Dear Alex,

Congratulations! We are pleased to invite you to the Y2K1 Stanford Junior Robotics Summer Program.
*   Your thoughtful application and exceptional*

*accomplishments convinced us that you have the intel-
lectual energy, talent, and imagination to thrive in our
high school robotics program. With over 5,000 appli-
cations to our program, your distinguished record of
academic excellence and personal achievement stood
out. We know you will be an outstanding contributing
member to the program.*

*The next exciting step is yours for the taking. Please
read through the enclosed package to learn more about
what is expected over the coming months. Whatever
decision you make, we request that you complete the
enclosed response form indicating your choice before
May 20, 2001.*

*Once again, congratulations and welcome to the Stan-
ford family.*

Sincerely,
Francesca Ricci
Director of the Stanford Junior Robotics Program

"Holy shit holy shit holy shit!" My hands started drum-
ming on the counter. Then I started jumping up and down. "I
made it in!" With all that had happened over the last several
months, I had completely forgotten about my application. I
got in! I had to tell—

I looked around. There was no one to tell. My dad was at
work. Mom was probably in LA again. Wylie was unreachable,
even if he was speaking to me. I sat back down and grabbed
the carrot I had abandoned earlier. It gave way with a satisfying
crunch. I chewed for a minute, staring in disbelief at the letter
before thumbing through the glossy magazine that came with it.
Two-months at Stanford working with one of the top robotics
teams in the country. This was going to be amazing.

call me him.

I thought about calling Roger and telling him about it. He'd be stoked. After all, he was the one who helped me with the programming that got my team first place in that robotics competition last year. Then I started thinking about Lamar and what he said at lunch. What did he mean, it didn't matter what he wanted? And what did he want to be, anyway? I couldn't understand doing anything other than what I wanted to do. Well, I guess within reason. I mean, look what doing anything I wanted has gotten me. Basically, alone and hating myself. Maybe there was something to be said for having your choices made for you. Ugh, life was confusing. I could feel my buzz fading.

I made my way upstairs to my room, after deciding I'd email Roger. That way I wouldn't have to talk about all the other stuff going on in my life. I tossed the Stanford envelope onto my bed and switched on my computer. While it booted up, I turned on the TV and booted up my PlayStation so I could escape into Legend of Zelda. When my computer came online, I navigated to my AOL account. I had an email. I hardly ever got emails. It was from Wylie.

13

Wylie

Atley Hall, Los Angeles — Day 3

Daily Journal Prompt: Expectations

So this is my first journal entry during my stay in Atley Hall—the transgender treatment center run by Dr. Springall. I've been here for three days now and I have to say, this is so freaking amazing! I've already gotten to meet other kids my age who are just like me. It makes me feel like I'm not such a freak. Oh yeah, and they give everyone in the program a laptop to do these journal entries and communicate with our therapists and stuff. I get to take this home? Are you serious???

Anyway. Ok. Expectations...expectations...

Well, nothing about this place was what I expected. You know how you get a picture in your head about how something's going to be, and then usually, some things are different, but not others? I mean, don't get me wrong, this place is fantastic, it's just...I guess I was expecting some kind of big institution with white walls and white linoleum floors and a bunch of crazy people walking around all Girl, Interrupted-style.

Dr. Springall had a good laugh when I told him that. He said that he didn't want his patients feeling like they were somehow crazy or deficient in some way, even though technically, the psychiatric overlords that make up diagnoses say that I have "gender identity disorder." That's what my chart said when I snuck a peak when my therapist, Shannon, left the room for a minute. Anyway, Atley Hall is actually an old Victorian house somewhere near UCLA. There's never more than 6 residents here at one time, and nobody is walking around in a straight-jacket.

I guess I expect that I will learn more about what being transgender really means and how I can transition. Shannon says that there are different ways people can transition and not everyone transitions the same way. Like, she says I've kind of transitioned socially because of the way I dress and expect people to call me by male pronouns—he/his/him. I'd never really thought about it like that. I actually felt like I was trying to trick people. It was confusing, actually liking it when people believed I was a guy, but somehow feeling like I was...I don't know...lying? But Shannon says that it's not lying, and that gender is about how you feel in your head, not what's between your legs. So, if I feel like a guy, then I am a guy. I don't know. It's still a little confusing to me. Anyway, what I'm really interested in is transitioning medically, meaning I get to take testosterone to make me look more masculine. They say I can't do it right now, because of my age, but maybe in a couple of years. We'll see. I wish it could be now.

I expect that I'll make new friends here. I've already met three transgender kids about my age. There's Nicole, an MTF resident who started the program the day before I did. She always wears a nylon tracksuit with basketball shoes and likes to run down the stairs. And back up. And back down. It's her exercise program, she says. It's cool—at least she doesn't do it at like 6 am. Then there's Echo. She's 18 and says that she's queer. Actually, Echo wants people to use they/them/their pronouns, which is weird to me, but I'll try to remember that. Half of their head is shaved and the other half is long. The nails on the hand on their long-haired side are long and painted pink. The nails on their other hand are short and painted black. They wear a mix of guy and girl clothes. Like yesterday, they wore a skirt with a guy's dress shirt and combat boots. They say that its fascist to be forced to pick a gender. And then there's Skylar. He just started yesterday and he's like me—FTM transgender. He's 15 and likes video games and drawing. He says he wants to develop video games and even has an idea for a story-type game. I think we might end up good friends.

I hope these are enough expectations, cuz it's time for dinner.

Late!

Ok, therapy journal entry—done. Time to have some fun.

I closed my laptop and set it on the small, wooden desk next to my bed. My room was on the small side, with room enough for a single bed, a desk and matching wooden chair, and a squat, two-drawer dresser. There was a wood-framed mirror mounted on top of the dresser, which, right now, reflected an awful floral wallpaper, a version of which could be found in every room of the house. A green throw-rug covered most of the hardwood floor. There was no carpet in the house. Through the closed door, I could hear the telltale swish of tracksuit pants and pounding footsteps outside. Nicole.

Most days have been pretty much the same here. Some version of wake-up, eat breakfast, go to group activities, talk to your therapist or have free-time, depending on the day, then lunch, more group activities, study time, dinner, then free-time. At some point each day, we're supposed to journal at least once. It's supposed to help us process things that happen in our lives.

Upstairs is a series of rooms connected by a long, u-shaped hallway that straddled a stairway. There were six rooms up here and mine was at the very end of the right side of the "u." I made my way downstairs, dodging Nicole, who actually passed me twice, sweat pouring down her face. In the dining room, silverware clattered down on the table next to ceramic plates of different colors. I liked the purple one because it reminded me of the color of the sky when we would go camping when I was younger, so I tried to claim that every night. Sometimes Echo would beat me to it, just to screw with me. Not in a bad way, just to be funny. They could be intimidating to be around, but actually, they were pretty cool.

I passed by the living room and through a narrow, floral-papered hallway that led to the dining room. Skylar was there, setting the table. "Hey, Skylar."

He jumped about a foot in the air, dropping what was left of the silverware in his hands. "You scared the crap out of me!"

I bent down to help him pick up the rest of the silverware. I felt bad that I startled him, but damn, I thought he was looking right at me. "Sorry, man." I handed over the spoons he had yet to place on the table.

He finished the job as Claire, the woman who did all the cooking and generally kept an eye on us at night, came in from the kitchen carrying a pan of what looked to be meatloaf.

"Well, good evening, Wylie." She was always cheerful and greeted us all whenever she saw us. "Would you be a dear and go grab the bowl of potatoes on the counter? Thanks."

As I was going through the narrow doorway that led from the dining room into the kitchen, Echo came through with a bowl of salad, nearly dumping it on me.

"Yo, watch it!" Echo bobbled the bowl and was about to drop it, but I caught it before it fell and handed it off to Claire, who placed it safely on the table.

"Maybe you should wear a bell, Wylie." Echo gave me one of their sarcastic smiles before returning to the kitchen.

Maybe I should—apparently nobody sees me here. I followed them into the kitchen and found the bowl of potatoes. I gave Echo a wide berth as they passed by with three different kinds of salad dressing in their arms. I was used to doing all the cooking at home. No one else helped out, so I didn't have to worry about running into people or scaring the crap out of them, like I seemed to be doing tonight.

"All right, all right, let's get down to business my young friends." Claire clapped her hands together before spreading them out again, as if trying to hug everyone in the room at the same time. "Let's eat. Nicole, the stairs will be there all night. Come join us." She shouted so that Nicole could hear over her own footsteps.

I sat down at the purple plate, Skylar sat next to me at the red plate. Echo chose yellow across from me, Claire, green. Nicole was left with the blue plate on the other side of me. Echo slid a thick piece of meatloaf onto their plate and I plopped a large scoop of mashed potatoes onto mine. There was always

159

enough food to eat here, even with so many people. I never went hungry.

Halfway through dinner, Skylar leaned over and asked, "Hey, you want to play some *Donkey Kong* after dinner?"

While Atley Hall was cool enough to supply us with a PS2 and a bunch of games, none of the games involved player-on-player violence. So we were left with games like *Super Mario Brothers*, *Tony Hawk's Pro Skater* (my personal favorite, of course), and *Donkey Kong*. Since I didn't have a PS2, or any other gaming console at home, any video game was a novelty, so I took full advantage. We'd already played together this morning, since it wasn't a therapy day for either of us.

Group activities today were interesting. We all had to write a mini autobiography of our ideal lives, told by our 99-year-old selves. Then we had to read them out loud to everyone. I wrote about my life as a pro skater and how I dominated the X-Games for over a decade. I married a hot, pro-skater-chick and we adopted two kids who could skate as soon as they could walk. We bought a huge house near the beach with all of our competition winnings and sponsorships. We were so rich that I could buy my mom and two brothers houses too. We also started a unisex skate clothing line that was majorly successful, which allowed us to start a bunch of non-profit indoor skate parks where we held skate camps and after-school programs for kids. My family finally accepted me and loved me.

Skylar developed a highly-successful series of first-person POV fantasy video games that he started designing in high-school. He and his boyfriend, Justin Timberlake (what can I say, the guy dreams big!) lived in Venice in a big, modern-style house with a private movie/gaming theater where they invite all their famous friends to come screen movies and play video games.

Nicole was a WNBA star and broke the men's and women's record for most points scored in a single game. She lived with her husband in Georgia where they raised Chinese Crested dogs and pot-bellied pigs.

Echo was a famous actor who used their fame to bring awareness to serious issues, like gender inequality. They were notoriously out-spoken and frequently arrested while leading civil disobedience campaigns against the sexist, patriarchal system. While they had hoped to marry and settle down someday, they could never find a mate with a passion equal to their own—on any level.

While we all dreamed of leading very different lives, I did notice one similarity—we all wanted to be famous in some way.

We were all just about done with dessert—chocolate cream pie—when there was a knock on the door. Claire left the table and returned with—

"Grandpa Frank!" I jumped out of my chair, nearly knocking it over, and gave him a huge hug. "What are you doing here?"

Claire interjected, "Why don't you two head to the living room for some privacy. We'll take care of the dishes."

I led my grandpa to the living room and we sat down on the overstuffed brown couch. He looked tired and more frail than I remembered him. It had been months since I saw him last.

"Now, I never get a full story from your mother." He started. "But your brother Mason called me and told me that you ran away and now you're here." His hand waved around the room, shaking. "I'm here to see for myself what's going on and make sure you're ok." He looked me in the eyes. "Are you ok?"

I was so happy to see him sitting here with me. Of all of my small family, Grandpa Frank was my favorite. He *got* me. "Yeah grandpa, I'm ok. Maybe even good." I fiddled with the chain that held my wallet to my pants.

He nodded his head, which shook almost as much as his hands. "Well I'm glad to hear that. You know, I don't really understand what you're going through. I'm old. But it doesn't mean I don't love you. I want you to pick up the phone and call me when you're sad, or mad, or glad. I want to hear from you. Understand?"

He wasn't mad, just emphatic. And I loved him for that. "Yeah, I understand."

He reached over to a bag on the coffee table and handed it to me. "This is for you."

I reached in and pulled out a brand new pair of guys jeans, a black belt, two black t-shirts, socks, and a new pair of shoes just like the ones I had been wearing that were Jared's two years ago.

"Mason helped me pick these out for you. I hope they're the right size."

I felt tears prickling my eyes. I'd never had new clothes—not guy-clothes, anyway. I felt like my heart would burst. It was such a change from the emptiness that I'd been feeling lately. These clothes meant love—acceptance. It meant so much to me that he and Mason supported me.

"Thank you." I whispered. The words seemed monumentally inadequate to express what I felt.

"Well, you deserve to be who you are. And you deserve to wear shoes without holes in them. Give 'em here." He motioned towards my feet.

I kicked off Jared's old shoes, revealing mud-stained, previously white socks.

"Those too." He held out his hands.

I pulled off the socks, stuffed them in the old shoes and handed them to him, a little embarrassed at the smell wafting from them. I pulled on the new socks and laced up my new shoes, feeling more like myself than I ever had.

"You haven't answered my question." Shannon sat across from me at her desk, legs crossed, tapping the back of her pen on her yellow pad.

I had been staring at the clock on the wall for several minutes, watching the second hand tick across the face. I hated ticking clocks. They set my nerves on edge. But just then, I was hoping the sound would fill the silence and be an acceptable substitute for my voice. Guess not.

"Why did you tell them that you lied about the officer touching you?" She read her notes again. "Maybe a better question is, why didn't you tell someone in the first place?"

I thought back to that morning. About being held down on the ground. About Skinny's hands on me. I crossed my leg across the other one and watched as my left foot flopped up and down on top of my right knee. It helped keep me from crying. Not only was I not allowed to have drugs, I was experiencing the hell that is PMS. I wondered for a moment how I could induce my own hysterectomy. Seemed painful. But was it more painful than feeling all…this?

"I don't know."

"I think you do."

I slid my foot back down to the floor. "Well, then one of us is wrong."

Shannon smiled. "Ok, let's turn it around a bit. Let's say

you were skating to school and you saw a man with his hand on a little girl's crotch. What would you do?"

I shrugged. "Probably hit him in the head with my board."

"Why?"

"Dude, because it's wrong. He's got no business touching that little girl."

She put her pen down and faced me directly. "Exactly. No more right than that officer had touching you. So what was it, Wylie? Why did you not feel you could fight for you? Do you not feel like you're worth it?"

I felt the tears at the back of my eyes again. Dammit! Why was she pushing this? Why did it matter? The second hand continued its forced march across the numbers on the clock. Tick. Tick. Tick. Talk.

"Wylie?"

"What?"

"Are you worth fighting for?"

"Fuck. Yes! Alright? But geez—do you want me to hit the cop upside his head?"

"No, of course not." She sat forward, leaning her forearms on her thighs. "But, I'm still curious as to why you didn't tell someone."

"Shit." I whispered, looking down at my new shoes. Tears spilled out, leaving darker black spots on my shirt. "Because then I'd have to explain to whoever what happened. I'd have to tell them my name and why they were searching me to begin with. And why it was such a big deal that I don't have a bulge in my pants. I'd have to tell them what they said to me. And then they'd want to know why I dress like this and why I try to look like a guy, and why and why and why? Because I'm a freak and nobody knows what to do with me." I wiped my eyes with the back of my arm. "Does *that* satisfy your curiosity?"

Shannon's face softened. She reached over across her desk and grabbed a box of tissues. She pulled a couple out and handed them to me. I took them and blew my nose. A wad of snot slid out of the tissues and down my arm.

"Can you tell me why you think you're a freak?"

I wiped the slime off my hand and tossed the tissue into the basket by the door. "Has anyone ever told you that you ask too many questions?"

"Yes. Has anyone ever told you that you use deflection as a coping mechanism?"

"No."

"Why are you a freak?"

I made an outline of my self with my hands, from head to toe. "Hello? Do you not see this?"

She leaned back in her chair and looked at me. "I see a transgender boy. One of many who have sat on that same couch. I see a smart, talented, resourceful young man who is letting other people's words define him. And I see him ready to define himself."

Atley Hall, Los Angeles — Day 10

Daily Journal Prompt: Things I Struggle With
I struggle with these writing assignments ....(Sorry Shannon, I know these are supposed to help us process the things that happen in our lives, but sometimes, it's just hard to have feelings all the time.)

alksjdhfaskjd falsdfh aszdryahksjdfh aiusxzdjtf nai-uskzxjdthmaf. Fuck.

Ok. Today I'm struggling with my family. Nothing

new there. I haven't had much contact with them since I was in the hospital. I think Reyna got some kind of court order to be my guardian, which is how I got to be here. I know my mom is pissed. Actually, I think my whole family is seriously pissed at Reyna for "butting into our lives" as Mason told me. I saw them today, briefly. Dr. Springall got them to come in for a family session, without me. I think he's trying to get them onboard with who I am. I think that might be one of the things that has to happen in order for me to go back home to them. Otherwise, I'll live with the Keens when I get done here. Based on the fact that my mom wouldn't talk to me, it sounds like she's not really onboard just yet. Jared at least gave me a hug. Mason talked with me for a minute and told me a little about what's been going on. Roy left. He said he couldn't deal with my mom and her "head case kid" (I'm guessing he means me). I'm not sad that he's gone. He's a dick and honestly, more of a head case than any of us.

I feel like I'm causing everyone around me pain though, and that sucks. Why does me being me have to be so goddamn hard on everyone else? And why can't my mom be an adult for once? Why can't she just get over herself and love me for me? Why can't she even talk to me?

I think I know what Alex is probably feeling right now with me not talking to him. I'm being childish, just like my mom. The thing is—I don't know what to say to him. I want my friend back. And I want him to know how much it hurt to see him with Desiree. Does he not understand that that's a basic violation of guy-code? And beyond that, does he not understand how hard it is for me to feel like I can be normal and find a girlfriend?

All I want to do right now is get high and skate. But, since I "have a history of drug abuse" they won't even give me a xannie to calm me down. And the most I can do without supervision is skate around on the concrete patio out back. I wish there was a pool. I'd drain it and skate my ass off right now.

"So, how's your mom doing?" Shannon swung her chair away from her computer. She was wearing a dark purple pencil skirt with a lighter purple flowy, sleeveless top. Her shoes were off, as they frequently were during our sessions.

I was wearing my signature color—black. I didn't like colors. Well, I didn't understand colors, really. They represented feminine clothes to me. I didn't know how to incorporate color into my masculine identity. Not that it was a legitimate problem, since I wasn't going shopping for a new wardrobe any time soon. Anyway, I loved my new clothes Grandpa Frank got me. I finally felt like I was being myself—not playing dress-up with my brothers' clothes.

"How would I know?" I hadn't talked to her. She brushed past me when she was here last week. "She's not exactly calling me everyday."

"And how does that make you feel?" She tucked her feet up under her legs.

I rolled my eyes. Enough with the feelings already! Isn't she old enough to know that feelings are highly over-rated?

"It makes me feel like my mom's not talking to me." I stared past her, out the window. There was a big shade tree out there, but all I could see was the top because we were on the second floor of the medical building.

"Wylie, that's not a feeling, it's an observation."

And that's very observant of you. I guess I should know by now that she never lets me off the hook when it comes to feelings. Fine. I'll play, but only because it means I can get what I want—puberty blockers.

"How does it make me feel that my mom won't talk to me?"

"Yes."

"It makes me *feel* like she doesn't like me. And like she's being a big baby."

"You know Wylie, her behavior has everything to do with her, and nothing to do with you. And yes, it is a childish reaction to the situation. The truth is, your mom is unable to process her feelings on this and she has no tools in her toolbox for communicating the complex emotions going on insider her. So, in reality, your mom is, emotionally at least, a child."

Suddenly in my mind, my mom became a Lego figurine, complete with yellow hardhat and empty red toolbox, a sad mouth line painted just below her little line nose. "Why can't she just grow up?"

She ran her hand through her hair, flipping it so that it parted on the other side. "Well, dealing with emotions and communicating like an adult are not things that just automatically happen when you turn a certain age. Those are behaviors that are learned and some people just don't have the role models they need to acquire those skills."

"Like me." I sighed and stretched my whole body. "And that's why you keep making me talk about my feelings."

"Exactly. We're filling your toolbox so you have what you

need to work through challenging situations as you go through life."

I closed my eyes. The tick of the clock formed the back-beat to a little institutional symphony beyond the closed door, complete with hushed murmurs, squeaky shoes on stained linoleum, fingernails tapping on plastic keyboards, ringing phones, and fax machines. All those tools that are supposed to make our lives easier, but really, people always seem to be stressed out and unhappy.

"I know you don't like to feel things, Wylie. Not everyone does all the time. But feelings are what make life interesting. Yes, they can hurt, but they can also help us experience some of the most amazing things life has to offer. Happiness. Love. Ecstasy. Without the down, you can't feel the up. Feelings aren't going to kill you. Running away from them may."

Oh, here we go. The *drug* talk again. I couldn't take another just-say-no lecture. "Ok, I get it. Drugs are bad. Feelings are good. Can we move on?"

Shannon paused for a moment and clicked her pen. "Sure. Let's talk about why you're angry right now."

"I'm not angry." I laid down on the couch and put my arm over my eyes to shade them from the harsh fluorescent lights.

"It sounds like you're angry."

"What difference does it make?"

"It's ok to be angry you know."

"Yep. All the feelings are good. I may have mentioned that a second ago." I wanted to open my eyes to check the time, but I didn't want to make eye contact with her.

"Your sarcasm is just another way of running away." I heard her shuffling some papers. "What's got you so afraid to feel today?"

169

When is this going to end? I sat up. "Look, I don't want to be angry at you. You're a really nice lady and I know you're just doing your job. But you know what? In my experience, the world is overwhelming. There's just too much bad shit happening. And sometimes, it hurts so bad that I just want to take the pain away. What's so wrong with that?"

"Occasionally taking a break from pain is healthy. But you've got a pattern of running away at just about every turn. We want to instill new habits in you. Healthier habits, so that you don't have to run away."

"This is crap. Everyone runs away." My dad ran away to who-the-fuck-knows-where. Alex ran away with Desiree. My mom runs away to TV, food—even drugs. Why is it ok for her to run to prescription drugs? It's like physician-sanctioned escape.

"I don't want to talk about everyone. I want to talk about you." Her chair squeaked as it turned across the small room. Open your eyes. Let's try something."

"What the fuck are you doing?"

Echo's voice startled me so bad I missed my next handhold on the white, vine-tangled lattice and nearly fell down to the thorny bushes below. It was after midnight. All the lights were out in the house, so I figured everyone was sleeping. Heart thumping, I found a place for my right hand and pressed my sweaty forehead into the splintery wood.

"Dude, are you trying to kill me to death?" I climbed the last several feet to the landing outside my bedroom window, shed my backpack and board, and laid down on the roof with a thud. I could feel the rough shake shingles on my outstretched arms.

"Kill you to death?" Echo got up from their perch outside their own window and climbed over to sit next to me. "Are you high?"

"Yep, about fifteen feet high." *There were so many stars tonight.* I felt as if I could float up to meet them.

"You idiot. Are you trying to get yourself kicked out of here?"

I didn't answer. I knew Atley Hall had a strict 'No Drug' policy. It wasn't like I wanted to be kicked out. Far from it. I've just been cooped up and controlled for so long. I was going a little crazy. Plus, therapy had been pretty intense this morning. I just needed to blow off some steam.

The wail of a police siren in the distance broke through the silence, waking the neighborhood dogs who howled in answer. The air was still. Warm, even for April.

"Hello?" Echo leaned over and waved a hand in front of my face. "Earth to fellow-freak."

"I'm not a freak." Shannon told me so. That was days ago. A day I went to bed feeling good about myself.

"Don't kid yourself." Echo picked at one of the roof tiles next to them. "We're all freaks here. We'll never be the majority. We'll never be understood by the world we live in. The sooner you accept that, the happier you'll be. Embrace the freak."

Embrace the freak. I hated that word. Would I always feel like there was something inherently defective about me?

"Don't you get tired?" I let the question fade. Sighing, I turned to look at Echo. The moon glinted off of the silver spike dangling from their ear. They had shaved the side of their head again recently. How did they get to be so brave? I mean, it's one thing for me to try to look like a guy. Echo doesn't try to conform to people's expectations. The "binary agenda" as they called it. I felt like that was the bravest thing. Especially because I knew what it was like—how much it hurt— to have people constantly asking, 'are you a boy or a girl?'

Echo laid back so that their head was touching mine. They smelled like pachouli and cinnamon—Echo loved cinnamon TicTacs. We laid like that for a while, my eyelids growing heavy.

"Yeah." They reached for my hand. "I get tired."

This was new. The hand-holding. Theirs was soft. Mine was clammy.

"The thing is—you can't escape the pain. It's in you. You can try and shove it down all you want, but one day, you'll feel it. All those emotions that you pushed down with drugs, alcohol, and sarcasm will emerge with the intensity of Mt. Saint Helens." Echo squeezed my hand.

"Is that why you're here?" They'd never talked about it. I figured they could do anything they wanted—like get on hormones or have surgery—because they were 18. And they seemed like they had it all together. Why did they need therapy?

"You could say that." They turned their face towards mine.

I started giggling.

"My pain is somehow funny to you?" They pulled their face away.

"No—I...It's just that your face..." I couldn't stop the giggling now.

"My face is *that* funny." They sat up. "Nice. Not sure why I waste my time on you." They dropped my hand and started to get up, startling some small creature in the tree over-hanging the corner of the house. It scurried to safety among the dying leaves.

Shit.

"No. No." I reached up for them, doing my best to swallow the giggles. "It's just that up close, you know, you looked like

172

those crazy cyclopes from Greek mythology. The ones who forged the thunderbolts of Zeus."

They considered me for a moment before sitting back down. "I guess I've been called worse things than a cyclopian monster." They smiled the bitter-sweet smile of one who can still look on the bright side of pain.

I'd never noticed how one of their front teeth slightly overlapped the other. I found it somehow charming, this lack of perfection. I wondered what they looked like under all the make-up, realizing that it was the mask they used to keep the world from their pain. The make-up, humor, sarcasm, drugs—all masks—shields to protect us from a world that feared us.

Us. Why were we such a threat?

Echo again reached for my hands, their metal bangle bracelets clinking like delicate wind-chimes. Another siren, this one closer, whined its way through the otherwise quiet streets. Echo brought my right hand to their forearm, just below the cuffs of their gray henley, which were slid up towards their elbows. They pulled their hand away. My fingers ran along their forearm, tracing thin ridges that ran like the cross members of a train track leading to their wrist.

"This is my pain." They whispered.

I looked up at Echo's face, partially hidden by the long locks of hair on the right side of their head. They were so beautiful. Beautiful in their uniqueness. Vulnerable in their pain. I leaned forward and kissed their lips. I felt them smile, slightly, then the wetness of their tongue. My world was softness, wrapped in cinnamon.

I don't know how long we kissed before I pulled back a little. When our lips parted, our foreheads converged to maintain the contact. Eyes, still closed. My heart pumped with an energy unlike any I'd ever known. My body consumed with a contentedness I hadn't felt in years. This wasn't like kissing Desiree, who now seemed miles away. This was like finding my own soul.

To: akeen1@aol.com
Subject: Hey
From: skaterwylie@aol.com

Hey.

So, my therapist said I should write to you to tell you how I'm "feeling." There's lots of feeling going on here, which sometimes is ok, but other times it totally sucks.

So here goes...

I feel hurt by what you did with Desiree in San Clemente. I know you said you're sorry. Alot. Don't worry, your mom's even told me how sorry you are. I get it. I wanted to say though, that it's really hard for me to trust people and it's really hard for me to get close to girls. So when my best friend snuck off with the first girl I'd ever kissed and started messing around with her, man, it was like getting shot through the heart with a shotgun.

I don't need you to apologize again. I know that life is about making choices and that those choices have consequences. And I'm for-sure the KING of questionable choices these days. We all make mistakes. Shannon (my therapist) says that's how we learn the best lessons. Well, I'm learning all kinds of lessons. One of them is that you're a good friend, despite stabbing me in the heart with a broken skateboard (sorry man, sometimes I just need to draw it out a little).

I want my friend back. I miss you.

Wylie

14

Alex

To: skaterwylie@aol.com
Subject: Hey
From: akeen1@aol.com

Hey man!

I screwed up and I know that. Please believe me when I say, I will NEVER betray you like that again.

I've missed you too. School's been lame without you around.

How is it there? Can I come visit now that you're talking to me again?

Write me back. (When did you get an email address?)
Alex

P.S. Did you know you're competing with Lamar to be valedictorian?

To: akeen1@aol.com
Subject: Hey
From: skaterwylie@aol.com

A—

   This place is amazing. I don't know how to thank your mom for getting me in here. Like I said, we have to explore our feelings a lot here, but it's not always bad. I've met some really cool people who are trans or queer, which makes me feel less like the freak my family thinks I am.

   What are you doing hanging out with Lamar? Yeah, we've gotten the best grades in our classes since—forever. It's just easy for me, especially because I have a photographic memory. My biggest problem is participation. I have to be careful what classes I ditch. Lol.

   Yes, please come visit. This weekend??? I want you to meet Echo.

Wylie

P.S. Bring weed, or we are not friends. (Kidding.) (Kind of...) ;-)

♠ ♥ ♣ ♦

"I'm glad to see you're making new friends, bud." My dad turned on his indicator to make a right turn, just past Del Taco.

My stomach growled. Lamar had invited me over for dinner. We'd been hanging out more since he "broke up" with Cam and Chase. So yeah, Lamar is officially my second "Evil Empire" friend. And what, it only took me like four months? Yay me.

"And I'm pleased to see that your friends are so diverse." He navigated us through the upscale shopping center and beyond, through one of the ubiquitous orange groves that lined so many of the streets here. "I have to say, I was a bit worried about the homogeneity of this area when we moved."

I stared out the window and rolled my eyes. He's just happy I'm not moping around the house. Wait, that was unfair. I know my dad has always supported me. He's honestly like the best dad I've ever seen. It's just that I've just been in such a bad mood for a while now. Good things are happening though. I needed to snap out of this. It's just a little weird having your whole life scrutinized.

We approached a corner where clusters of orange trees flanked a large wall sign that read "Hillcrest Estates." Lamar lived in the nicest neighborhood I'd seen in SoCal. Even nicer than ours. Every house was two stories and had perfectly man-icured lawns. Lamar's house sat at the end of a cul-de-sac. Nobody was outside. No kids playing. No one mowing lawns. Nothing like my neighborhood here, or in San Francisco.

A dark blue Mercedes Benz sedan sat in the driveway in front of a two-car garage, just like Lamar said. I was no expert, but I didn't think ACLU lawyers made that much money. Maybe I was wrong. I realized that I was frequently wrong about things these days.

My dad slid our jeep into the driveway next to the Benz. "I'll pick you up at 7:30. Ok?"

I opened the door, grabbed my backpack and jumped out. "Yeah that's cool."

"Be polite!" His voice was swallowed by the slamming of the door.

Geez, does he really have to remind me to be polite? The Jeep's engine roared away, leaving me alone in the eerily-quiet neighborhood. The wind howled through the alleyway between Lamar's house and the one next to it. We'd been having Santa Ana winds all week and I'd had about enough of the hot, dry weather. My lips were cracked open and it was almost impossible to skate, between the winds and all the palm fronds and other tree branches all over the place.

I walked up the long brick-lined concrete path that led from the driveway to the large front porch. A brown wicker table and loveseat with a maroon seat cushion occupied the space to the right of the door. A fat gray cat occupied the loveseat. The cat peered at me through one eye. I guess I wasn't enough of a threat to open both eyes. I pushed the white button to the left of the door and heard a deep bell ring through the house. A few seconds later, footsteps rumbled down stairs and Lamar opened the door.

"Hey, come on in." He motioned for me to come in. As I entered the foyer, a tall, elegant-looking woman appeared in the hall leading towards the back of the house.

"Is this Alex?" She brushed her hands on the black apron she was wearing and came towards me.

Lamar looked at me and rolled his eyes, like *who else would it be?* Then answered, "Yes mom, this is Alex. Alex, meet my mom."

"Welcome, Alex. You can call me Michelle." She shook my hand. "I've just pulled some crostini out of the oven to hold you over until dinner. Please, make yourself at home."

Crostini? Who makes crostini?

Lamar led the way back to the kitchen. "You're going to love this stuff. My mom's a great cook."

"And you're sweet for saying so." Michelle piped up from behind us. "Grab a plate and head to the game room. Dinner will be out in about half an hour when your father gets home."

"Thanks mom." Lamar gave his mom a kiss on the cheek on his way into the kitchen.

We took our plates of crunchy bread slices and scoops of a tomato, onion, and basil mixture and Lamar led me back to another room with a massive television and black leather couch on one side of the room, a pool table in the middle, and a card table and dartboard on the other side of the room. I followed, a little confused. I wasn't sure who this person was, but he was not the Lamar I was used to. He was so *polite*. And he hadn't called me a fool once.

We ate our appetizers while watching *Rounders* on HBO. It was one of Lamar's favorite movies. I could understand why—the main character, played by Matt Damon, drops out of law school to become a big-time poker player. I'm not exactly sure if that's what Lamar wants to be, but I couldn't stop thinking about our conversation the other day.

"Hey, you know the other day when you told me how your family wants you to go to law school and all that?" I shoved a bite of crostini into my mouth and crunched down on it, waiting for Lamar's reply.

He shrugged. "Yeah."

"Well, I still don't know what *you* want to do with *your* life."

The television suddenly got super loud as Matt Damon and Ed Norton's characters were getting their asses kicked by a bunch of cops because they discovered Worm was cheating. Lamar turned it down. "Not that it matters, but I wanted to be an actor."

"Really?" I guess it's not a difficult leap when I considered the different versions of Lamar I've seen. I wondered which was the most "real."

Lamar nodded. "Like I said, not that it matters."

"Why not?" I mean, yeah, maybe it's not the most practical

of vocations, but geez, if you've got a dream, you might as well follow it. Isn't that what everyone was saying now—*follow your bliss*?

"My mom says everyone has got to have a purpose in life and they must make a difference in the world." He crunched up one of the crostini crusts like a cigarette butt on his plate. "She says our family's got a gift for the law and we should use that gift to make the world a better place."

Seemed a little fascist to me. Why do some parents insist on making their kids into mini-me's? "Dude, actors can make a difference in the world. I mean, you could play roles in film or stage that really make people think about things. Like Denzel Washington in *Malcolm X*. Or Ed Norton in *American History X*. They educated their audiences, who probably didn't even know it was happening. Who knows how many minds were changed by those films? My dad always says that the truth tastes better when it's served with a dose of fiction."

Lamar was quiet. I wasn't sure if he was thinking about what I said, or was just engrossed in the movie.

Then, from beyond the game room, his mom's voice rang out, "Boys, time for dinner."

We gathered our plates and brought them back down to the kitchen. Lamar's mom was bringing a tray of what looked like lasagna out to the dining room table. She set it down next to a big silver bowl of salad. The table was set for four people, but it could have easily fit two more. Between the elaborate chandelier, the perfect-looking food, and the fancy table settings, the place looked like it should be on the cover of a magazine. How did his mom have time to do all this? I'd have to ask Lamar later. His family was nothing like I imagined. I mean, I knew his parents were attorneys, but I just imagined they ordered out a lot and kept late hours. His mom's like half-Ally

McBeal and half-Martha Stewart (only way less white, of course).

Lamar's dad was on the phone in the living room, sounding heated. All I could see was the back of his body. He was shorter than me, maybe the same height, but stocky. He wore a black, tailored suit, his grey-socked feet sinking into the plush, cream-colored carpet. "Listen Marvin, I don't care what they told you. I want those documents on my desk in the morning. If I am not setting my coffee down next to those documents at 9:06 am, then I had better be reading a motion for sanctions against our illustrious and inebriated opposing counsel at 9:07 am. Understand?"

He pressed the button to hang up the phone, only to press it again and start dialing another number.

"Honey, enough. Dinner's on the table." Michelle called from the kitchen.

Lamar's dad waved his hand as if to swat a fly away from his head.

I sat down in the plush cream chair next to Lamar and placed the black cloth napkin on my lap, feeling more like I was in one of the fancy restaurants we used to go to in the City, not in my friend's dining room. The smell of tomato sauce and melted cheese made my stomach rumble even more. I wished Lamar's dad would hurry up.

"Finally." Michelle said, hands on hips at the head of the dining room table. "Isaiah, I swear you'd forget you had a family if we didn't remind you from time to time."

Lamar's dad plopped down across from me. Michelle sat down next to him, picked up his plate and almost filled it with a generous helping of lasagna. Waiting my turn, I nearly choked on a mouthful of water. Sparkling. I never liked sparkling water. It felt dry—never able to quench a thirst.

"You don't look like my daughter." Lamar's dad directed the statement at me.

I wasn't sure if he was serious or not. "Um, no sir?" I was a little intimidated.

He laughed. "I'm joking young man. You're Alex. Welcome to Chateau Jones." He waved his fork in a circle around his head before plunging it into the cheesy mess on his plate.

I took the silver salad bowl from Lamar. "Thanks Mr. Jones."

"Call me Isaiah. Please." He said, not exactly between bites.

I nodded, placing a pile of field greens on my plate. Lamar slopped a heap of lasagna on my plate—the sauce running into the salad. I couldn't wait to dig in.

"This is really good, Michelle." It felt kinda weird calling her that.

"I told you she was a good cook." Lamar sipped his dry water.

"Thank you Alex. I'm glad you like it." Michelle poured some red wine for herself and Isaiah. "Lanika called me this morning. She made law review." Her smile revealed a mouth full of perfectly-straight, white teeth.

"Was there any doubt?" Isaiah answered, checking his watch.

"I wish you two would stop this nonsense. You need to apologize." Michelle sipped her wine, eyebrows raised above the bulbous glass.

"This isn't the time, Michelle." Isaiah said, before shoveling more lasagna into his mouth.

I hated it when my parents fought, which wasn't often. Watching other people's parents fight was even more uncomfortable. I stabbed at a baby tomato that rolled across my plate. Why doesn't anyone cut these things?

"Hey dad, will you be able to make it to my play next Friday? Jeremy broke his leg, so I get to play Oberon."

"I don't know why you insist on wasting your time on that, Lamar." Isaiah took a gulp of his wine. "And I won't watch my son prance around onstage for a school that can't see fit to produce something written by a black man."

"Or woman." Michelle added. "Besides, you need to focus on your studies."

Lamar put his fork down. "Focus on my studies? Are you kidding? I've got one of the highest GPAs in school. And how is it my fault you moved to white suburbia? How many people here do you think are gonna come to *Roots, the Junior High School Musical*?"

"That's enough." Isaiah's voice boomed, as his fist pounded the table. Michelle's hand darted out to steady her wine glass, which was on the verge of tipping over. The red fluid sloshed around, but remained in the glass. She looked shaken though.

I felt Lamar shrink down into his seat. I understood. His story was written.

15

Wylie

Atley Hall, Los Angeles — Day 15

Daily Journal Prompt: What are 5 Things That Make You Incredibly Happy?

Echo makes me incredibly happy. I feel safe with them, but also challenged. They know so much and is so experienced. Sometimes I just want to lick their brain. (But not in a creepy way...)

Aces (my skateboard) because it's the first, well, only thing, that I've built with my own two hands that has been useful. Well, I guess my clock worked, but it was ugly as F—. Aces is my ticket to freedom.

The fact that Alex and I are friends again makes me incredibly happy. I can't wait to see him.

Thinking about making a difference in the world. I feel like I was born to do something great and make a positive impact. I just don't know what that is. I feel a little jealous about Echo in that respect—they know what they're going to do and how to do it.

The thought of being able to transition. I mean, yeah, I know I've transitioned socially, but the thought of going on puberty blockers, or better still—testosterone, oh man, I can almost feel the facial stubble. While I've been here, my breasts have started to get puffy. That makes me sad because now I don't feel like I can go shirtless and still "pass." I'm worried that my mom won't consent to the treatment though. I guess worried is putting it mildly. I'm terrified. What if my boobs keep growing? I don't know when I could afford top surgery.

The amber light flickered on my desktop. It was late. My ass was tired. I had wanted to finish reading my Algebra II book and get my homework done by the end of the night. That represented the last of my work for the year, except for the final exam, of course. Dr. Springall's staff had arranged to have all of my assignments available to me so I could complete them on my own time. I rather liked the idea that I was done before all of my peers. This independent study option had its perks.

From my laptop came the sound of a squeaky door closing. I looked over to see that Echo had entered our AOL chatroom. A small, gray box appeared on the bottom right hand corner of my screen.

EchoEchoEcho: hey, you big jerk. ;-)

A smile played on my lips. I pushed my Algebra II book aside and brought my laptop closer to me.

SkaterWylie: what's up captain lam-o?

EchoEchoEcho: are you done with that kids work yet?
SkaterWylie: i'd hardly call quantum physics 'kids work.'

EchoEchoEcho: ugh, whatever. when can I come over?

The clock downstairs began its incessant hourly chiming to mark the 11th hour. I could hear animalistic snores coming from Nicole's room next to me. She wore herself out on those stairs today. I couldn't say I blamed her. Group therapy was rough today, particularly for her. We had gotten onto the topic of bullying.

"White girl, you think you got it bad in your life? Please." Nicole shook her head and wagged her finger back and forth.

Echo look pissed. "Don't you dare impose your gendered labels on me. And when did this become a competition?"

Matt admonished in his soft voice, "Friends, please. Remember our group rules. This is a safe space. We should all create a safe haven for each other to express themselves. And we should be careful to remember to use our friends' desired nouns and pronouns."

Echo sat with their arms crossed, starring daggers at Nicole.

"May I continue?" Nicole asked, her voice oozing with attitude.

Matt spread his hands out in front of him—a motion to continue. The small room felt claustrophobic. Not only was it stiflingly hot because the air conditioning had gone out (again), everything was in shades of tan—like the DMV and every other medical facility I'd ever been in. They say it's supposed to be soothing. But at this point in our collective evolution, it's just associated with institutionalized apathy. Let's get some color in here people. Some freaking variety.

Nicole continued with her story. "I was shooting hoops at the court down the street from my apartment building, over on 22nd. It was the afternoon. My school had gotten out early that day. Parent-teacher kind of stuff. Most folks was at work." She spread her fingers out on her lap, one hand on each leg, and rubbed the tops of her thighs. She always did this when she was nervous. It made me nervous.

"Anyway, these three wanna-be gang-banger types comes into the gate, says they wanna play. The tall one grabbed the ball from me and tossed it to one of his buddies—a short moth-erfucker with a goatee and a foul attitude—fouler than the others. They kept passing the ball between them. I could tell they didn't really want to play. I was getting uneasy 'cuz of the way they were looking at me—studying me. They was circling me, passing the ball, all silent-like until the short one started asking me questions. You know the ones. 'You a homo?' 'You a dike?' 'Yo, you pretty tall for a sister.'" Nicole swallowed hard. "I asked them to pass my ball back. I said, 'if you wanna play, let's play. You wanna be a jackass, you can leave.' The other one, he was a sloppy-type, fat. I remember his stained-ass wife-beater. Holes everywhere. Anyway, he had the ball and he rushed me. At the last minute, he slammed the ball into my face. All I saw was black. I staggered backward, but they must've tripped me because then I was on the hard ground." Nicole paused and licked her lips, hands rubbing back and forth on her thighs, like she needed to warm herself. "So then, they was on me, kicking me in the head, stomping on my hand, one of them—I think it was that goatee'd bastard—he was on top of me, punching my face like a jackhammer. I couldn't get up. He just kept punching me and punching me while the others laughed." Nicole's voice started shaking. I knew what it was like to be in a fight, but not to get the living shit kicked out of you by three guys. She took a deep breath and let it out through pursed lips. "I—I think someone must have called the cops because I heard sirens coming closer. The beating stopped, but then they took turns—" Nicole's voice cracked. "—they took turns pissing on me."

My stomach turned. I couldn't believe people would do such a thing. Nicole was one of the sweetest people I'd met. Intense, for sure, but she had a beautiful heart, though she seemed to try hard to protect it. I can't say I blamed her at all for that. I looked over at Skylar. He had tears running down his face. I know he hadn't been physically beaten, but we had all had slurs slung at us and come close to the heartache that Nicole was feeling.

"The police came. Asked me what happened. Got me an ambulance. They was nice and all, but I didn't want to go in no ambulance because that shit's expensive. You know? My momma don't work enough hours to cover that kind of business. So they cleaned me up as best they could. Drove me home. I got in that shower and washed the blood and the piss off my body. Watched the rust-colored water run down that pipe. I could barely see anything because my eyes was swelling up. When I got out of the shower, I couldn't recognize myself in the mirror. When my mom got home, she didn't recognize me neither. When I told her 'momma, it's me' she broke down and cried. So we both on the floor crying when there's a knock at the door. It's the police. They say they think they caught those brothers 'cuz they was out bragging' about they beat the shit out of some tranny."

"Thank god they caught those fuckers." Echo's anger was no longer directed at Nicole, it was now directed at the guys who beat her. "I hope they got what was coming to them."

Nicole just shook her head. She was rocking back and forth now, still rubbing her hands on her thighs. I thought she might just wear a hole through the tops of her track pants.

"They say they want me to come down to the station. They want me to identify them. But I'm like, if I do that. If I ID them, they just gonna come back and finish what they started."

"So you didn't go?" Echo was astonished. "What the—"

"Echo." Matt shook his head. "We don't walk in others' shoes. We don't judge."

Nicole continued. "We didn't go to the police station. My momma took me to the hospital. I didn't want to go. We didn't have the money for that. But she said I shouldn't worry about that and that I was worth every penny she had. That's how I ended up here. The doctors knew Dr. Springall. And someone, I don't know who, paid my way here."

I wondered who paid Nicole's tuition here. I didn't know who was paying mine. I suspected that the Keens were, but I wasn't certain of that. Echo's parents were well-off. They said their parents paid for them to be there. Echo said their parents didn't know what else to do with them. At any rate, today was emotionally-draining for everyone.

SkaterWylie: give me 37 seconds?

No return message. But 30-some-odd seconds later, there was a soft knock on my door, and Echo snuck into my room for the fifth night in a row.

Atley Hall, Los Angeles — Day 27

Daily Journal Prompt: Write a Letter of Forgiveness to Someone Who Has Caused You Pain

Ah hell. Really? So many choices...I've already for-
given Alex, shouldn't that count for something?

Cam can still fuck off. So can Desiree and Brianna. So
can my mom.

Alright, here goes...

Dear Dad,

It's been five years since you left. Why did you go? Where
did you go? You just went to work one morning and
never came back. Did mom know? Because she didn't
seem all that surprised that you didn't come home that
night. I've missed you. Jared and Mason probably do
too, but they never talk about you.

My therapist says that you didn't leave because of us
and that you love us. I like to think that, but I don't
understand how you can love someone and just abandon
them. Anyway, I could really use a father-figure right
now. One who truly loves me no matter what. I'd like to
think that you would still love me—and even like me—as
a boy. I would have liked you to teach me how to work
on cars and how to shave. I would have liked to have
someone cheering me on when I skate. I would have
liked to talk to you about Alex and Desiree and have
you say something—anything—that would make me feel
better.

Even though I don't understand why you left, I do
forgive you for leaving. When I'm old enough, I'll try to
find you. But I won't be mad.

Your son,
Wylie

191

Patient: Wylie (Willow) Masterson

Age: 14
DOB: 5/17/85
Diagnosis: Gender Identity Disorder
Narrative: Wylie is a female-to-male transgender resident, recent run-away with a history of drug abuse. Partially socially transitioned, presents as male, except with family. Recent issue with alleged sexual harassment by police and opiate overdose. Late onset puberty. Currently under guardianship with Reyna Keen, mother of best friend. Observations of family in hospital setting: Family includes mother, actively in denial and hampered by religious dogma, father (out of the picture), older brother, Mason (age 17), most sympathetic, older brother, Jared (age 16), confused and angry—

"Here we are, now." The lilt of Dr. Springall's voice just outside the door startled me. I snapped the chart closed and slid into my seat just as he opened the door and my family walked in. First Mason, then Jared, then my mom. Dr. Springall followed them in and closed the door.

"You cut your hair." Mason remarked as he hugged me tight. "Looks good."

I had the back and one side cut to a short boy-style cut, leaving my bangs chin-length and parted to one side. I loved it, but was nervous to show it to my family. Just a few words from Mason put me at ease. "Thanks."

"Yeah, dude, looks good." Jared was not as convincing, but it felt good that he was making an effort. I don't think he'd ever called me 'dude' before.

I looked over at my mom, who just looked away and sat

down closest to Dr. Springall's seat. My heart sank. What did I expect? An overnight change of heart?

Everyone was on edge. I'm not sure who this was going to be hardest for—me or them. I had worked all week with Shannon and Dr. Springall about how to communicate what I wanted from my family. Today was the big day. No drugs. No running away. Shannon said that it helps to be able to separate myself from any outcome. The purpose was to be able to make my voice heard. The rest was up to them. I had to make myself not care whether they accepted me or my terms. Not as easy in practice. I mean, they're my family. Shouldn't they want to do things that are healthy for me?

Dr. Springall sat down in his chair, my closed chart in hand. "Right, how is everyone today?" His gaze passed over each of us, resting on my mom, who refused to make eye contact with anyone.

"Mom!" Mason's voice had gotten deeper. He almost sounded like our dad.

She acted startled and looked at Mason, then at Dr. Springall. "Oh, well, you know. Making it through." She wrang her hands. "You know Roy left us last week. All of this was just too much for him. So now, I'm alone." She sighed. "Except for my boys, of course." Her gaze swept over Mason and Jared, but did not include me.

Mason rolled his eyes.

Jared glared at the floor. "Yeah, he was supposed to be teaching me how to drive." He glanced over at me. "He said he was going to buy me a car. And you ruined it."

What? I jumped up. "Me? How is that ass-wipe leaving *my* fault?" This was not going as planned. We were supposed to sit down together and everyone was going to listen to what I needed to say. We were all going to be calm.

Jared rose up out of his chair. He stood a good four-inches taller than me. "He left because of all of your mental issues."

"Hey! Knock it off, Jared." Mason was about to come between us but Dr. Springall got up and moved towards Jared. "Right. Ok, let's all sit down and remain calm. We like to maintain a blame-free space here." He touched Jared on the shoulder. Jared shrugged him off and sat down, arms crossed, glaring at the floor.

"Good. Now, Wylie has some things he'd like to say to each of you and I'd like it if everyone would listen with an open heart and allow him to say what he needs to say before responding. Can everyone agree to that?"

"Yes." Mason said.

Jared and my mom nodded, but said nothing.

Dr. Springall sat back down and motioned for me to start. "Go ahead Wylie."

My heart was still racing. I tried the deep breath exercise Shannon taught me, but felt really self-conscious. *Ok, here goes.* "I know this is hard for you guys to understand and accept. But, I'm a guy. Ever since I understood that there was a concept of gender, I felt like a male—not a female." I looked at my mom, trying to will her to look at me. "This isn't a phase that I'm going to grow out of. And I'm not a freak or a mental case." I looked at Jared, who was actually paying attention. "There are others like me all over the world. I've met some of them here. And I need you to understand that I will no longer answer to the name Willow. If we're going to be a family, I need you to call me Wylie and use male pronouns." I saw Mason nodding his head in encouragement, which gave me a sense of solidarity, like I was not alone in this—for once. "Jared, I'm not doing this to hurt anyone. I'm just trying to be me. I know we haven't always gotten along all the time, but I need my brothers to stand with me." He nodded. "Mom." She looked up. "I need you to let me dress in the clothes I feel comfortable in. I can't be one person for you and another for everyone else." She nodded her head, slowly. "And, I need you to sign off on puberty blockers for me."

"What?" The head nodding stopped.

"Mom, wait—"

"I won't have them experimenting with your body—"

Dr. Springall interjected, "Ms. Masterson, we agreed to let Wylie say everything he needs to say, right? Now let's let him finish."

Surprisingly, that shut her up.

I took a deep breath and let it out again. "You don't have to worry, mom, these blockers won't do anything permanent to me. People use them all the time. It'll just stop me from—" It was embarrassing talking about this in front of my brothers, "—you know—growing into a woman." I decided to stop there and not talk about going on testosterone or having surgeries. I didn't think she could handle it.

"I don't know Will—" She corrected herself, "Wylie."

Score one for me!

"Mom, this is what I want. And if you won't help me, I'm not coming home."

She just looked down at the ground again. The chasm of silence between us grew as I began to give up hope. Then, she said the words that made the whole world right again.

"Ok. I'll consent." When she looked up, I could see the tears smearing her mascara down her cheeks.

I was elated. Relieved. Yet, in a way, heartbroken for the woman who brought me into this crazy world.

"You'll feel a little pinch." The nurse swiped an alcohol pad across my upper glute. I laid on my stomach on the clinic table, the thin sanitary paper crinkling underneath me and sticking to my ever-sweaty hands. It's not that I was nervous. Far from it. I'd been waiting for this day for what seemed like forever.

I barely slept last night. After Echo left, I just tossed and turned in my bed. By the time morning came, the sheets were off one corner of the mattress and I felt like a zombie—albeit, an excited zombie, if such a thing was possible. When I did sleep, I dreamed again of graduating from high school with a goatee, delivering my valedictorian speech (because, of course) with a voice as deep as Darth Vader's.

As grateful as I was to be going on puberty blockers, my deepest wish was that I could go on testosterone. Maybe they would screw up or change their minds and give me that coveted male hormone instead. Could I hack into their computer system and change the order? Hmmm. Not a bad idea...

I felt the needle push through my flesh, deep into my muscle. A slight burn as the medication entered my body. Lupron, it was called. This magic solution would stop my breasts from developing, stop my hips from widening, and eventually, stop the monthly devil's waterfall. To say this 'little pinch' brought me relief would be the understatement of the century.

"All done." The nurse applied a bandaid to my ass and dropped the syringe in the red sharps container by the sink. "Not so bad, right?"

I pulled my jeans up before swinging my legs down. "Not bad? Freaking awesome." I buckled my belt and slid off the table, noticing a small ache in the injection site. I would take that over a period any day.

"You'll go to your local doctor once a month for injections. Let us know if you have any of the side effects listed in this packet." She handed me three pieces of yellow paper stapled together with the word LUPRON printed across the top. "Any questions?"

I folded the papers in half long-ways and stuck them in my back pocket. I shook my head.

"Alright, you're done." She peeled the glove from her right hand and held it out to me. "Congratulations, Wylie." I shook her dry, powder-coated hand, feeling elated—as if I'd gone through some sort of right-of-passage.

Echo was waiting for me when I got back to the house. They were the only one. Everyone else was out.

"Congrats Wylie." They kissed my cheek. "I have a surprise for you." They took my hand and led me up the stairs. When we got up to the top of the landing, they turned and said, "close your eyes."

"Why?" I thought briefly that they might push me down the stairs. Not sure why. Sometimes, odd situations just pop into my brain.

"Because I said so, you big jerk. Just do it."

I complied and let the world fade away as I hid behind closed lids. I felt their soft hand on my wrist as they led me forward. I heard a door open. We moved forward. "Stay here."

I wondered what they were doing that required all the dramatics. This was totally out of character. I heard a door close and the soft sound of Echo's uncharacteristically bare feet on the wood floor. I felt their body next to me, then their warm breath on my ear, "you can open your eyes now."

The afternoon light poured through the open window, making it hard for my eyes to adjust. When I could finally focus, I saw that Echo had somehow procured a cupcake with blue frosting, a balloon that said, "It's a Boy" on it, and a card.

My heart melted. I didn't have anyone else to celebrate this pretty monumental event with. I turned to Echo and put my arms around their waist. "You didn't have to do this."

They kissed me and lightly bit my bottom lip. "I know. And I hate myself for perpetuating the myth of the binary by celebrating your first steps into manhood, but if that's what makes you happy, I want to support you." They kissed me on the nose. "Go open your card!"

I tore the baby-blue envelop open to reveal a homemade card with a hand-drawn image of what looked like me and Echo leaning forward and kissing, like those Precious Moments figurines. Inside the card, in big, black block letters, were the words: "I LOVE YOU. DON'T TURN INTO A DICK."

I stared at the card, a flurry of thoughts running through my mind. First, odd choice of sentiment for a greeting card. Second, they said they *love* me. Third, Precious Moments?

"If you hate it, don't say it. Just pretend." Echo was more nervous than I'd ever seen them. Actually, I'd never seen them nervous. What was up?

"No, I love it." I really did. I was just…shocked. We'd been hanging out almost constantly since that night on the roof, mostly talking and making out. They were the most interesting person I'd ever encountered and I couldn't get enough of them. "I love you too."

They took a step forward to the desk and unwrapped the cupcake, tearing the bottom off.

"Hey! What are you doing with my cupcake?"

"What makes you think this is *your* cupcake?" They took the bottom half of the cupcake and put it on top, sandwiching the blue frosting in between the cake pieces.

198

I stepped forward and took it from them. "Because it's not your signature color." I took a bite. The cake was moist, and the blue buttercream frosting squeezed out the side and onto my fingers.

Echo stuck their tongue out and licked the frosting from my fingers, then their lips. "Perhaps I should change my signature color." They kissed me again, their tongue dipping deep into my mouth. I put the rest of the dessert back on the table and guided us towards the bed.

Atley Hall, Los Angeles — Day 33

Daily Journal Prompt: Look in the Mirror. Pretend Your Looking at Your Best Friend. What 5 Qualities About That Person in the Mirror do You Love the Most?

Dear Diary,

Sometimes people don't like me because I am soooo good looking. :-)

What's a guy to do?

I still feel goofy doing these. In case you hadn't figured it out.

This is hard, because normally, I think about everything that's wrong about me, like how much pain I cause my family because I can't fake being a girl. And how scared I am that high school will be the same as junior high and I'll always be known as the freak. I wish I was fearless, like Echo. But this isn't the assignment...

Ok. I'm looking in the mirror. I guess I'm not really bad looking. But that seems pretty superficial. I just wish I had a guy's body.

Why do I keep going back to the negatives? Focus Wylie.

Alright…

I love that I'm athletic. I mean, in all honesty, I'm an amazing skater. And that is pretty rad.

I love that I'm smart. Smart is sexy, right? That's why Echo and I are so good together.

I love that I'm learning to deal with life stuff better than my family. It feels kind of monumental that I might be overcoming unhealthy patterns that have been passed on in our DNA.

Shit, this is hard. I don't actually think I'm a good person. What makes a good person? Because I kinda feel like I'm an asshole. It's not like I don't care about people. I do. I really do. It's just, so many have ended up hurting me. I guess I have trust issues. I don't like following rules. I don't make friends very easily. I use drugs. I'm insecure. Aloof. These are all things that others say are "bad" characteristics. Like, I feel like I should be forced to wear one of those shirts that say, "I'm the guy your parents warned you about."

Sorry Shannon, the results are in—I'm not a very good human.

Later.

16

Alex

"So I have a question for you. How does someone who smokes as much weed as you do end up being valedictorian of our 9th grade class?"

Wylie laughed. "I don't know man. It's not like I was trying to be the top of my class." He shrugged. "This stuff just comes really easy to me."

I shook my head. "Well, congrats on that."

"It's not for sure yet, man, but thanks." Wylie sat across from me, swinging back and forth on a bench swing on the back porch of Atley House. He looked good. Happy, even. It was a relief to see him like this. Honestly, it was a relief to see him at all.

"I think Lamar's less than happy to share the title with you, but he'll get over it." Hopefully his parents would too. Geez, talk about pressure. It was a wonder Lamar didn't implode.

"Yeah, so what happened with all that?" Wylie pushed off the wooden porch lightly to move the swing. "Why are you guys suddenly besties?"

Was he jealous? "I don't know. I think he's just outgrown

Cam and Tracky's crap." I flicked an ant off my pant leg and watched it fly off the deck into the bed of pink geraniums. "He's not a bad guy, you know."

"Lamar?" Wylie's right leg swung in a lazy circle, his left leg was tucked underneath him. He fiddled with the laces on his shoe. "I know." His admission seemed reluctant. "It *was* kinda bullshit that he stood with them when they turned on me. And what? It took him *months* to come around?" Wylie shook his head.

"Look, maybe you would have done things different, but you gotta give him credit for figuring it out eventually."

Wylie seemed to ponder that for a while. Next door young children played, their shrieks climbing over the fence, filling the silence.

"Did you know about Cam's dad?" I figured he did, but who knows what they shared.

"How he died and stuff? Yeah." Wylie switched feet and pushed off to get the swing started again. "I didn't know him when it happened, but yeah, Cam said his dad had a heart attack or something while they were driving home from school one day. Cam had to go home early because he felt sick, and his mom was out of town or something. His dad left work to come get him and he just died. Cam had to push his dad's leg off the accelerator, but they still ended up crashing into a parked car. He felt like it was his fault. Like if he had just stayed at school, his dad would still be alive."

"Shit." I shook my head. So much made sense now. Still no excuse to be a complete jerk to people, but I had a lot more compassion for the guy, knowing all this.

"I have some good news." I'd wanted to tell him about this ever since I got the letter.

"Better than me being valedictorian?" There it was. That sarcastic tone and smile I had missed these past months.

"Yeah, man. Way better." I pulled the folded letter out of my back pocket. "I got into this amazing robotics class at Stanford." I handed him the letter. "Check this out." I watched as he read the acceptance, my excitement renewed. "What do you think?"

"Alex, this is awesome. Why didn't you tell me you entered?" He handed the letter back.

I refolded the paper and slid it back into my pocket. "Honestly, I forgot about it with the move and all. I applied before we came here."

"So, do you have a project that you're going to work on? Or, like, how does it work?"

It was cool to see Wylie so excited about my project. I was a little worried he would feel left out. But I didn't want him to be left out. It would be so rad if he could come too, but that wasn't an option. At least, not this year. "Actually, I have no idea what I'll be working on. I guess there are several project options, but they don't disclose the details until you get there." Just trying to imagine what we'd be doing was getting me excited all over again. "I'm hoping that my project will have something to do with incorporating AI with a humanoid form."

"Oh yeah! Like Data from Star Trek: Next Generation." Wylie stopped swinging. He planted both feet on the ground.

"Exactly. I love the idea of turning science-fiction into reality. And besides, wouldn't it be awesome to have, like, this super brilliant friend that you could hang out with and have access to all the knowledge of the entire planet accessible to you?"

"What, I'm not brilliant enough for you?" Wylie feigned being hurt.

"No." I shook my head—all serious. "You're definitely not."

We both busted up laughing at that.

"Hey, so tell me about Echo. What's she like?" He had just mentioned her once in an email, but never elaborated. I wondered if she was a strong enough influence to get Wylie to forget Desiree. I still felt like a monumental dick about all that.

A smile played on Wylie's lips, but quickly faded. "Well, it's 'they' actually. And I think they're mad at me right now."

"'They?' Like instead of 'she?'"

"Yeah. They don't like that we have to make a decision between two arbitrary constructs." Wylie stretched up to look at something inside the house before settling back down into the swing. "They want to have sex." He looked down at his hands. "With me. Aaaand I wouldn't let them."

"Dude! Why not?" I instantly regretted that. "I'm sorry. I mean, tell me about it."

The silence stretched so long I thought I'd totally blown it. Again.

Wylie picked at some dirt under his fingernails. He wouldn't look at me. "It's just that I feel really uncomfortable with—" He waved his hands over his crotch. "—the state of *things* down there."

Oh man, that totally sucks. I couldn't wait to cross "devirginize" off my to-do list. I couldn't imagine the conflict he must have. I mean, I know he *wants* to have sex, but to want it and be afraid to show himself, that just blows. I didn't know what to say.

"So, anyway. Yeah. They had planned it after I got my first shot. They were so sweet with the balloon and the homemade card and the cupcake." He finally looked up at me. "But when they tried to take my jeans off, I just—" His voice faded. "—I just couldn't do it." He flopped over so that he was half-laying on the bench swing, his eyes closed.

"Man, that must really be difficult." I felt like I was impersonating a therapist, but it was all I could think to say.

"It's impossible." Was his muffled reply. "And now they're being all weird around me. They think I don't love them."

Damn. And I thought my love life was complicated. "Have you talked to her about it?"

Just then the screen door screeched open and a brunette girl burst through. "Talked to her about what?"

Wylie popped up to a seated position, a look of panic on his face. "My mom. About the testosterone."

"Ah yes, your mother. God's gift to—" She looked down and tapped on her chin. "—what *is* she God's gift to?" She shook her head. "I can't come up with anything."

She turned to me, then I saw that half her head was shaved. "Hi. I'm Echo.

Crap. 'They.' Not 'she.'

Echo reached out to shake my hand. Silver rings adorned each finger. "You must be Alex. Wylie's told me lots about you." They turned to Wylie, leaned over and gave him a kiss on the nose. "Hey baby."

Wylie flipped his bangs aside and scooted over so they could sit next to him.

"Speaking of mom's, I *am* a fan of yours, Alex." Echo reached over and slipped their hand into Wylie's. They wore a black military-style button down shirt with the sleeves rolled to their elbows. Below the cuffs, I could see thin lines running cross-ways down their forearms with surgical precision. Most were white, but there were two fresh cuts—red and angry-looking. I wondered if Wylie noticed.

"Uh, yeah, she's pretty great, I guess." Not that I'd spent a lot of time with her of late. Since Wylie came here, she's been spending more and more time in LA. I was beginning to think we should've moved here instead. She's getting more involved in things, like she did in San Francisco. I liked it better then, because I actually got to be a part of it. But now, with her gone and Wylie here and my dad working so much, it's been really lonely. Sometimes I wished we had never left SF. Maybe Pete wouldn't have turned into a douche and we would still be friends. But then, I wouldn't have gotten to meet Wylie. On the other hand, maybe I'd still feel like I actually *had* parents. I was getting irritated. Everyone else seemed to be getting the best parts of my parents. I only warranted left-overs. "Why, in particular, are you a fan?"

"I just love the work she's doing here with the AIDS population. She's becoming a true advocate for a population people are trying to pretend don't exist. She even said she'd put me in contact with a director who's doing a documentary on kids growing up with HIV. I want to be in films and really make a difference in the world. This could be my big first-step." They leaned over and put their head on Wylie's shoulder.

Yep, sounds like my mom—champion of the downtrodden. It certainly looked like Echo loved Wylie. They didn't seem mad at him. I kinda wished I had more time alone with Wylie so I could find out more about his relationship with Echo.

"So where do you live when you're not a resident here?" I asked.

Echo swung their leg in circles like Wylie had earlier. "Well, I had been living with my parents. But they don't really understand me, so it's been kind of hard to stay there. I've got some friends that have a place downtown, so I might stay there for a while so I can get on my feet and start auditioning for roles." They lifted their head from Wylie's shoulder and flipped their long fire-engine-red hair back with their hand. "I'd like to go to film school at some point. My parents said they's pay for it, but they want me to live at home and I just can't handle them anymore."

They caught me staring at their arm and quickly covered up the new cuts with their other hand. I looked at Wylie to see if he noticed, but he was watching their face.

I nodded my head and eyed their arm. "What's the deal with the scars?"

Echo looked offended. "No sensitivity necessary here, just please, feel free to charge in and ask questions."

I didn't mean to offend, I just didn't understand the whole cutting thing. "I'm sorry. I'm just, you know, trying to understand."

Echo stood. "Maybe it's not for you to understand."

"Well, why do you leave them showing if you're ashamed of them?"

"I—" They looked at Wylie. "—a little help?"

"Dude, just leave it, ok?" Wylie implored.

"Fine." I put my hands up in surrender. "I give up. Sorry for being curious."

"Whatever." Echo left in a huff, muttering "Prick" under their breath before slamming the door.

17

Wylie

Atley Hall, Los Angeles — 3 Days To Go

Daily Journal Prompt: I hope that...

I guess I hope that my family will be a little more understanding. Dr. Springall convinced them to come and have some sessions with him, then we all sat around and talked together. It was weird, but, actually a little bit cool. My mom cried a lot, but she agreed to call me Wylie and use male pronouns when she refers to me. Mason said she was really fighting Dr. Springall, but when he said that I almost died because I wasn't being heard, she kind of got it. So, I hope that when I go back home, I can dress how I want and not have to change in the bushes every day.

I also hope to never get my freaking period ever again because I started taking puberty-blockers. YES!!!! Shannon says that if I keep up with my therapy sessions and monthly check-ins with Dr. Springall, I can be *considered for testosterone when I turn 17. It's going to be a loooooonnngggg two years. :-(*

I hope that high school will be different, and that the teachers will call me Wylie and use male pronouns. It's funny, I never thought language would have such a crucial impact on my life. I mean, it's just grammar, one of the most boring classes you can take.

I hope that I can win more skate comps so that I can save up for hormones and surgery. To be anatomically-correct would be such a relief. I feel bad about Echo and stuff. I know they've been frustrated that I won't let them see me without my pants on, or touch me there. (No one's reading this, right???) I don't touch myself there. I don't even like to look at myself down there. I don't want anyone else seeing me like that. So yeah, I'll probably be a virgin until I can afford surgery. Dammit. I wish I could just wake up and have it all done.

Later.

"I can't believe you're leaving tomorrow." Echo brushed my bangs off of my forehead and kissed it.

We were laying in their bed. It was almost midnight and the house was quiet, except for the scraping of the tree branch on the glass and the light rush of wind intruding under the open window. The lamp was on, but Echo had draped a thin scarf over it so that it cast a red light on the walls.

Their lips traced the line of my nose, down to my lips. A hint of cinnamon on their tongue. Would I ever be able to eat cinnamon and not get turned on? As much as I wanted to leave here and get back to my life and my friends, I was also scared.

I'd made good friends here. Especially Echo. I would miss not seeing them every day. I'd miss kissing them and talking to them about things that got my mind excited. The best thing was—they thought I was brilliant too.

Echo's kiss was always welcome, but ever since that night, it was also a source of anxiety. There would always come this point when they would tug at my belt and all of the excitement that I felt was completely shut down. The crappy thing about it is, I didn't actually understand what I was anxious about. I felt ridiculous because it wasn't like they expected me to have a dick or anything. They knew who I was, which, to be honest, was probably the safest thing. If I was going to go all the way with someone, Echo should be the one.

"What's wrong?" Echo pulled their face away from mine, their eyes narrowed.

"Nothing." I brought my head up to try and capture their lips again. I didn't want a fight.

They put their hand on my chest and pushed back. "Don't tell me it's nothing. You're not even here."

I really, REALLY didn't want to argue with Echo. Not tonight. Not our last night together. "I'm sorry. It's just that I'm gonna miss you."

"I know, moron, that's why you should be here right now." They grabbed my wrist and put my hand on their chest. "Here, this should help." They leaned back over to me and kissed me deeply, their fingers wound into my hair.

Echo moaned. An electric current ran from my lips to my crotch, sending that familiar feeling I got sometimes in my sleep. Those times when I woke up with the blanket bunched up between my legs and my pulse racing. I wanted that. Dammit, I wanted that so bad I could have screamed. The trouble was. Well, obviously there was lots of trouble. I didn't know how to make that feeling happen. I felt their other hand begin wandering down my chest to my stomach. I could feel my body backing away. The lower their hand went, the farther I got—both in my mind and in the bed—until finally, I fell off the edge.

Echo sat up and stared at the door. We both held our breath, hoping the noise didn't wake anyone. We weren't actually supposed to be in other people's rooms at night. We heard nothing. "Wylie, what the fuck?" Echo whispered, staring down at me sprawled on the floor. "And don't tell me you're running away from me because you miss me."

I could feel the heat rising to my face. Tears pricked at the corners of my eyes. I felt like a complete idiot. Why was I so lame at this? At this rate, I really *was* going to be a virgin until I could afford surgery. When would that be? After college? The tears won out over my resolve never to cry again. They streamed in silence down my face, leaving dark green dots on the braided rug.

"It's ok if you want to break up with me." I whispered, hating myself for my weakness. I stood up to go.

"Wylie wait." They reached out and grabbed my arm. "I'm sorry. I...I'm probably pressuring you too much." They pulled on my forearm to get me to turn around. "Please." They patted the bed beside them. "Come sit?"

I didn't see the point. I was destined to be a 30-year-old virgin. The freak that can't get off. The guy that cries in bed because he's too scared to take his clothes off. I started sobbing, my stomach boiling with the acid of anxiety.

"Hey. Shhhh." Echo put their arm around my shoulders and drew me close. "I'm sorry." They whispered. "Dammit. I'm such an unmitigated ass."

If I wasn't so distraught, I would find their ability to sound smart while they were berating themself to be extremely charming. I didn't want them to feel bad though. It wasn't their fault.

Echo tilted my chin up with their left hand so that they could look at my face. "I'm sorry I pressured you. That was way uncool of me."

"No." I shook my head. "It's my fault. I just can't...do... *that*."

"I keep forgetting you're so young. Or maybe, you don't really feel that way towards me?" They looked down at their hand with the chipped black nail polish.

"I'll be 15 tomorrow. I'm not a child." Except that right then, I did feel like a child. How could I explain this to them? "I totally feel like that towards you. I love you. It's just me. I hate the way my body is down there. Instead of being on an 'on-button' it's an 'off-button.'"

Echo looked up at me. "I love your body. I want to see you. I want to feel you. Don't you understand that?" They reached up and put their hand to my face, gently pulling my cheek towards them. "You're beautiful." They leaned in and kissed me.

I pulled away. "What's the point of this? It's just the same story every time. We both get excited and then you want more and then I feel like throwing up."

Now Echo looked like they were going to cry. "I didn't mean—"

"You just got done saying you shouldn't be pressuring me and then you start kissing me again. Are you even listening to me?" I slipped out from their embrace and got up.

"I wasn't trying to pressure you. I just wanted to kiss you." Now *they* were crying.

"But it's never really just a kiss anymore, is it? There's always a goal." I turned to leave. "I'm sorry I can't help you achieve your goals."

♠ ♥ ♣ ♦

"You're awfully quiet today, Wylie." Shannon swiveled back and forth in her chair. It was Saturday—my last day. She was in jeans and a white t-shirt, a light purple cashmere sweater draped over her shoulders. "Are we back to silent sessions again?"

I was exhausted. I didn't sleep at all after leaving Echo's room last night. They didn't come to breakfast. I was worried. And angry. And sad. All of the emotions. And they weren't good.

"Can you tell me how you're feeling about going home today?"

Like throwing up, actually. I didn't want to leave Echo on bad terms. I was afraid that my mom would go back on her word to let me stay on puberty blockers. I was worried that I might be forever in puberty limbo because I couldn't afford testosterone treatments. I was terrified that I wouldn't ever find love again, but even more terrified if I did, because it would mean more struggle with my lack of anatomical correctness. All of these thoughts swirled around in my mind like dirty bathwater trying to make its way down the drain, blocked by a giant glob of hair and slimy soap residue.

"Wylie?" Her chair squeaked as she leaned forward to grab her mug. She always drank tea, but she never pulled the tea bag out of the mug. The little white tag fluttered at the end of its string when she set her cup down under the A/C vent.

"Do you think I'll make it through this?" That was the real question. I could see where I wanted to be. See the man I wanted to become. It was far off at the end of the horizon—that point in space where the boundary between earth and sky is not defined by a solid line, but rather, by a hazy band where everything and nothing is possible. The problem with that place is that you never actually get there, no matter how far you travel or how hard you try. And what you can't usually see are all the obstacles that can slow you down or swallow you up. But I saw those obstacles, too. They were infinite. And they were overwhelming me.

Shannon gazed at me over her pale green mug. Steam rose from the cup as she took a sip, then swallowed it. "Do *you* think you'll make it through?"

I looked down at my hands. I really needed to cut my nails. They were getting too long—making my hands look too feminine. "I hope so."

"What makes you think you won't?" She picked the string attached to her teabag and dunked it twice before setting the string down on the other side of the mug. She took another sip.

The big hand on the clock advanced another minute. I wouldn't miss that damn clock. Screw it. Let's stop beating around the bush. "My mom, for one. My inability to have sex is another." There—pure honesty, Shannon—and I didn't even make you work for it.

She set the mug down. "Those sound like pretty strong obstacles for you. Tell me, how will your mom stop you from making it through?"

"She could go back on her promise to use my pronouns or my real name." I ticked that obstacle off on one finger, then queued up another. "She could make it so that I don't get my shots." Another finger. "She could force me to wear girl-clothes again."

Shannon stood up, her chair groaning like she weighed three-hundred pounds, instead of the one-twenty she probably weighed, and crossed the office to the door. Hanging

215

from the door was a full-length mirror—the kind you could get at Target with the cheap, black-plastic frame. She lifted the mirror slightly and pulled it from the small nail that held it in place. Crossing the office again, she set the mirror down in front of me.

"Look in the mirror, Wylie, and tell me: Is this a person that can be forced into anything?"

I stared at myself in that mirror. My reflection, only slightly warped, gave me pause. I didn't see a girl pretending to be a boy, like I used to. I could finally see myself that way I felt—male. And honestly, I felt strong in that moment. I saw a person that tried hard to be themselves, even if only in limited circumstances. I saw that my acts of self-preservation were not acts of cowardice. They were simply a means to an end that I could live with.

"You are a strong, intelligent individual. More than capable of making up your own mind about what is and is not ok when it comes to how people treat you. I know that you can make it through anything that life throws at you. You have to be willing to stand up for yourself and what you believe in. I know it can be scary, especially when it means standing up to adults. I also want you to know that you have options." She leaned the mirror up against her gray filing cabinet and sat back down.

"No matter what happens when you go home. Know that you have options. You have me. You have Dr. Keen. You have the friends you made here. You have the means to reach out to us and get the help you need if you are not getting that help at home. No more running away. You've got this."

I nodded my head, slowly.

"I'm serious, Wylie. I want to hear you say, 'I've got this.'"

I suddenly felt like I was in a Tony Robbins seminar.

"Say the words, Wylie."

"Alright." Exasperated. "I got this."

Shannon smiled. "Thank you. Now." She leaned forward. "Let's talk about sex. Why don't you think you can be intimate with another person?"

I laid back on the couch and closed my eyes. This was not a conversation I wanted to have with the lights on. But I truly did want to figure out why I couldn't get comfortable with my body. I also wasn't sure how to discuss it without bringing Echo into it. We tried hard to keep people from knowing we were anything more than friends. I guess I could just change the name to protect the not-so-innocent.

"Well, I mean, it's not even just with other people." I draped my arm over my eyes. "I can't make myself, you know, get off. It physically makes me ill to go down there."

"So what I'm hearing is that it makes you sick to masturbate. Am I correct?"

"Yeah. So when I'm with someone else and they want to go down there, it's the same thing. There's always this constant reminder that 'all-parts-are-not-included.'"

"I see." I heard her take a sip of her tea, then the soft scrape of ceramic on the matte-glass coaster on her desk. "You know, for some people, it helps to use different words for your anatomy—for example, an individual might call their clitoris a penis."

"What?" I stifled a laugh.

"Why is that so far-fetched? Did you know that the penis and clitoris are made from the same materials? And that we all exhibit the same anatomy until we're about nine-weeks old? If you can be born with a vagina and identify as male, how is that so different than calling your clitoris a penis?"

That kind of made sense. I mean, they're just words. We

create them. So we should be able to use them in the way that makes the most sense to us.

"Think it over. And know that your body is designed to bring you pleasure, either alone or with others. The key is to do things in your own time. You should never feel obligated to go further than what feels comfortable to you, no matter what anyone else says or does."

"Can we just pretend we sang to you already and just skip to the blowing part?" Echo stood next to Claire, who was holding a round, German chocolate cake in both hands, 15 candles undulating with the breeze coming through the front door. I was glad to see Echo had finally emerged from their room. I was afraid they wouldn't be here to say goodbye. I didn't want to leave with last night hanging over us.

"Nonsense. Ignore the sourpuss and sing to our dear friend." Claire led everyone in singing a discordant Happy Birthday to me while Echo acted as snide musical director, complete with invisible baton and dour facial expression. Skylar, Alex, Nicole, Reyna, and of course, Claire, took part in helping me blow the candles out. My wish? Well, it didn't come true, so what difference does it make?

This was one of two birthday parties I would have that day. Part birthday celebration, part graduation from the program. Shannon, Dr. Springall and a couple of the other therapists stopped by to wish me well in my journey between bites of cake and ice cream. It felt weird to be leaving this place. But, I felt confident today. I was 15 now. Two more years and I could start taking testosterone. Three more years and I could be approved for surgery. The challenge: how to pay for it.

I tried not to think of these things while I said goodbye to my new friends. Or when Echo pulled me into their room for one last time. Our kiss was deep and slow—an attempt to prolong a moment and avoid the inevitable. Every emotion that we had felt together this past month was contained in that kiss. It tasted of chocolate cake and caramel frosting and vanilla bean ice cream, but still I detected that spicy hint of cinnamon underneath it all. I ran my hand along their ear—the one with the silver spike, and felt the soft stubble of their buzz cut on my fingertips.

"I'm sorry." They whispered, pulling away almost imperceptibly. They leaned their forehead against mine and exhaled. We stood there like that for a moment before they slipped a folded up piece of paper into my pocket. "Don't open it until you get home."

I didn't like the sound of that. "Why can't I read it now?" I opened my eyes so that I could see them.

"Just promise me, ok?" There were tears in the corner of their eyes. I felt an uneasiness in the pit of my stomach, all jumbled up with a feeling of loss that I was never going to see Echo again. "Please?"

I didn't want to argue with them. Not again. "Ok." I assured them. "I promise."

"Surprise!!!!"

I nearly jumped out of my skin. Standing there in my living room was my mom, Jared, Mason, Grandpa Frank, and Lamar. They had each released handfuls of rainbow confetti, which floated and flickered down into the carpet. The first thing that came to my mind was, 'who gets to vacuum that?'

A giant rainbow sign wishing me a 'Happy Birthday' hung just below the ceiling where the living room and hallway met. Reyna and Alex pushed me through the door and into the next party. I had been obsessing over the note in my pocket for two and a half hours, the folded mass pressing against that tender spot on my ass where they gave me my injection. I wanted nothing more than to run to my room and open the letter, but there everyone was, waiting to celebrate me.

This was so weird.

Mason was the first to cross the room and hug me. "Happy Birthday, Wylie." His strong arms felt good around me. I felt safe.

Next came Jared, who actually said, "I missed you little bro."

Grandpa Frank, looking as frail as the last time I saw him, hobbled over and shook my hand. He leaned on his cane for balance. "Happy birthday, young man."

"Thanks Grandpa." I reached out and hugged him as tight as I dared, feeling the sharp edges of his shoulder blades under his light blue, button-down shirt. The scents of Old Spice and pipe tobacco filled my nostrils. He never smoked in our house, but he always smelled like it.

Alex grabbed my backpack from me and took it to my room. Reyna scooted past us to say hello to my mom. I don't know if they ever talked after the hospital, but my mom was polite. Even still, there was a coldness that passed between them that was unmistakable.

My mom looked down at me, her manner, tentative. "Happy Birthday, Wylie. It's good to have you home." She hugged me. A full hug. It lasted longer than was comfortable with, but I took it to mean she was sorry. My apprehension about coming home faded, at least a little bit. It actually seemed like maybe things would be ok. That I had worried for nothing and that I could finally be me, the real me, in every aspect of my life.

Lamar came up last. He had shaved his head. No more massive afro. He looked so different. More mature. He reached out to shake my hand. I took it. "Happy Birthday, fool." He paused and made a point to look me in the eyes. "And, I'm sorry." I believed he meant it.

Dinner was a six-foot submarine sandwich from Togos, lettuce and onion spilling out over the ham and turkey filling. There were Doritos and coleslaw and celery with cream cheese. My second cake of the day was a spiral ice cream cake with mint ice cream and chocolate cake from Baskin Robbins (convenient, since they occupied the same store space). I sat on the ottoman my mom had sat on when the police interrogated me before I ran away. It seemed like such a long time ago. I didn't feel like the same person I was back then.

As I tried to shove a piece of that gigantic sandwich into my face, I couldn't remember the last time my family had eaten together. It was strange to see them all talking and smiling with my friends. Even my mom seemed to enjoy it and was holding a conversation with Reyna—about what, I couldn't imagine. Alex and Lamar were engaged in some debate with my brothers, but I was thinking only about that note from Echo. I couldn't wait any longer. I set my plate down next to me and got up, intending to go to the bathroom where I wouldn't be disturbed. I could finally read the letter and ease the dread I was feeling.

"Wil—" My mom stopped, closed her eyes, then smiled. "—Wylie, where are you going? We've got presents to open."

"Yeah, I just need to go to the bathroom." I started for the hallway. "I'll be right back."

I walked down the hall, pulling the letter from my back pocket. Closing the door, I flicked on the bathroom light. I placed the toilet seat down and sat on the fluffy pink seat cover. Unfolding the letter, I recognized Echo's signature block letters filling the college-ruled page.

Dear Wylie,

I want you to know that I'm sorry for making you feel pressured last night. And the other night. And any other night you may have felt it and not told me. I can get pretty intense sometimes, especially when I have strong feelings about something. Or someone. I love you, Wylie—so much. It kills me that I caused you pain. Can you forgive me? Wait, don't answer that yet, because I might need to ask for it again. This was a hard decision for me to come to, but I think it's for the best. Despite my strong feelings, or maybe because of them, I think we should break up. My life is in Los Angeles and yours is in Riverview—two hours and forever away.

On my left wrist, underneath that studded leather cuff you loved, is a healing scab in the shape of your name. You will always be a part of me. Please don't write to me yet. Maybe in a month or two. I need to heal. If you ever find yourself in LA, look for me in Hollywood, in person or on the Walk of Fame. We're destined for greatness, you and I.

Remember, soulmates can never be torn apart.

Echo

I read it three more times through tear-filled eyes before folding it and returning it to my back pocket. I pushed on my pocket, into the injection site, preferring that ache to the crushing of my heart.

"Wylie, you ok in there?" It was Alex.

I wiped the tears from my eyes and tried to find my voice. "Yeah." I croaked. "Be out in a second." I got up and ran some water, splashing the cold liquid on my face. I knew without looking in the mirror that my eyes would be puffy. My face felt like it was a million degrees. My body was heavy, but empty. I'd never been broken up with. Probably because I never had a girlfriend. My hands gripped the white tiled counter top. I'd heard the cliché. Better to have loved and lost—that whole thing. My guess is that that person never loved and had their heart stomped on.

One more splash of water on my face, and I was ready to face my friends and family. I looked at my reflection in the mirror and told myself: "I got this."

When I opened the door, Alex was still standing there. "You ok, man?"

I hated it when people asked you if you were ok when you're clearly not ok, and all that effort you spent trying to seem ok is basically destroyed and you start crying almost immediately. I shook my head and walked back into the bathroom. Alex followed. "Dude, what happened?"

I reached into my back pocket, pulled out the letter and handed it to him. Then I soaked a washcloth with water and stuck it on my eyes. That always helped me stop crying. I hoped it would also keep my eyes from looking so puffy.

Alex read the letter. "They *carved* your name into their wrist? Dude, that's scary."

I didn't answer. I had to admit though, it wasn't the most healthy of choices. But I loved them and now I would never see them again.

"I'm sorry man. I know getting dumped is the worst." He folded the note back up and handed it to me.

"Yeah." I threw the washcloth into the sink. "It sucks." I sighed. "On the one hand, I feel really crappy, like I'll never find anyone as cool as them. On the other hand, it kind of gives me hope that there are actually people that would want to be with me."

"Yeah, totally man." Alex smiled.

Despite the hole in my gut, I was still grateful to be home. And to have my friends back. "So, who organized this whole soiree?"

"It was actually your mom's idea." Alex looked as incredulous as I felt.

"Seriously?"

"Yeah man, she called my mom and asked if we would come and if there was anyone else she should invite. It's kinda funny watching her try to be nice to my mom. I still think she's pretty mad at her."

"Yeah, that seems clear." Wow. I couldn't believe my mom had changed her tune so fast. Well, I guess it wasn't that fast, but at any rate, I was glad to know she was trying.

It was the next to last day of school and for the first time in my life, I got to leave the house in the clothes I chose to wear. They weren't even hand-me-downs either. My mom bought me all new boxers for my birthday and a bunch of Axe deodorant and body spray. Jared got me a new black Offspring t-shirt. I had my new jeans and shoes Grandpa Frank got me last month. Finally—no hiding behind a bush to shed a skin that never fit. No trying to hide who I was.

I can't describe how amazing this day felt. I was back home, bombing down the hill on Aces, the wind in my hair and Propaghandi in my ears. Lamar got me a portable CD player and three skate-punk CDs. Alex added to my collection with the entire Metallica collection. It only took 15-years to gain the freedom to be me and, despite the ache in my heart for having lost Echo, I felt like my life was actually on track. I didn't care so much about the run down houses in my neighborhood, with their fire-hazard-brown yards. I barely saw them.

I emailed Echo last night. I know they told me not to, but I couldn't help it. I'd been obsessing over everything all night and I couldn't sleep. I didn't ask them to reconsider or anything—that seemed unfair. I did ask them if they would come to my graduation. They had been there for some of the most important milestones of my life these past few weeks. It seemed wrong that they would miss this one. I was proud of my accomplishment and I wanted them to see me on that stage, making my valedictorian speech in front of everyone. Admittedly, I did hope that maybe we'd get to talk. And maybe they'd agree that a trial long-distance thing might be a better option than just cutting the most beautiful relationship in the history of the world off so early in its life. And maybe we'd be able to finish where we left off. I didn't say any of that in the email, of course. I do have *some* self-respect.

The sun was heating up the streets already as I rounded the corner to Alex's street. Barely 7 am and it felt like it was already 85 degrees. I skid to a halt in front of Alex's house. The scrape of my board on asphalt tore through the quiet morning just as his front door opened and he appeared. He slid what looked like a PowerBar into the pocket of his cargo pants and shut the door.

"One more day." Alex smiled and cinched his backpack onto his back. With a running start, he mounted his board and took off, with a good lead on me. One more day. I wasn't sure what this summer would hold for me. But, with Alex going off to Stanford for that robotics camp and me newly single, I'd have lots of time to skate. I had started looking at local competitions online. I noticed some boards up that advertised comps, but I also needed to pick up some mags. I had one goal: get signed.

I pumped my right foot on the concrete so I could catch up with Alex. He was coasting now, so it didn't take long. "Hey, you got plans this afternoon?"

Alex shrugged. "What do you have in mind?"

"Shopping."

"Shopping?" He looked at me sideways.

"I need something to wear tomorrow." I explained. "Something nice."

"Something nice. You got a date?" He teased.

"Something like that."

"Yeah, I'll go." Alex glided around the bend and onto the next street. Traffic was picking up as people were taking their kids to school and heading to work.

"So, I emailed Echo last night." I said, over the sound of engines accelerating from a stop.

Alex's head dropped. "Dude, no. Tell me you didn't."

"What? It's not like I begged them to get back together. I just wanted them to come tomorrow. To see us graduate." I rationalized. "That's respectable, right?"

"Whatever man." He swerved around a pothole. "If you ask me, they did you a favor. Let it go. There are plenty of well-adjusted skater chicks out there waiting for you. This is your year to explore."

That stung a little. I still didn't think he got how difficult this was for me. We skated on, past the high school we would be attending together next year, and into the parking lot of Chaparral Junior High. One more day.

"Your final exams are being passed out now. Please place them face down on your desks and do not turn them over until I instruct you." Ms. Davidson walked past me and slipped a note on my desk.

> *It's good to have you back, Mr. Masterson. While I can't confirm your valedictorian award, if your past performance is any indication of your work today, I am confident we will see you on that stage tomorrow night. Best be prepared.*
>
> *~TD*

Between that note and the email I got back from Echo first period, I was so ridiculously happy I could barely sit still. They said they'd come to the graduation ceremony and "maybe, just maybe" accompany me to Alex's party afterwards. I tried to concentrate on what Ms. Davidson was saying, but all I could think about was Echo. A rumbling was beginning in my stomach like a breaking wave radiating out to every part of my body.

Alex leaned over from the row next to me and whispered, "Dude, what's with the goofy grin on your face?"

I tried to stifle it, but I couldn't. Shannon would say that I shouldn't. She said that we spend so much of our lives giving full energy to sadness that we won't let ourselves give full energy to our happiness. It's a crime, she says, to give the good times short shrift. That morning, I don't think I could have stifled it if I tried.

I sailed through my Algebra II final, remembering my last night of studying before Echo came to visit. We spent hours together talking, making out, and falling asleep in each others' arms, being careful to wake before anyone else was up. I wondered if I could find a way to stay in LA this summer. There was such an amazing skate scene there. It would be off the hook.

To say that fifth period was less than a joy would be a monumental understatement. Mr. Kaplan let us come up individually to see our final grade while everyone watched some boring history documentary about the Crusades.

"Dude, come on Mr. K." I pleaded. "B+? But I aced every test. I got an A on my research paper. How can you give me a B+?

"Wylie, it's good to see you back in class, but I'm afraid you missed out on some group projects, and of course, you knew that a large percentage of your grade was participation." He stacked the papers on his desk and removed his glasses to look at me directly.

I dropped my voice to a whisper. "Please, Mr. K. Didn't they explain to you that this was like, a medical necessity?"

"I'm sorry, Wylie, I understand that this was not entirely in your control. But this is how the real world works. If you want a full paycheck when you work, you have to show up everyday."

This was a disaster and he was lecturing me about real-world lessons. I stood there, staring at my shoes, willing him to give into my plea.

Mr. Kaplan leaned forward. "Can I give you a little advice, Wylie?" He didn't wait for a response. "Your life does not hinge on getting straight-A's. A B+ is a perfectly respectable grade in an AP class and worth an A for GPA purposes. You've done well. Relax and try to enjoy that."

"Looks good." Alex looked with approval at the flat-front black Dockers I had paired with a white button-down dress shirt. "You gonna wear a tie?"

I looked at myself in the mirror, flipping my chin-length bangs to the side and tried to imagine some Miami-Vice-worthy scruff on my face. We were at JC Penney at the mall. In the guys' section. I was a little nervous that I was going to get called out for being in the men's dressing room. I'd gotten a couple double-takes already. But with Alex there, I think it made it look more like I was a guy. And it helped calm me.

I liked what I saw in my reflection. "Doesn't the dress code say guys have to wear one?"

"Yeah." He shrugged. "But you don't seem to be one for following rules all that much."

True. I looked back at the mirror. I looked more masculine, yes. But I also looked—square. A tie would only enhance that effect.

"I have an idea." Alex got up from the fake-leather ottoman he was perched on. "Go change."

"What do you have in mind?"

"Just go change."

I retreated to the beige dressing room, locked the door with the brass hook, and shed the dress clothes to the 80's greatest hits played on the piano.

While I changed, Alex stood outside. "Oh hey, I forgot to tell you, I got an email from my mom. She's bringing Echo here tonight so they can go to our graduation."

"Really? That's great news." I wondered how they were gonna get here. I re-emerged from the dressing room, my casual-dress-clad self, with new clothes in hand. Alex took them and put them on the go-back rack.

"But —?"

"Come on." Alex grabbed my t-shirt sleeve and dragged me out of the store, across the crowded mall, dodging harried mothers and screaming children. Destination: Macy's. I groaned inside.

I'd never been in this place before. It was clean and modern. Symphony music streamed from the invisible speakers. I didn't think I could afford even a pair of socks from this place. I felt uncomfortable. Alex seemed at home here though, knowing exactly where he wanted to go. He pulled pants from shelves and shirts from racks before leading me over to the dressing rooms.

"Here." He handed me the clothes. "Try these."

I felt the fabrics in my hand. They were soft. Not like the crunchy, itchy stuff I tried on before. I slid on a pair of actual dress pants like you'd wear to an office, then one of the dress shirts from the hanger. There were two. A black one and a silvery one. I unbuttoned the silvery one and put it on, enjoying the silky feel of the fabric on my skin. Once I was buttoned and tucked, I looked in the mirror.

Holy crap.

I felt a chill run through my entire body. I ran my hand through my hair to bring it out of my face. The collar of the shirt opened wide, while the rest of it fit just right, without bunching a lot when I tucked it into the flat-front trousers.

"That's more like it." I said, to no one in particular, as I unlocked the silver doorknob on the gray dressing room door and walked out to look for Alex.

He was standing just outside the dressing room, black sports coat over one shoulder. "Damn!"

Chills again.

"That's what I'm talking about." He handed me the dress coat. "Try this on."

I complied. It felt heavy, but not overly-restricting. I held my hands out to my sides and turned to face Alex.

"Hell yeah." He turned me around to face the mirror. "This is what you're wearing."

I stared at the rockstar version of myself. I imagined myself on that stage, confidently giving a speech that would be remembered and quoted for years to come. Honestly, I still wasn't quite sure what I was going to say, but damn, I would look good saying it. If I squinted, I could see Johnny Depp looking back at me.

The price tag of the jacket caught my eye—$75. My heart skipped. How much was all this going to cost?

"You alright man?"

I started sweating. "Yeah. Good." I walked towards the dressing room. "Just gonna change."

As I peeled off the coat and shirt, I found the rest of the price tags. My rockstar outfit was going to cost me $150. I looked at the hand-me-down clothes sitting in a pile on the floor, then at my boxer-clad reflection. Who was I trying to fool? The scarecrow staring back at me was a far cry from Johnny Depp. I was just a poor, confused nobody who dreamed of busting out of obscurity. How can I hope to afford hormones and surgery if the first thing I do when I get a little money is buy clothes? What was I thinking? But wait, don't they all say 'fake it 'til you make it?'

A knock on the door startled me out of my sad musings. "You ok?" It was Alex.

I scurried to put on my pants. "Yeah. Be right out." I shrugged into the rest of my clothes and headed out to meet him.

"Where's your stuff?"

I'd left the new clothes in the dressing room.

"I don't know man. It's a lot of money." I headed for the exit.

Alex scrambled to catch up to me. "Dude, wait." He grabbed my shoulder.

"What?" I spun around to confront him. I was more embarrassed than mad, which made it all the worse.

"Come on man, you looked great in those clothes. A besides, everything is on sale." He turned to head back towards the dressing room.

I stayed where I was.

Alex turned back to me. "Trust me. This stuff'll end up costing you the same as you would have spent on that lame-ass JC Penny stuff." He turned and walked into the dressing room and came back out moments later with the three items I had tried on.

He was right. Once the checker rang everything up, it was like $90. It was still a lot of money, but it wasn't as bad. I deserved to look my best when I stand up on that stage and tell the world who Wylie Masterson is and what he can do. I still had $150 left from my winnings. A few thousand more poker games, or better yet-skate competitions, and I would be able to afford to fully transition.

"Wylie, phone's for you." Jared yelled from the kitchen.

I got up from my desk where I had been chatting online

with Echo. They were at the Keen's house. I wanted to be there so badly it hurt. I walked down the long hallway from my room to the kitchen and took the phone from Jared.

"Hello."

"Is this Willow Masterson?" The nasally voice on the other side of the line inquired.

I cringed. "Sure."

"Ms. Masterson, this is your Principal, Dr. Edwards. How are you this evening?"

My inner monologue went something like this: *Wishing you would stop calling me that, but also hoping you have good news for me, otherwise, why would you be calling?*

"I'm fine," was all I could say.

"Good. Good. Well, I wanted to congratulate you on being Chaparral Class of 2001 co-valedictorian. You share this honor with Lamar Jones. On behalf of the teachers and staff, we invite you to prepare a speech for tomorrow's commencement ceremony."

Damn. Well, I guess if I had to share the spotlight, at least it could be shared with a friend. I couldn't blame Lamar. He was wicked smart. I'm guessing my B+ in AP History made that possible. Oh well. I still got to speak. "Alright, thank you for letting me know."

"Yes, well, we'll see you tomorrow evening. Congratulations again." Principal Edwards hung up with a click and I was left with a dial tone buzzing in my ear.

Guess it's time to finish that speech. I walked back to my room and let Echo know. They said they were proud of me and that they would see me tomorrow. I told them I loved them. They didn't reply.

"I want a green one." I handed the gold cap and gown back to Mrs. Olsen, the Attendance Secretary. She was manning the L-P table. The gym was buzzing with the sound of excited students ready to throw caps into the air and head to whatever graduation parties were on the docket for the night. The pre-graduation formalities were almost more than we could bear.

Mrs. Olsen looked at my school ID sitting in front of her. If ever there was an appropriate image of a "quizzical brow," this woman had it. "Gold gowns are for young ladies, green gowns are for young men. You are Willow Masterson, yes?"

I rolled my eyes. She knew who I was. After three years of cutting classes, we'd had plenty of conversations. "Yeah, technically, but..."

"Then this is for you." She shoved the plastic-wrapped gold square back into my hands. "Next please."

I was holding up the "elemenopee" line. Mrs. Olsen was having none of it.

"No, wait." I stood my ground—my new Chuck Taylors peaking out underneath the dope new trousers Alex and I shopped for together. "I know that's what my ID says, but, look at me," I spread my arms wide, "do I really look like I should be wearing a gold gown here?"

"Maybe you don't recognize young Wylie Masterson, co-valedictorian of Chaparral Class of 2001." Alex chimed in from the G-K line next to me.

Mrs. Olsen was not impressed. "I'm sorry. Rules are rules. Each student is assigned a cap and gown and you were assigned a gold gown, so a gold gown you will have."

Dammit! What is the deal with the rigid rule-following all the time? Do they remove the areas of the brain that govern creativity and compassion when you get hired on as a school administrator? I was starting to sweat through my shirt. There was no way in hell I was giving my valedictorian speech looking like a canary.

"Forget it." I turned to walk away, when Mrs. Olsen piped up—

"No gown, no walking. That is the dress code." She picked up the golden packet and held it up to me once more.

"Just take the stupid thing and let us get on with it." Stacey Peterson was standing behind me, her black patent-leather pump-clad foot tapping impatiently on the shiny wood floor. She was one of Brianna's friends—the one who ratted me out to her and turned her against me.

I wanted little more than to grind my heel into her pointy toe box, but instead, I took a deep breath and let it out. I turned back to the table. "Look, Mrs. O. I know we haven't been the best of friends here and I'm sorry about that. I've had a lot going on in my life. And maybe I didn't win the best attendance award. And maybe I didn't treat you with the respect that you deserved. I'm sorry. But, if you could, maybe just this once, bend a rule that really doesn't mean that much in the grand scheme of things, and let me have a green gown, I would genuinely appreciate it."

Her face softened. Was this really going to work? Shannon had suggested that I might win more friends if I took responsibility for my actions and treated them how I would like to be treated. Not bad advice, really. Though I knew it was harder in practice.

"Willow—"

My heart sank.

"—it's nice to see that you've matured in your time here. But you will get nowhere in life if you cannot live by the rules. Do yourself a favor and go with the flow for once. Your parents are out there in the auditorium waiting to see you walk across that stage and begin the next phase of your life. Make them proud." She set the cap and gown down on the table. "Next."

Alex leaned over to me. "Dude, you can wear mine."

I left the gown there and walked away. While I appreciated Alex's loyalty and willingness to sacrifice his gown for me, he'd done enough for me. This was his "big day" too. And if he didn't walk, John and Reyna wouldn't get to experience this milestone for their own son. They all deserved this.

"Nah man, it's ok. Don't worry about it. Enjoy the forced frivolity." I waved goodbye to Alex and made my way over to the waiting area for those of us that would be on the stage. We would walk out first before all the other graduates. It was me and Lamar, as co-valedictorians, then Ms. Davidson, who was voted teacher of the year for our class, then Vice-Principal Sprag, Principal Talbot, and some old guy in a light gray suit I'd never seen before.

Lamar looked almost regal in his green gown and goofy-ass cap. "You are looking fly today, my friend."

"Thanks man. I can't wait for all this crap to be over."

All the other students were lining up alphabetically in rows, talking and primping as if this was the best day of their lives. I was embarrassed to admit it, but I had been looking forward to this day for a long time. Finally, I would be able to stand on a stage and have people see me and listen to what I had to say, for once. After my exchange with Mrs. Olsen, I was feeling invisible.

"What's got you down, fool? We are about to bring this house down!"

"Wylie, Lamar, congratulations on your well-earned achievements here." Ms. Davidson patted us both on the shoulder. "I know you'll both do big things in this world."

"Thanks Ms. Davidson." Lamar gave her a big smile.

Just then, Mrs. Sprag waddled over. "Miss Masterson, where is your gown? It's almost time to go onstage."

Out of the corner of my eye, I thought I saw Ms. Davidson cringe.

"I —" I didn't know what to say. Sprag was always intimidating and I wasn't sure what tactic, if any, would work in getting her to let me skirt the rules and give me a green gown.

"Well?" She glanced over at the side doors of the auditorium as they groaned open to let us out.

"I tried to get one, but they were out. So I thought I would just, you know, opt out of the dress."

"Opt out? Don't be ridiculous." She stomped over to a box by the long white tables and pulled out a gold cap and gown package. She stomped back and handed it to me. "Hurry. It's time to go."

"Well, if there are extras, can I get a green one? Please?"

"Miss Masterson—"

Ms. Davidson interjected. "Mr."

Sprag looked confused. "What?"

Ms. Davidson looked at me and smiled.

I stood a little taller. "My name is Wylie. And I need a green gown."

"Miss Masterson," she spat out the 'Miss' as she would a curse, "we don't have time for this. You'll wear the gown associated with your gender or you will sit out today's commencement."

"Mrs. Sprag, surely we could make an exception for Wylie. After all, it's just a color." Ms. Davidson had always called me Wylie, ever since the first day of school when I told her that's what I wanted to be called. No questions. Just respect. She always showed everyone respect. It didn't matter if they're students or teachers. It's little wonder she won teacher of the year.

"Teresa, please take your place in line. We're falling behind schedule."

Ms. Davidson didn't move.

"Will you be joining us in your proper attire?" Sprag glared at me. "Or will you take your place with the spectators?"

The gym was near silent as the students waited to march to the auditorium. My heart raced. Sweat fell in rivulets down my spine. So those were my choices—ghost or impostor. I thought about Echo and how they were always railing against the myth of binary oppositions. What would they do in this situation? It felt like everyone's eyes were on me and Mrs. Sprag—wondering how this was all going to play out.

I looked up into her small, brown eyes. "Neither." I tossed the plastic-wrapped commencement wear at her feet and walked out the way I had come in.

"Wylie— " Ms. Davidson called out.

Sprag cut her off, "She's made her choice. Now let's go folks. We're 5 minutes late."

When I reached the door, my heart was pounding, but I felt good. Clear—but not invisible. I heard footsteps pounding on the floor and Sprag shout, "Mr. Jones! Return to your place immediately!"

"Wylie, hold up." Lamar stopped short. "What are you doing?"

"I'm not playing their game anymore, Lamar." I pushed the metal handle on the door to release it. Bright sunlight streamed in, nearly blinding me. "Go on and give your speech. You've earned it. I'll see you later tonight."

"Will you hold up a minute, fool?" He grabbed my arm. "I've got an idea."

238

♠ ♥ ♣ ♦

"As teacher of the year, I have the honor of introducing to you one of our co-valedictorians, Lamar Jones. Now, I've had the pleasure of working with Mr. Jones these past three years and have watched him grow into a gifted young actor with the mind of an engineer. I will personally be sad to see him leave us, but know that in all things, he will exceed our expectations."

Ms. Davidson turned and held her hand out to Lamar, inviting him up to the podium. She shook his hand and whispered something in his ear before she returned to her seat. Lamar smiled and trained his gaze on me.

That was my cue. My heart raced. I had that feeling I got standing at the edge of a half-pipe before I dropped in. I wiped my sweaty hands on my pants, turned the knobs and flipped the switches in the order Lamar had told me back in the gym. A red light illuminated next to the microphone that extended about two feet from the four-foot by three-foot sound panel. There was a faint buzz, then, the opening chords to Metallica's *Unforgiven*.

"Thank you Ms. Davidson." Lamar cleared his throat. "My parents always taught me to stand up for what is right. This is me, standing up."

From where I sat, perched on a stool in the control booth eight-feet above the audience at the back of the auditorium, I could see everything. Lamar, standing there—motionless. The administrators sitting straight-backed behind him giving furtive glances at him, their watches, and each other. Did they think he had stage fright? The man who had people weeping after his performance of King Lear last year? Nope. He was playing his best role yet.

239

I leaned forward and bent the mic towards me. This was it. I was going to deliver my commencement speech—guerilla-style.

"Students of Chaparral Junior High, parents, teachers, and admini-sheeple, I am Wylie Masterson, co-valedictorian of the class of 2001."

The administrators' furtive glances became blatant looks of panic and confusion. The square caps of the student graduates rotated back and forth, trying to find the source of the music and voice that hijacked the PA system. Echo's flaming red hair made it easy for me to pick them out of the audience. They looked up towards the control booth and smiled that crooked-toothed smile I loved. Mason followed Echo's line of sight and spotted me. He gave a wry smile and nodded his head up and down, like, 'awe yeah, son.' I smiled back. Here we go.

"You know…" I looked down at Sprag. "All I wanted was a green robe."

Sprag's pinched face turned a deep crimson as her eyes found mine. I hoped someone was recording this, because that look was one—I swear—would cheer me up out of the deepest funk for years to come.

New blood joins this earth
And quickly he's subdued

I let the words of the song speak for me about the challenges a man faces trying to become himself in a world that is constantly fighting against him.

On stage, Sprag was trying to pull Lamar from the podium. His mother stood below. It looked like she was lecturing him. Or was she lecturing Sprag? He just stood there, eyes focused on me, gripping the podium. Most of the 9th grade class was standing now. Some watching the spectacle on stage, others turned to look up at me. Cam had his arms raised, giving the classic rock horn hands sign as he tried to engage the rest of the students in a mosh session.

An insistent knocking came from the door behind me. "Masterson, cease this activity at once!"

I ignored them and turned the music down.

"It seems like these past three years here have been a constant fight for me. Fighting to be the person I know I am. Fighting to find my place. Fighting to understand why life happens the way it does—why it's easier for some people and harder for others. I know this struggle isn't unique to me. To a certain extent, each of us is fighting for something. Whether it's the fight to be seen as something other than a dumb kid, the fight to get through the day without having an emotional break-down or the fight to give your valedictorian speech—every day is a fight for us."

The knocking behind me graduated to pounding and shouting: "get out of there this minute!" and "how did he get in there?' And "where are the goddamn keys, Jim?"

I didn't care. What were they going to do to me? Suspend me? Too late, suckers. I'm already out. Down below, Lamar had pried the microphone from the podium and was running up and down the stage, dodging Sprag and campus security. He slid the mic to Ms. Davidson, who slipped it into the sleeve of her long, black robe.

I felt a rumbling under my feet. Alex had moved towards the stage and was pounding on the floor. Mason, Jared, and Echo stood up to face me. Echo blew a kiss. My mom shifted in her seat for a moment before she joined them. She was crying, but it kind of looked like she might be...proud, too?

Gradually, the people around my family started to rise, creating a wave of motion that extended out to the rest of the audience. Some looked pissed; dragging younger children down aisles and out side exits. A few graduates followed. Most stayed. More and more people were stomping their feet on the auditorium floor—the sound, like a perpetual roll of thunder. My heart felt like it was about to explode. People were actually listening to me. I couldn't waste this chance. I crumpled up the lined paper in front of me—the one that held the words anyone could say. I needed to say the words only *I* could say.

"You've heard people say, 'it gets better.' Maybe that's true. I don't know. I've seen plenty of people who've given up the fight. For them, it didn't get better. They got beaten down until they just couldn't keep going. I get it. I understand how that happens. You feel like change is hopeless. You feel like every choice you make leads you down this path that gets darker and darker each day. You feel like there's no one there to walk beside you and catch you when you trip up. And you just keep walking until you disappear."

The stomping faded. I looked up and saw a procession of green and yellow caps making their way up the aisles, led by Alex and Lamar. Mason and Jared pushed their way out to join them. They stopped in the aisle-way beneath the control booth. I rose from the stool so I could see more than just the tops of their caps. I slid open the window panel that separated me from the rest of the auditorium. I wanted to see the faces of the people who previously only stared through me. The people who saw me as a freak. And those who saw me as a friend.

"I get it. Because, you see, I almost gave up this year. I made some really dumb choices and would have died underneath a bridge if my brother hadn't found me. But what I learned from those dumb choices is this—I do have people that are willing to walk beside me. To help me find my path. To fight for me when I don't have the strength to fight for myself."

I gazed out into the crowd below. Brianna stood with her friends, who were whispering and laughing in her ear. She waved them off. Jared wiped a tear away with the back of his hand. Mason stood next to him, arms crossed, staring back at me, nodding his head in solidarity. My heart swelled with the comforting realization that they would fight for me. I looked at the faces of the rest of the audience. Did they have people that would fight for them? Did they know it? I didn't know anyone cared enough whether I lived or died until I almost did.

"The thing is, I think we've all felt exhausted and alone. I think we've all felt in some way that it wouldn't matter if we lived or died. But each of us matters. And whether you know it or not, you're not alone. Sometimes, you just need to ask for help."

I thought about how hard it was for me to ask for help. Not as easy as it sounds. I thought about my sessions with Shannon, realizing even when people did try to help me, I fought them. I felt in that moment the shame of hypocrisy. I knew I had to be better than that.

"Life is about making choices. Some of those choices make our lives better. I think that some of our choices might even make the world a better place. In my limited experience, the best choice we can make for ourselves—and for the world—is to be the best person possible—'the best version of ourselves,' as Ms. Davidson likes to say. Shout out to Ms. Davidson for being one of those adults that are actually on our side!"

Whistles and applause broke out below. A sea of green and yellow caps undulated in front of me as the students stomped their feet again.

Ms. Davidson was still on stage. I watched as she slipped the microphone out of her sleeve. "You're the reason I do this—all of you. Make me proud, Wylie."

Sprag stalked over and snatched the microphone from Ms. Davidson.

I took a breath. Keys jangled outside. Quickly, I jammed a chair under the doorknob, then returned to the mic, keenly aware that only 2 inches of plywood stood between me and an irate A/V tech.

"Miss Masterson, that is enough." Sprag pushed her way up the left aisle. She stood, one hand on the microphone, the other on her hip, about twenty-feet from me. That's as close as she could get because the students refused to let her pass. I was surprised to see that Cam was one of the students locked arm-in-arm with Lamar and other students to keep her away.

"No." I stared straight at Sprag. "It's not enough." I knew what I had to do. I had to stop hiding. Stop being afraid that nobody would like me for me. Stop worrying that no girl would like me if they knew who I was.

Just then, the door behind me flew open, the chair slid across the room and slammed into the wall under the orange counter, bounced back and hit me in the leg. That would leave a bruise.

"Finally." Sprag waved her hand. "Get her out of there."

In an instant, Chase snatched the mic away from Sprag and ran towards the stage. Sprag's face was a hilarious mixture of shock and anger. Someone's hand was on my shoulder, pulling me back. I shrugged it off. Before they could drag me away, I leapt onto the counter between the sound panel and the light panel. I stepped up onto the half-wall that separated the control booth from the rest of the auditorium.

Below, I could see Mason and Jared pushing forward

towards me. I thought about jumping. It wasn't as far down as dropping into a half-pipe, but I didn't have a board and I didn't want to risk breaking a leg. Crouching down, I lowered myself into Mason's up-stretched arms. With his hands around my waist, he eased me to the ground. I was in a sea of bodies—all reaching out to touch me, all talking at once. Alex and Lamar squeezed through them. Lamar shrugged his gown off and put it around my shoulders.

At that moment, the rear doors to the auditorium burst open. Six campus security guards poured through.

"Shit." I looked around to see what my options for escape might be.

"Come on." Jared grabbed my arm and led me towards the front of the auditorium with Alex and Lamar surrounding me. I glanced back and saw Mason leading some other students in a surge towards the guards closest to us. When I turned back around, the principal and superintendent were descending the stairs at the side of the stage, followed closely by Ms. Davidson.

We were three feet in front of the stage when the principal stepped in front of us. "This ends now Miss Masterson."

"George, I don't—" Ms. Davidson winked at me, then collapsed onto the floor. The two men knelt down beside her, giving Jared the chance he needed to lift me onto the stage.

Alex hopped up, took off his cap and placed it on my head. "You've earned this, man."

Chase scrambled up from his hiding spot below and handed me the mic he swiped from Sprag. I felt the weight of it in my hand as I looked out at the audience. The principal and superintendent helped Ms. Davidson off the floor. I only had a few seconds.

"Anyway, yeah. So, I think we can only be the best version

of ourselves when we live true to who we are—being proud of the person we were born and the person into whom we've developed. They say you can't please everyone. I say that the only person you need to please is yourself. Because, if you can't look in the mirror and see someone you truly like, what's the freaking point? So the next time someone asks you 'what do you want to be when you grow up?' Tell them this...Tell them you want to be happy."

I took another deep breath to try and calm the tremors in my body and keep my voice from shaking. Some of the students were making their way towards the stage, wiping tears from their faces. Others smiled up at me as they guarded the stage. Lamar took up his place in front of me and began pounding his fists on the stage. More joined in.

"As we take the next step into our high school years, I challenge each of us to look in the mirror and make the choices we need to make to be the persons we like—love, even. Because I know I don't want to die with regrets. I want to die knowing I lived true to myself."

The entire building seemed to be pounding, taking the place of my own heartbeat. I felt more alive than ever. Looking out over the audience I located Sprag. I brought the mic closer to my mouth, and, in the loudest voice I could summon, proclaimed to the world, "My name is Wylie Masterson. Call me *him*."

Acknowledgments

Writing can be a lonely endeavor, but I believe it should never be one performed in complete isolation. Sometimes you must bring others into the utter torment and ecstasy that is writing, so as to make the story what it ought to be. This book would not have come to be without the support of my tribe of writers and misfits.

First and foremost, I give a soul-felt thanks to my wife and biggest fan, Christy, for giving me the space to find my voice both literally and figuratively, the patience to review this chapter "just one more time," and calling bullshit when I declared myself "not a writer."

I must also thank Janet Rendall, my aunt and the OG Author in the family, who knew I was a writer before I did and encouraged me to take the leap and join her at my first writers' conference. Without her, I would not have met: Alyson Gines, Jenny Davis, Kristen Washburn, and Tawnya Bragg - four-fifths of the AJKR writing ~~menagerie~~ group. For a creative bunch, we were sure unoriginal in coming up with a group name! No matter. I thank you each for listening to some of the best and worst writing I've done, encouraging me, guiding me, and sharing your lives (peanut butter M&Ms, cookie dough, pizza, and tequila) with me.

To my agent, Eric Myers, thank you for taking a personal interest, expressing genuine excitement for my work, and going to bat for me so many times with publishing houses across the country.

I'd like to give a special thanks to the Santa Barbara Writers' Conference organizers and participants for the magic that you create each summer, particularly my fellow Pirates, including, Lorelei Armstrong, the Pirate Queen, for your practiced guidance in helping me adequately illustrate Wiley's triumph; Stephen Vessels, for telling me I had the chops to be a writer (and gets my dark humor); Robin Winter, for your careful ear and wise, detailed feedback; Norm Thoeming, for knowing exactly what a scene needs; Trey Dowell, for ongoing lessons on how to write with powerful brevity; and Avery Faeth, for showing me what it truly means to write with courage.

If we have met and you have not been named here specifically, know that you played a part in shaping who I am and how I observe the world, which informs everything I create. You may have given me a different perspective, a clever turn-of-phrase, a memorable character, a smile, a philosophy to consider, or a position to rage against. I am grateful to you for sharing your truth with me.

Finally, I would be criminally remiss if I did not take time to acknowledge those in the LGBTQ+ community who have made it possible for me to not only live who I am out loud, but also to write this book. I hope that with it, I have done something worthy of your sacrifices.

About the author

River Braun is the author of the young adult novel *call me him*. Having gone through puberty twice and worked with a national organization assisting with at-risk LGBTQ+ youth, River feels uniquely qualified to write about the emotional turmoil that is growing up in a world where it can feel impossible to find the love and support we crave. He believes that art can help transcend perceived boundaries between "others" — and that is what he strives to do in his novels. His goal: to write the stories he needed as a young person. He lives unconventionally with the love of his life aboard their sailboat *Plot Twist* somewhere on the seven seas. You can visit River online at www.riverbraun.com.

Made in the USA
Monee, IL
08 December 2021